# WAKE WOOD

K. A. John lives on the Gower Peninsula in Wales with her husband, cat and whichever of her three children chooses to visit. A full time writer with several pseudonyms, she also writes historical fiction as Catrin Collier and crime as Katherine John.

# K.A. JOHN

# WAKE WOOD

Published by Hammer Books 2011

2 4 6 8 10 9 7 5 3 1

First published in Great Britain in 2011 by
Hammer Books
Random House, 20 Vauxhall Bridge Road,
London SW1V 2SA

www.randomhouse.co.uk

Addresses for companies within The Random House Group Limited can be found at: www.randomhouse.co.uk/offices.htm

The Random House Group Limited Reg. No. 954009

A CIP catalogue record for this book
is available from the British Library

ISBN 9780099556183

Typeset by SX Composing DTP, Rayleigh, Essex
Printed and bound by CPI Group (UK) Ltd, Croydon, CR0 4YY

# WAKE WOOD

The dead should never be woken

# One

Alice Daley felt extremely pleased with herself as she left home to walk to school on her own for the very first time in her life. It was her ninth birthday. Only one more year before she reached double figures. Then she'd be *really* grown-up, although she doubted that she could feel any more grown-up than she did at that moment.

She stopped at the gate, turned and looked back at her mother framed in the front doorway, before glancing up at her father who was leaning out of the bedroom window. She gave one last, perfunctory wave – the goodbye wave of an adult.

Alice had won two arguments that morning, both by stating her case calmly, logically and sensibly as her father had taught her. The first with her mother, who'd wanted to walk her to school – as if she were still a child. The second with her father, who hadn't wanted her to take her birthday present to show her classmates.

She looked down at the hamster in the cage she was carrying.

'Of course you want to meet all my friends, don't you . . . ?' She hesitated. 'I think I'll call you Howie. Do you like the name, Howie? I think Howie the hamster sounds good.'

The small creature poked his nose inquisitively through the bars and looked up at her. Alice stroked his nose with her thumb and carried on walking, but she slowed her step when she reached the high wooden gates that walled off her father's veterinary surgery and yard. She set the hamster cage down, carefully looked up and read the brass plaque affixed to the door.

VETERINARY CLINIC, PATRICK DALEY, MRCVS.

She adored her father, was proud of him, and she nursed an ambition to work alongside him. Both her parents had told her that she was good with animals and, false modesty aside, she knew they were right. From an early age she'd watched her father soothe and calm sick, injured and terrified animals and had tried to emulate his technique. He'd warned her that the university course was long, but told her that if she worked and studied hard, one day her name would be up there beside his on the brass plaque.

Her smile broadened as she imagined it.

ALICE DALEY, MRCVS.

The gates towered over her. She clutched her packed lunch and debated whether or not to enter the yard. Her father had told her about his latest patient when he'd given her the hamster for her birthday. He'd been called to an emergency in the early hours. A 'big noisy dog' had needed life-saving surgery.

In her experience, big noisy dogs, even ones recovering from an operation, were hungry. And her mother had packed her an extra – and entirely unnecessary –

sandwich on the grounds that 'nine-year-olds needed to eat more'.

She glanced at her watch. She could spare ten minutes.

Humming the last song she'd learned in school softly under her breath, she stood on tiptoe and reached up to the combination lock. She entered the numbers – her father's, mother's and her own combined birth dates, so none of them would forget it. Then she braced herself.

The gates were heavy, even for her father. Alice leaned against one of them with all the weight and strength she could muster, and then she still struggled to open it wide enough for her to slip through. The hinges creaked and groaned when the gate eventually swung back.

The pens in the yard were empty, her father's patients still bedded down in their inner cages. She headed for the last pen on the right. It was the largest, the one reserved for the biggest dogs.

Alice fingered the new silver chain around her neck, a birthday present from her mother, before opening the latch on the pen. She whistled.

'Come and see what I've brought you.' She unclipped her lunch box, fumbled at the tie on the plastic bag that held her sandwiches, tore open the extra one and took out the slice of ham.

There was still no sign of the dog. She stepped inside and shouted, 'Come on, slowcoach. I know Daddy's made you better. Aren't you hungry?'

The first she saw of the massive German shepherd was his eyes. He peered out of the opening that led to the inner cage and eyed her suspiciously.

'There you are. Look what I have.' She held out the ham.

The dog continued to stare at her. Suddenly, without warning, his mood changed. His ears flicked back; he snarled, bared his teeth and sprang into attack mode. Growling savagely, he knocked Alice to the ground and closed his jaws on her neck.

Alice screamed. Just once. There was no time for more.

The dog clamped his teeth tightly together, breaking into and tearing Alice's fragile, delicate skin. He bit down viciously, tore a lump from her soft flesh and spat it aside. Alice saw droplets of blood flying through the air. The pain was excruciating.

The world darkened. Bright morning turned to grey-tinged night. As the light faded Alice heard footsteps. She looked up . . . saw her daddy and, behind him, her mummy. They were running . . . She closed her eyes, knowing that now she would be all right.

# Two

Few people had reason to visit Wake Wood other than those who lived four-hour drive away from the bright lights and hustle of the city. The tiny Irish town was no more than a speck on the map in the midst of acres of thick woods interspersed with clearings of agricultural land, accessed by narrow winding lanes that connected the isolated hamlets, farms and small-holdings that surrounded it.

Rural life did not mean ignorance of the times and modern technology. When farming revenues fell, more than one Wake Wood farmer made use of the government subsidies that were available to those who were prepared to site wind farms on their land

No one denied the turbines stood taller than the surrounding trees and – every bit as brash, noisy and incongruous as their detractors had feared they would be – along the edge of the wood that bordered the town limits.

'A blight on the landscape', or so the detractors who'd fought against their advent said. 'A necessary accessory to combat carbon emissions,' declared the bureaucrats and Green Party members, who were happy to place the turbines anywhere except within sight or earshot of their own homes.

'A much needed and welcome source of income,' the locals agreed when they saw their bank balances climbing out of the red. The small number of tourists and travellers who'd ventured deep enough into the countryside to discover Wake Wood before the wind farm had been erected generally had recalled little about the place afterwards. Later, they remembered the wind farm and little else.

Guide books that covered the area highlighted the ancient woods surrounding the town and mentioned a prehistoric circle of tall, thin standing stones, its origin long since lost in the mists of time. But the delights of Wake Wood were only available to the day tripper. No hotel, motel or even humble bed and breakfast within a thirty-mile radius had made it on to any lists of recommended places to stay, for the simple reason there were none.

The local farmers had never been exactly content with their income from farming, but neither had they been desperate enough to increase it by offering bed and breakfast to nosy outsiders who would inevitably ask questions. The inhabitants of Wake Wood were used to the place and the strange noises that echoed through the woods late at night – and occasionally even during the day. Things happened in the town that they realised would appear odd to visitors, and the last thing they wanted was strangers poking and prying into the town's affairs.

As for those tourists who did drive through the town,

the most common opinion was 'A small town lost in a time warp'. Some might add 'picturesque' or 'quaint' to their description. Those with an imagination activated by Stephen King's horror films set in rural communities on the other side of the Atlantic labelled it 'creepy'. More mundane and observant travellers occasionally remarked that Wake Wood was in its death throes. Over half the business premises in the main street had their doors and windows boarded up. A smaller proportion of unoccupied houses had also been sealed against vandals, and as for the remainder, few residents appeared to possess the money or inclination to maintain their homes in a good state of repair.

Yet despite the dire state of cattle and arable farming – the only real labour-intensive industry in the town – people remained tied to the place. Their reasons for staying were a mystery to the casual traveller. But not to those who'd been born there.

Wake Wood was more than just another small Irish town, more even than home. It was an ancient place full of secrets that had to be carefully guarded from one generation to the next if the close-knit society was to survive in anything resembling its present guise.

The one thing every person in the place agreed on was that they had to be very careful of the invitations they extended when necessity dictated they add skills or professionals to their community.

To quote Mick and Peggy O'Shea, whose families had farmed in Wake Wood for generations, 'People who come to Wake Wood have to be "right".'

The O'Sheas didn't have to define 'right'. Not to their neighbours. 'Right' was something all natives recognised when they saw it, and they saw it rarely outside of themselves. They were certainly quick to mark its absence. But suspicious as they were, all of them had to accept that from time to time they needed the new blood of 'incomers' to keep the town alive.

In living memory, very few people had moved into Wake Wood, settled into the town and adopted its ways. Far more had tried and failed.

So if anybody had told Patrick Daley at the time he qualified that he would end up not only living in Wake Wood, but trapped in the town with no prospect of ever escaping, he would have laughed at them. But that would have been before sheer desperation had led him to reply to Arthur's advertisement.

*Due to ill health of present owner, full and free partnership in thriving rural and farming practice in small west-coast Irish town offered to qualified young veterinary not afraid of hard work. Excellent prospects and remuneration will be given to the right applicant.*

Two years before he'd had a loving wife he adored, a beautiful young daughter, a covetable Georgian town house – complete with original features – and a growing city veterinary practice. In short, everything a man with his qualifications could wish for, except the knowledge that the happiest days of his life were coming to an end and all he'd be left with was a yearning to recapture them.

And now – now he was alone, lonely and adrift in

Wake Wood. But, if everything went according to his carefully laid plans, not for much longer.

A night gale howled around his isolated stone cottage, rattling the doors and windows and hurling the branches of the surrounding trees against the walls. When he'd spoken to Arthur earlier that evening, his partner had warned him to expect wild weather.

Arthur had been right. He shivered as a draught cut across the landing. The living room would have been warm and cosy with its open log fire but he was sitting in the master bedroom, which he deliberately kept cool.

He was sick with apprehension. He'd spent months preparing for the events he'd set in motion. But had he planned for every eventuality? Failure would sentence him to a lifetime of loneliness. But could he – would he – find the courage to do what was necessary when the moment came?

He moved restlessly from his chair and went to the window. If his plan didn't succeed he'd lose everything he cherished except his memories. Memories of his precious loving family . . . his wife Louise . . .

As a young man, he hadn't believed in love at first sight until he'd seen Louise. One glance across the crowded student-union bar of the university during Louise's first week in college had been enough. He'd lost his heart. If she'd asked him to be her slave he would have sacrificed everything he had, including himself, to her without question. To quote one of his closest friends, Louise had 'touched him with the barmy wand'.

Wherever Louise had gone, male heads had turned. But it hadn't been her long blonde hair or stunning slim figure that had captivated Patrick. It had been her dark blue eyes. Every time he'd gazed into them he'd felt as though he were drowning.

The most amazing miracle was that after crawling around campus in her wake for an entire month, she'd suddenly noticed him. They'd moved in together at the beginning of her second term, lived together for the next three years until they both graduated from their respective courses, and married the week after they'd been given their diplomas.

They'd made so many plans. He'd wanted his own veterinary practice in a historical and beautiful old city, Louise her own pharmacy. They both wanted a rambling old house, dogs rather than dog, cats rather than cat, maybe horses – dependent on spare time – but one definite ambition was a large family. At least four children, possibly six.

They'd soon discovered real life meant compromise. The house they'd bought with the maximum mortgage the bank would allow had been beautiful, old and rambling. It had also been in need of expensive renovation that had ruled out any prospect of them taking a holiday for three years. But on the plus side, it had had a yard and outbuildings that Patrick soon had converted into a surgery.

The pharmacy had never materialised. Louise had accepted a position with a high-street chain of chemists – a temporary job while she'd looked for suitable premises to set up her own place. But pregnancy had tempered Louise's ambitions. There'd been no point in starting up a time-consuming business just as she was about to embark on motherhood.

Patrick had set up his practice, worked hard, and by the time their daughter Alice had arrived he'd been making a comfortable living – so comfortable it had enabled Louise to give up work and become a full-time mother, wife and homemaker.

Alice had proved to be the best gift either of them had ever been given, so small, slight and fascinating, yet a combination of them both. She'd inherited his colouring and Louise's beauty. Her skin had been as white as porcelain, her eyes large, dark, questioning, intelligent – just like Louise's but brown, not blue. Her beautiful hair had been long, like strands of silk, but black, not blonde.

Alice, so fragile, so vulnerable – the first of the children they had planned, and, because of Louise's medical problems, their last.

Crippled by an emotional pain that transcended anything physical, Patrick returned to his chair. Oblivious to his surroundings and the temperature, he stared into his open veterinary instrument box.

He picked up a scalpel and ran his thumb along the edge, drawing a thin red line that dripped blood. It didn't even hurt at first. The blade was sharp enough to cut cleanly through soft pink skin. Slice the fat beneath it, sever and divide nerves and tensed, hard muscle . . .

But would he find the will and the strength to wield it? He'd soon find out. The waiting was almost over. He listened to the water flowing in the shower in the bathroom. A soft, steady murmur below the wails of the wind, accompanied by the occasional splash as a body moved beneath the spray.

It had been months since he'd shared the house with someone. Long, desolate months, but if he succeeded he wouldn't be alone again. Not in his lifetime.

Soon the water would be switched off . . . and then . . .

He listened hard with every fibre of his being. Was it his imagination or was there really a tapping? Was someone knocking at his door? He checked his watch. Surely not at this hour. Not straight after the ceremony.

His business partner, Arthur, was his nearest neighbour, and he was miles away. Besides, Arthur had been with him, helping and supporting him throughout the ceremony. Surely now Arthur and all the others would respect his privacy.

The sound appeared to be coming from somewhere above him. Birds on the roof? In this gale? Or a banshee? If it was, now would be the time to look up and discover whether they really were old hags or exquisite young fairies.

He steeled himself, leaned back and stared. A skeletal tree branch was bouncing wildly on the skylight, hitting it intermittently and lightly. So lightly, the sound was reminiscent of a child's fingers drumming against glass – or the wings of a small plastic bird . . .

He almost smiled. A sad ghost of a smile. He didn't need prompting to recall his last moment of pure happiness. That magical early-morning hour of Alice's ninth birthday. Would he – could he – have savoured it more if he'd known what was to come?

He closed his eyes and turned back the days. More excited than Alice, he hadn't even been able to wait for her to wake naturally on her birthday morning. He'd dangled a wind-up bird he'd found in a joke shop from his bedroom window down to hers, a floor below. The bird's wings had beaten against the glass. Tap . . . tapping . . . tap . . . tapping . . . the same light staccato the branch was pounding now against the skylight.

He creased his face against the pain, as Alice's voice – sweet, high-pitched in excitement – echoed in his memory.

'Mum . . . Dad . . .' First her shout, then a thud as her feet had hit the floor when she'd leapt out of bed. A light patter as she'd raced to the window. He and Louise had stayed up until the early hours, blowing up balloons and stringing them and the banner he'd ordered from the signwriter across the garden outside Alice's window.

HAPPY NINTH BIRTHDAY, ALICE.

He hadn't been there, but he'd imagined the look on his daughter's face when she'd seen it for the first time.

When he'd heard Alice racing up to the master bedroom, he'd pulled the bird back in through the window and returned to bed, jumping in and covering himself with the duvet seconds before she'd burst in.

Alice had never moved slowly. She'd only had one speed – headlong – always in a rush as if somehow she'd sensed that time, for her, was in short supply.

She'd dived on to the bed and landed on top of him, her black shoulder-length hair flying behind her, her dark eyes glittering with excitement.

He'd hastily stuffed the bird under his pillow and hugged her, revelling in the feel of her slight body pressed against his. Flesh of his flesh. Her heart beating against his, her skin soft, velvet smooth, he'd caressed her face and run his hands through her fringe, combing it back from her forehead with his fingers.

Overwhelmed by love, he'd held her at arm's length so he could look into her eyes. 'Do you like the banner?'

Alice had kissed his cheek and returned his hug, wrapping her small arms around his chest. 'You and Mum are silly.'

'Really?' He'd feigned indignation.

'I heard you moving around, making noises in the night. What were you and Mum working on so late apart from balloons and "happy birthday" signs?'

'I had a night call. A great big hairy dog sick with a blocked intestine, which is . . .' he'd tickled her stomach through her ruffled turquoise pyjama top, 'exactly here. He was your kind of dog. Big and noisy!'

Alice had giggled. 'I'm not big and I'm not noisy. But I am nine years old from today.' Her smile had been irresistible, disarming. He'd have given her the world if it had been his to give and she knew it. 'So . . .' she'd wheedled.

'It's no use trying to charm me, honey,' he'd teased. 'You know Mum's rule about birthday presents. No gifts to be given or opened until after school.'

Her face had fallen.

'Is that OK?' he'd checked, knowing it wasn't and fighting to keep a straight face.

'It's OK.' She'd shrugged her thin shoulders in resignation.

'So go to your room and get dressed, slowcoach.' He'd rested his arm lightly on the package under the duvet.

She'd left the bed, only to turn back quickly at the door. 'What's that lump under the covers on your bed?' she'd demanded.

'What lump?' He'd tried to sound innocent but Alice had been having none of it.

'This lump.' She'd returned and patted it.

He'd pulled away the duvet to reveal the parcel he'd hidden beneath an enormous bag. She'd trembled, transfixed by excitement.

'Go on, open it.' He'd been as impatient to see her reaction to the surprise he'd prepared for her as she'd been to unwrap her present.

She'd returned to the bed, lifted off the paper cover he'd made, and had revealed a large cage, full of hamster toys and surmounted by a hooped plastic tunnel that could be used as a carrying handle for the cage.

The milk-and-honey-coloured occupant had pushed his nose through the bars and peered curiously up at her.

'Dad, he's gorgeous. Can I take him to school?'

'I don't think that's a good idea.'

'I'll take care of him. He'll be with me the whole time,' she'd wheedled.

'The cage is heavy.'

'Not for me. Please, Dad.' Another bear hug. One that took his breath away.

'I'll think about it.'

Alice had opened the cage, lifted out her present and cradled him gently in the palms of her hands. The tiny creature had looked up at her, whiskers twitching, eyes wide, trusting and unafraid.

'He loves you already.'

'And I love him, Dad.' She'd lifted him high, brushing his fur against her cheek. It had been an image Patrick had cherished. But time had been ticking on.

'You'd better get dressed and go downstairs for breakfast before your mother shouts at both of us.'

She'd returned the hamster to the cage, closed it and looked plaintively at him.

'All right,' he'd relented. 'But carry him carefully.'

'I promise, Dad.' She'd carried the cage out, but not before she'd blown him a 'thank you' kiss from the door.

Tired from his interrupted night, he'd left the bed, gone into the bathroom, cleaned his teeth and showered under scalding water for ten blissful minutes. When he'd heard Louise and Alice's voices in the hall, he'd stopped drying himself, had grabbed his towelling robe and run down the stairs, trailing water on the carpet. Louise had been holding out Alice's jacket, waiting for her to slip her arms into the sleeves.

'That's a beautiful silver chain you're wearing,' he'd complimented archly, knowing just how much effort it had cost Louise to track down a chain similar to one

Alice had admired in a book illustration.

'Isn't it?' Alice had fingered it. 'Mum gave it me. I love it.'

Louise had frowned when Alice had put on her jacket. 'I still don't see why I can't walk you to school.'

'That would be ridiculous,' Alice had dismissed. 'No other nine-year-olds in my class are walked to school by their mothers. Please, stop nagging me, Mum. I'll be fine.'

Louise had turned to him, mutely appealing for help, but he'd known better than to step into a disagreement between mother and daughter.

Conceding she'd lost the argument, Louise had handed Alice her lunch box and opened the front door. 'All right, Alice, you can walk yourself to school, but I warn you: nine-year-olds have an extra sandwich in their lunch. And they have to eat it.'

Alice had picked up her lunch box and the hamster cage and stepped outside. 'I'll never manage it. I'm not any bigger than I was yesterday and neither is my appetite. Bye, Mum. Bye, Dad.'

He'd run back up the stairs, picked up a paper envelope from the dressing table, opened the bedroom window and shouted, 'Hey, birthday girl.'

He'd waited until she'd looked up at him before tearing the envelope open and shaking the contents over her.

The confetti had cascaded down, a shower of glittering multicoloured rain.

And that's how he liked to remember his daughter. Standing outside the house she'd been carried into as a newborn, while glitter floated and sparkled around her like fairy dust.

'Have a great day, honey.'

Beaming, Alice had smiled and waved up at him and then at Louise, before turning and walking down the garden path. Below him, Louise had taken her time to close the front door. He'd suspected that she too had been watching Alice and regretting – just a little – the speed at which their daughter had been growing up.

He'd been lying on the bed when Louise had brought two cups of coffee upstairs. She'd placed them on the bedside cabinet before looking down on him.

'You had a busy night, Patrick. You must be tired.'

He'd reached up and grabbed her arm, pulling her down on top of him. 'Not that tired.'

He had begun to unbutton her shirt. She'd smiled the slow lazy smile he loved.

Coffee forgotten, they'd rolled over on the bed, kissing, stroking, fondling one another, and slowly undressing, taking their pleasure at a leisurely pace, secure in the knowledge that each knew the other's body as intimately as their own.

And that's why he'd never forgiven himself. While he'd been kissing Louise's breasts, thighs and mouth, thinking only of his own and Louise's satisfaction, Alice had stopped outside the massive wooden gates that walled off his surgery and the yard in front of it.

He'd relived the sequence of events so often it had entered his nightmares. Him grabbing his trousers, thrusting them on, zipping them as he ran, charging down the stairs barefoot, out through the door into the yard. Seeing the gate ajar. Rushing in and finding the dog's pen open and the dog worrying and tearing at Alice's bloodied, inert body. Him fighting the dog, pushing the animal aside.

Carrying Alice out of the pen and locking the dog in, so he could deal with it later.

Scooping up and holding what was left of his daughter close to his chest, desperately willing strength and life into her broken body. He hadn't needed to look at Alice's face or into her eyes, or check her vital signs. He'd already known. But his mind had refused to accept the evidence of the images that had rotated in a kaleidoscope of horror around him.

Louise talking at speed into her mobile phone. Blood pouring from Alice's head and facial wounds, soaking his chest, flooding on to the ground. More blood dripping from minor wounds on Alice's hands. One of her shoes lying stained and abandoned in the yard. Such a small, inconsequential thing given the trauma of the moment; but he'd noted it, along with the bite marks and imprint of teeth that marred his daughter's neck, legs and frail body. She'd been plastered in blood and tissue mixed with the dog's saliva.

But worst of all, her throat, torn wide open, her carotid artery severed. Still dripping blood.

Charging out of the yard holding Alice in his arms, heading towards blue flashing lights. The raucous, head-and-ear-splitting din of sirens. He'd run towards them wanting help. His mind still refusing to accept the evidence of his eyes, right up until the moment cool, dry, capable, latex-gloved hands tried to wrest Alice from him.

He'd refused to hand his daughter over. Curling his body around hers, he'd knelt on the pavement, hugging her, keeping her close, willing her to be alive again.

Because he hadn't been able to bear the thought of losing her.

Not to anyone. Not even to Louise, who'd crouched beside him, her tears falling on his arm, diluting Alice's blood.

That morning had marked the beginning of his nightmare. He'd relived it every second of every day since. And now – *now* – he wanted it to end.

But was he brave enough to finish what he'd begun?

# Three

After Alice's death, Patrick felt as though he'd entered a surreal, grey-tinged world where nothing was real and nothing mattered. What was the point of eating . . . speaking . . . moving . . . sleeping . . . breathing . . . when everything and everyone, even those he loved the most, would disappear into the black void of death?

No longer capable of feeling anything except the all-consuming pain of Alice's loss, he and Louise remained side by side purely from habit. Together, yet separate, rarely communicating unless necessity forced them to, they drifted through bleak days and nights where everyone wore sad expressions and spoke in hushed tones.

All he and, he sensed, Louise wanted was to be left alone to grieve and remember, yet they were forced to make decisions.

Alice had gone from their lives for ever, but her remains had to be dealt with. What kind of funeral did they want? Did he and Louise want a grave? Or cremation and scattered ashes? A private or public affair? Open to all comers or invitation only?

Unable to bear the thought of destroying what little they had left of their daughter, Patrick decided on a grave. If Louise wanted to cremate Alice's body she didn't voice her opinion. He hoped his decision would end the need for conversation, as well as give him and Louise a physical place where they could mourn Alice. But there were more questions, so many more.

Did they want floral tributes or donations in Alice's memory that could be used to create a more lasting and charitable memorial? The service – humanist or religious? And if religious, which denomination? Then there were hymns and music to be chosen. And even when the service had been decided there was the grave itself – did they want to mark it with a monumental sculpture or simple headstone?

The smallest of steps involved making a choice. Patrick began answering 'yes' or 'no' without listening to the questions, simply because he didn't want to have to think or utter another word.

The funeral director was professional and sympathetic; family and friends supportive. But Patrick didn't want professional advice, sympathy or support. All he wanted was Alice, beautiful, alive and well again, as she'd been on the morning of her ninth birthday, before she'd left the house. But that was the one thing he couldn't have.

And still everything in his life – and, he suspected, Louise's – revolved around Alice. Even the marble angel they picked out to mark Alice's grave had been chosen because it resembled their daughter.

Although he wished he could be buried alongside Alice, Patrick survived his daughter's funeral. Afterwards, he recollected it only as a series of disconnected images, most of them hazy.

Alice lying pale and still in the white wood coffin they had chosen, covered by a pristine white silk and lace shroud; the worst of her injuries concealed by the undertaker's make-up that had transformed her lively, beautiful face into a grotesque mask.

Louise signing the pink card she attached to the heart-shaped floral tribute of pink and white rosebuds they placed on Alice's coffin.

*To our darling Alice, all our love now and ever. Mum and Dad.*

Riding in the back of the mourners' car, following the hearse that carried Alice's coffin to the church and later the cemetery. Shaking the hands of the seemingly endless stream of people who attended her funeral. Standing around in the hotel room where a buffet was served afterwards, making small talk to friends and relations, unable to meet Louise's eye for fear of breaking down.

Worst of all, returning home to a house so empty it echoed. Every room he walked into held heartbreaking reminders of Alice. The book of children's poetry carelessly discarded on the sofa where she'd last read it. Her coat still hanging on the rack in the hall. Her shoes on 'her' shelf in the cupboard under the stairs. Her toothbrush in the lion mug on the bathroom windowsill. And when he went to the window to look out at the garden, the sight of a football on the lawn, abandoned after their last game together, brought tears to his eyes.

Louise hadn't touched Alice's bedroom since that last morning. Her pyjamas lay where she'd thrown them on to her unmade bed. Her pillow still bore the imprint of her head. Her shelves were filled with her toys and the hamster in its cage.

Patrick took to waking in the early hours, mouth dry, heart thundering, blood coursing around his veins; believing he was lost in a nightmare. But one look at Louise's face, tear-stained even in sleep, was enough to return him to cold reality. He began to make what soon became nightly trips to Alice's room.

Their daughter was gone – for ever. He would never see her again, but there at least he could sit . . . and remember.

Practicalities dictated that life must go on. He and Louise needed a roof over their heads, food on the table, petrol for their cars; his surgery expenses had to be met. The mortgage and bills must be paid, which meant he had to work. Sick animals needed to be doctored, their pain assuaged.

Patrick returned to work a week after Alice's funeral and discovered that life was a little more bearable when he was occupied, although Alice was always in his thoughts. He saw her image wherever he went. He couldn't escape her. Nor did he want to.

It was different for Louise. She had given up work – and gladly – after Alice's birth, and now she wouldn't countenance his suggestion that she look for a temporary position to fill the void in her life. Without Alice to care for, she sank into a depression that culminated in indifference to her surroundings and to Patrick. Within a month, she retreated to a place where he could no longer reach her.

When one evening he returned from his surgery to the house – he hadn't been able to think of it as 'home' since Alice's death – three months after they'd buried Alice, to find the place cold and in darkness yet again, his breakfast dishes unwashed in the kitchen sink, and no sign of another breakfast or lunch having been eaten or an evening meal prepared, he went in search of Louise.

He knew where he'd find her. Since their return from Alice's funeral she'd haunted their daughter's bedroom by day, just as he haunted it by night. He left the landing light on and walked into the gloom. Louise was curled on the floor, her head resting on Alice's pillows, surrounded by Alice's toys, her arms wrapped tightly around Alice's pyjamas. The turquoise pyjamas he knew Louise hadn't washed since Alice had worn them last.

He braced himself for an argument. For the first time in his married life he'd made a life-changing decision without consulting Louise. But he'd done it to protect his own sanity as much as hers.

'We have to move out of this house and away from here, Louise,' he began forcefully.

'No!' Louise's face was streaked with tears he knew she was unaware of shedding. 'Here, I'm close to Alice—'

'No, you're not.' He felt a brute for interrupting and contradicting her. 'Alice isn't here. She'll never be here again,' he added savagely. 'All that's here is a museum

– a shrine you've made of her belongings. Clothes she'll never wear again. Toys she'll never play with. You're treating them as if they're relics. And that's not healthy.' He knelt beside Louise and cupped her face in his hands, forcing her to look at him. 'Don't you see, Louise? We have to leave this house and this city. Make a fresh start where no one knows us, or remembers Alice or what happened to her . . . to us.'

'No.' She silently mouthed the word.

'If we stay here we'll both go mad,' he prophesied.

She shook her head. He knew she didn't want to think about leaving the house, much less listen to the plans he'd made. But he persevered.

'I applied for a job, helping a disabled veterinary in a small country town, Wake Wood. I went there today for an interview and had a good look round. It's a pretty place,' he elaborated. 'Surrounded by woods and fields. It'll be a different kind of work from what I've been doing here. A challenge, treating more farm animals than pampered pets. There's a pharmacy in the town. It's been closed for a while because they had no one qualified to take it over. We could take a lease on the shop. Buy it, even. You could work again . . .'

'I can't leave this house. I can't, so please don't ask me to.' It was the longest sentence she'd spoken since Alice's death.

'I've been offered the job and I've already given my word that I'll take it,' he said flatly.

'You're leaving?' Her eyes were dark, bruised with misery.

'We're leaving, Louise. Together. I start in a month.'

'How could you . . . ?' She started crying. Silent tears that brought the realisation that he could feel something besides the pain of Alice's loss after all.

'I had no choice, Louise. This house and its memories are killing both of us.'

'But this house . . . your surgery . . .'

'I talked to an estate agent when I came back this afternoon,' he cut in impatiently. 'He's had an enquiry from a veterinary looking to set up here. If we sell this house and my surgery we'll raise enough to buy a cottage I saw in Wake Wood and the freehold of the pharmacy. Prices are lower there than here. You'll love the cottage, Louise. It's everything we dreamed of when we were in university. It's old, big enough to be called rambling, with ten rooms, nooks, crannies, and the original fireplaces. It has a huge garden, outbuildings, and it's surrounded by trees—'

'No.' She was vehement.

'Louise.' He continued to hold her head.

'No.' Her voice dropped to an almost inaudible whisper.

'If we don't move out of here we'll both go crazy.'

'Alice—'

'Alice will always be in our hearts and our memories,' he broke in. 'Nothing can change that.'

'We'll know no one in this town.'

'It's called Wake Wood,' he reminded her. 'And that's the attraction of the place. We'll make new friends. You'll like Arthur, my new partner. He introduced me to some of the locals. They're kind, helpful without being intrusive. Slightly reserved, the way most country people are.' Patrick wished he could believe that a move would dispel the numbing emptiness that had become their lives. But whether the move would culminate in success or failure was immaterial. He'd made the decision because he could no longer allow the past to outweigh the present and destroy what was left of their marriage.

Louise's voice was filled with pain and anguish. 'You really want us to move?'

'Yes.'

'To live in this Wake Wood,' she echoed despondently.

'Yes,' he affirmed, feigning a resolution he couldn't feel. 'Yes, Louise, I do. And it's time we started packing.'

Less than four weeks later they were ready to drive away from the house they had lived in all their married life. Patrick had spent most of his time during the preceding week nagging the estate agent and solicitor to expedite the sale of their property and the purchase of the cottage and pharmacy in Wake Wood.

Men from the removal firm had carried out the bulk of their furniture that morning and it was on its way to Wake Wood in a van. The back of Patrick's estate car was piled high with personal possessions neither he nor Louise could bear to entrust to strangers.

Patrick had been ready to leave for over an hour, but Louise was still busy. Careful to keep her back turned to him, she was stowing black bags behind the front seats of the car. Her body language told him that she resented him watching her.

He stepped into the hall and looked around. Stripped of his and Louise's possessions – and Alice's – the house appeared bleak and forlorn. He found it difficult to believe that they'd ever been happy within its walls . . . until he remembered Alice. He pictured her running down the stairs, calling out to him, laughing as she raced into the kitchen to thrust open the fridge door . . .

The vision was so real, so powerful; he backed out of the front door, slammed it shut and posted the keys through the letter box. He'd already given their other two sets to the estate agent.

Louise was sitting waiting for him in the passenger seat of the estate. He climbed into the driver's seat before turning the ignition and glancing across at her. She was staring directly ahead at the windscreen, sunk into the silent indifference that was now normal for her. He knew that despite his insistence that they start again without any mementoes of Alice, she'd smuggled most of Alice's possessions into the bags she'd loaded in the car.

She may have kept them, but he was determined not to give her an opportunity to unpack them. They would remain in the sacks. And one day – soon – he would carry the bags away where Louise would never find them again. Somewhere far from the new cottage and their new lives.

'All right?' he asked.

Louise nodded a reply.

A nod was better than nothing. He set off and concentrated on the road, trying not to think about anything in particular. Once or twice he was tempted to comment on the scenery but, anticipating Louise's lack of response, he kept his thoughts to himself.

Three hours later he negotiated a bend just beyond a narrow bridge. A large sign loomed on his right.

WELCOME TO WAKE WOOD.

He glanced instinctively in the rear-view mirror, forgetting that the car was packed so high the back window was blocked.

'The town centre's just ahead of us.'

If Louise heard him she gave no sign of it.

He slowed the car's speed. The field behind the sign sloped upwards to a thicket of close-growing dark woods. In the centre below the line of the trees, the one concession Wake Wood had made to modernity dominated the scenery: a wind farm with its massive turbines. The blades turned slowly and noisily, their din and appearance perversely at odds with what should have been a tranquil scene.

'Not much electricity being generated there,' he observed. He continued straight and entered the main street of the town.

The pharmacy was halfway down the commercial centre on the right-hand side. Its windows and door were boarded up and, judging from the water stains on the wood, had been for some time. He stopped the estate momentarily outside the building. The 'A' in the word PHARMACY over the door had come adrift and hung at a precarious angle.

Louise studied the building through the car window.

'It will need some work inside as well as out. Arthur

– my new partner – gave me the name of a firm of shopfitters who come highly recommended. I've made an appointment for us to meet them here tomorrow.'

'Tomorrow? I need time . . .'

'And you'll have it,' he assured her. 'It will take them at least a month to complete the refit. It will take us a couple of weeks to set up accounts with the suppliers and get stock delivered.'

Another nod.

He'd made progress. There had been times during the past month when Patrick had begun to wonder if he would ever get Louise to Wake Wood. Perhaps she'd be more enthusiastic once she actually met the fitters.

He checked the wing mirrors. The street yawned behind the car as empty as it was before them. Rain was falling, a light drizzle that had coated the windscreen with a fine mist. He pulled out again, driving past deserted pavements devoid of human or even animal life. The few shops that weren't boarded up displayed 'CLOSED' signs in their windows. No blinds or curtains twitched.

The only movement was the wings of the crows flocking around a television aerial. He loved animals but he'd never liked crows, regarding them as ugly, ragged birds. Scavengers of the worst kind.

'A murder of crows.'

'What?' He slowed the car and looked at Louise in amazement, wondering if he'd heard her correctly.

'A murder of crows,' she repeated. 'You know the old sayings. A storytelling of rooks, an unkindness of ravens, a tiding of magpies . . . A murder of crows.'

'If I ever knew them, I'd forgotten.' He was beset by a feeling of foreboding, but when he tried to quantify it, he couldn't. It had to be down to the ugly black birds, grey dismal weather and Louise's depression – nothing more. After all, what horrors could their future hold compared with those of their past?

Anxious to get Louise to their cottage, he drove on.

Their new home was in a beautiful spot, isolated but within easy driving distance of the town. The outside had been painted green; the garden was natural, laid to grass and surrounded by trees, the only sign of cultivation the recently mown lawns. Louise had seen it just once but she'd expressed no opinion on the place one way or the other.

Patrick had told her he'd bought it before he'd actually signed the papers to make it theirs. A small white lie. When she hadn't objected to the purported purchase he'd gone ahead and closed the deal. Like the shop, he hoped she'd develop enthusiasm once they moved in.

He handed Louise the keys to the house, left the car and went to inspect the garage and outbuildings he'd earmarked to convert into his surgery. When he looked back Louise had unlocked the front door. She was standing on the step, peering inside.

Their new beginning?

He turned back to the garage. Was it too much to wish for peace – of sorts – after the tragic loss of their only child?

Happiness was out of the question. A desire for peace was all he and Louise had left, and he clung to it with all the hope he could muster.

# Four

L ouise stood in front of the pharmacy window, staring at the rain streaking down the glass. It was relentless, the street as grey, dismal and deserted as when she and Patrick had driven into Wake Wood for the first time. They had been living in the town for nine bleak, sterile months and every day had dragged for her, interminable and never-ending.

She glanced around the shop: neat, clean, well stocked, the perfect small-town pharmacy. The locals had complimented them, commenting that she and Patrick had accomplished miracles in a short time. But the locals were wrong. She hadn't achieved anything; nor had she wanted to. It had been, and was still, a struggle to get out of bed in the mornings; to dress, to eat, to make any movement no matter how small, even to shower. If there'd been any miracles they were the result of Patrick's efforts, not hers. And he hadn't performed the only miracle she wanted.

She knew what he would say if she voiced her thoughts: 'No matter what the topic of conversation, Louise, you always return to Alice. As if I could forget our daughter any more than you can.'

Never a direct reproach, but she saw hints, whether

or not Patrick intended them, that she wasn't making the effort needed to adapt to their new life – that she preferred to live in the past, which she had to admit was true. As if she somehow blamed him for Alice's death, because if he'd been a baker or an engineer instead of a veterinary there wouldn't have been a sick, vicious dog in their yard.

She thrust her hands into the pockets of her white lab coat, turned and surveyed what Patrick had made her domain. The shopfitters had done a good professional job of clearing out the old-fashioned dark wood counters, flooring and shelving and installing bright, new pale beech and chrome fittings.

Patrick was determined to immerse himself in the life of Wake Wood. By asking around, he'd found cleaners for the pharmacy and their cottage and thrown himself into the veterinary practice he'd joined as a junior partner. But she couldn't help feeling that her husband was role-playing. Acting in a production that would soon end, although she couldn't have said how it would finish or even why it should. And when it did, they could return to . . .

What? Not their old house and old life, because another vet had moved into the house that had been theirs and set up practice in what had been Patrick's surgery. Normality? This was their new normality, or so Patrick continually told her. Their life from now on would be lived out in Wake Wood. But if that was the case, why did she feel as though she were merely marking time, waiting for something momentous to happen? Something huge, life-changing.

She crossed her arms tightly across her chest and hugged her secret close. Patrick was unaware of the black bags she'd secreted away from his prying eyes behind the door in the spare bedroom. He thought the room was empty, and at first glance it looked that way, although it held everything she'd brought from Alice's room at home.

*Home.*

That one word conjured so many images from the past – the only place Louise wanted to live. Alice kneeling on a chair, painting pictures on the kitchen table. Alice, her back turned to the hearth, reading a book by firelight in their living room. Alice hitting tennis balls against the side of the house. Alice running ahead of Louise as she walked her home from school, so that she could call into Patrick's surgery and see the animals he was doctoring. Alice curled in her bed last thing at night, listening to a story Louise was telling her.

Soon – very soon – she'd recreate Alice's bedroom in their Wake Wood house. She didn't know why she'd waited so long. Yes . . . she did. Fear of Patrick's disapproval. But once it was done, the only difference would be in the actual walls. Alice's room would become her sanctuary here, just as it had been her refuge and sanctuary before they'd moved.

She continued to stare at the raindrop-streaked window.

Why did it appear that some drops were massing and moving upwards, not downwards?

She heard the bell and the sound of the door opening

and closing behind her, followed by footsteps, but she didn't turn her head. She simply couldn't summon the energy required to communicate with a customer. It was easier to remain where she was, dwelling in the past, concentrating on recalling every tiny detail of Alice's room and how she would duplicate it in the cottage.

'Excuse me?'

Louise finally turned to an elderly woman wearing a brown wool cloche hat that clashed with her khaki mac. She was holding out a box of self-tanning lotion. Louise avoided eye contact but extended her hand to take the box.

The woman spoke with a local accent. 'Is this hypo-allergenic?'

It was a commonplace enquiry that sparked an uncontrollable reaction. Louise dropped the box, tried and failed to stop tears starting into her eyes and rushed to the door. 'Sorry. I . . .'

Abandoning the woman and the shop, she hurried down the street, sensing rather than seeing the faces peering out of the few open businesses as she passed. Curious, unsympathetic faces. The faces of people she still considered strangers after long, weary months in the town.

The room – Alice's room. She had to recreate it. She needed it, needed something to hold on to. Patrick was cruel. He should never have forced her to leave their old house. She'd been close to Alice within its walls because Alice had lived there, and a part of her had remained.

Alice wasn't in Wake Wood because she'd never even visited the place.

Why couldn't Patrick see that mothers and daughters needed one another – and desperately? Death couldn't alter that. She needed Alice and Alice still needed her. Now they were separated more than ever.

The rain had lightened to a drizzle. The farmhouse and outbuildings glistened pewter beyond the sea of muck and mud, criss-crossed by tractor tracks, that covered the farmyard. Patrick was standing in a pen at the far end of the open yard, preparing a cow for a Caesarean. He dipped a wide brush into a bucket of antiseptic and proceeded to scrub the animal's flank.

Arthur, the senior partner of the veterinary practice Patrick had joined, drove into the farmyard, parked his car to the left of the gate in front of a neat stack of black plastic-covered hay bales and turned off the ignition. He picked up his trilby and walking stick from the passenger seat, jammed the hat on to his head and stepped gingerly outside. He limped across the yard, avoiding soiling his shoes in the piles of mucky water that had collected in depressions in the concrete. He wasn't dressed for a farmyard or work, and wasn't carrying overalls or an instrument case.

The two farm workers, brothers, Ben and Tommy, who'd been watching Patrick minister to the cow from the far end of the pen, turned and waved to the visitor.

'Look lively, Patrick. The senior partner's coming to

check you out,' Tommy warned, tongue in cheek. 'He's late, considering how long you've been doing the job for him. But then, better late than never.'

'He's here to show you how it's done, Patrick,' Ben teased.

Arthur shouted, 'Hello there,' as he headed for the pen.

'And how are you doing today, Arthur?' Tommy asked.

'Fine, just fine, thank you, Tommy.' Arthur opened the gate to the pen, slipped inside, shut it and joined the two brothers at the back.

Patrick paused to wipe rain from his forehead with his forearm. 'Afternoon, boss.' He finished scrubbing the cow, picked up the syringe he'd loaded earlier and plunged it into the centre of the area of hide he'd sterilised.

The cow was already heavily anaesthetised, docile and placid. Patrick exchanged the syringe for a scalpel and slowly and carefully began to draw a fine line down the cow's side at right angles from its backbone. The black hide split, revealing layers of white fat separated by a swelling of bright red blood.

The incision Patrick was making widened as pressure was exerted from within the animal. The men watched as the purplish bulge of an amniotic sac extruded slightly through the gap. Blood spurted upwards. Patrick lifted his latex-gloved hand to brush it from his cheek, but all he succeeded in doing was smearing the mess over his forehead. Blinded by another spurt of blood, he looked for a clean spot on his sleeve that he could use to wipe his eyes. It wasn't easy to find one. His overalls were caked with tissue and muck.

'As you well know, I would like to be in there with Patrick,' Arthur expounded to Ben and Tommy, 'but it's my knee. It's not getting any better. That's why I brought in a younger man. And, as you see, I know how to pick one with a fine, steady hand.' Arthur waved his arm towards Patrick as his partner continued to draw the scalpel downwards.

Tommy nodded sagely. 'You found a good one there, Arthur, no mistake. He knows how to doctor beasts.'

Patrick glanced from Ben to Tommy. They were so alike, not just in looks and clothes but also voices – they could have been twins. 'Want to keep your hand in, boss?' he asked Arthur.

Arthur shook his head and smiled. 'Ah! If only I could.'

A phone rang. Arthur reached instinctively into his pocket but it was Patrick's mobile that was ringing. It was a critical moment in the operation. Still caught in the amniotic sac, the calf was visible through the gash in the mother's side. Ben came forward to give Patrick a hand.

'Steady there.' Patrick supported the sac. His phone stopped ringing. He didn't have to check the caller ID. He would phone Louise after he'd stitched up the cow, when the calf was on its feet and he'd made sure that the mother had taken to her offspring.

'You don't miss the blood and muck of the farmyard

then, Arthur?' Tommy grabbed the hip flask Arthur was handing him, unscrewed the top and took a deep pull of brandy.

Arthur shook his head and offered Tommy an open pack of cigarettes.

Patrick stopped Ben from reaching for the calf. 'Not yet, Ben,' he warned. 'Slow and careful does it.' Patrick inserted the scalpel into the gash he'd made in the animal's side and made an incision in the amniotic sac, slicing it through. Blood and fluid spurted out, adding to the film that coated his overalls, the wall behind him and the floor of the pen.

Ben winced and turned his head aside.

'Everything all right there, Patrick?' Tommy called out anxiously.

Patrick didn't answer. Frowning in concentration, he reached inside the incision he'd made in the cow's side. A squelching filled the air as he fought to get a grip on the calf. 'Here we go.' He pulled out the forelegs of the young animal. Slowly at first, then in a gush, the body emerged, squirming and wriggling in a stew of blood, amniotic fluid and afterbirth.

'There,' Arthur said proudly, as if he were the one who'd completed the operation. 'A new life and no harm done to mother or young one. It looks a fine calf too. Well done, Patrick.'

'Yes, well done,' Ben and Tommy echoed.

Patrick set the calf on the floor of the pen and pushed it towards its mother. The cow bent down and licked her offspring. It was a sight that Patrick had seen often but it never failed to thrill him, although he was too preoccupied by thoughts of Louise's telephone call to enjoy it.

He knew that if he'd answered her call there would have been more silence than conversation. Nine months into their new life in Wake Wood and still he was waiting for his wife to start living again. Would she ever? Could she without Alice?

Louise allowed Patrick's phone to ring four times before ending the call. She leaned against a wall and looked up and down the street before remembering she'd left the pharmacy unlocked and with a customer inside.

Retracing her steps, she hurried back. The pharmacy was empty. After a quick check that everything, especially the drugs cabinet and till, hadn't been touched, she closed the shop for the day. She emptied the till and placed the takings and float in her handbag. She went outside, shut the door and took her keys from her pocket.

What did it matter if she closed early? It wasn't as though the pharmacy was ever that busy, even after the doctor's surgery. If anyone wanted something desperately they'd return in the morning.

She inserted her key in the lock but started when she felt a tap on her shoulder. She turned her head to see Mary Brogan standing behind her.

Mary had been one of the first people to introduce herself when Louise and Patrick had moved into Wake Wood. Louise had estimated her neighbour's age as late thirties or early forties, but there was an air of girlish naivety and unworldliness about her. Mary dressed like a latter-day hippy in long flowing skirts, beads and scarves, and today was no exception.

Her waist-length hair was tied back from her face with a broad rust-coloured scarf that matched her dress and home-made tote bag. Her long green home-knitted cardigan was knee-length and far too large for her slim body. Her face was pale and drawn.

'Are you closing?' Mary stated the obvious.

'I was. Did you want something?'

'Yes. I'm sorry, but I was hoping to get something for a headache.'

Louise hesitated, fighting the impulse to walk away and say, 'I'm sorry but I've already locked the till.' But something in Mary's manner made her withdraw the key.

'Come in.' Louise opened the door and they entered the pharmacy together. 'A headache, you say, Miss Brogan. What kind? Stabbing, dull ache . . .' She looked along the shelf of painkillers that could be bought without a prescription.

'Please call me Mary. Don't mind me asking, Mrs Daley, but you're very pale,' Mary observed. 'Are you all right?'

'Yes.' Louise hadn't meant to snap. She took a box down from the shelf and gave it to Mary. 'These are mild but they work for most people.' She stiffened when she saw someone moving behind one of the cosmetic displays. Someone she was sure hadn't been there when she'd closed up minutes before.

A painfully thin, willowy adolescent girl, with long dark hair and a stone-coloured coat worn over a striped sweater and slacks, came into view. She glanced slyly at Louise from beneath her eyelids and murmured, 'Hello.'

'I didn't see anyone else come in.' Louise shivered as the temperature dropped suddenly and dramatically. It was as though someone had opened the door to a freezer and left it open. She looked to Mary in confusion. 'Are you together?'

'This is my niece, Deirdre. Come for a short visit to Wake Wood,' Mary explained.

'Hi there, Deirdre.' Louise forced a smile. She watched Deirdre take an asthma inhaler from her pocket. The girl tried to use it, but it clicked, unmistakeably empty. That didn't deter the girl. She continued to click it again . . . and again . . . and again.

Clearly uncomfortable with her niece's odd behaviour, Mary intervened. 'It looks like you need a refill, Deirdre.'

'May I?' Louise held out her hand to take the inhaler. Deirdre handed it to her with an awkward smile.

'Thank you.' Louise checked it.

Deirdre turned back to the shop and looked around at the walls and shelves crammed with health and beauty products. 'When did you do this place up? It's totally different to what it was. Much nicer and brighter. And so many more things to buy. Nice things, hair grips and cosmetics and scent.'

Louise struggled to keep her equanimity. 'It was finished just recently.'

'Not that recently,' Mary Brogan elaborated. 'It must be nine months or more by now.'

'Something like that.' Louise tried and failed to sound casual. So many months without Alice. So many.

'And in that time, you've worked wonders. Hasn't she, Deirdre?' Mary looked at her niece.

Louise held up Deirdre's inhaler. 'Ventolin, one hundred micrograms. Can I see your prescription, please?'

Mary glanced at Deirdre. Louise wondered if she'd actually seen or imagined guilty looks being exchanged.

Embarrassed, Mary began to rummage in her bag. 'I might have it in here. I always hang on to everything. It needs a good sort-out.' She lifted out a hairbrush, a purse and a pair of gloves.

Louise continued to watch Deirdre, then, realising she was staring, made an effort to be pleasant. 'So . . . how long are you visiting your aunt here in Wake Wood, Deirdre?'

Deirdre didn't answer, just continued to look around the shop. The young girl seemed odd, dislocated from her surroundings in some way, and Louise wondered if she had a problem communicating with people.

Mary finally extracted a prescription from her handbag. 'What a relief,' she said loudly. 'Here it is.'

Louise took the crumpled slip of paper from Mary. 'There's a Wake Wood address on this.'

'Mine,' Mary explained. 'The doctor wrote it out the last time Deirdre stayed with me.'

Louise read it and handed it back. 'It expired last year. Have you another?'

Mary looked at Deirdre and shook her head. 'No. But she needs the inhaler.'

'I can phone the doctor—'

'No,' Mary interrupted swiftly. 'No. Don't do that. There's no need to bother him. We'll manage somehow. Deirdre, time to go.'

The young girl went to the door. Headache forgotten, Mary dropped the packet of pills Louise had given her back on to the counter. They left the shop and walked quickly down the road, Mary's long skirt billowing in the breeze behind her. Two slender figures from another era.

Louise slipped her hand inside the collar of her polo-necked sweater. The shop suddenly seemed uncomfortably warm and stuffy.

# Five

Patrick had scheduled the cow's Caesarean for what he'd hoped would be the end of his working day, but he'd reckoned without a cat that had had its ear torn in a fight with a fox, and a horse with colic. He didn't finish until night had fallen, dark, misty and water-logged. The windscreen wipers on his estate could barely cope with the downpour and he found himself peering through a dense grey fog that obscured the trees as he headed up the lane that led to the cottage.

His blood ran cold when he saw the house in darkness apart from a single light that burned low in the master bedroom. He hadn't returned Louise's call. He could have if he'd wanted to. It would have been a simple matter to make time between doctoring the cat and the horse. But he just hadn't wanted to engage in another telephone call with his wife littered with strained silences.

He parked the car, lifted his instrument case from the passenger seat, turned up his collar and ran to the front door. Unlocking it, he dropped his case, switched on the landing light and climbed the stairs. The door to the spare room was ajar.

He stepped inside but didn't turn on the lamp. The

landing light illuminated all he wanted to see. They'd left the room bare when they'd moved in. Bare, that is, apart from the black sacks and red bag Louise had placed behind the door. Neither she nor he had ever mentioned them. Patrick wasn't even sure she was aware that he knew of their existence. The only emotion the bags had engendered in him until now was relief that Louise hadn't unpacked them.

But both the sacks and the bag had gone, and recently. The area where they'd been stacked the last time he'd looked was the only part of the floor free from dust balls.

He closed the door, crossed the landing and walked into the bedroom they shared. Louise had emptied the sacks and bag on the carpet beside their bed. She lay in a muddle of Alice's belongings, clutching Alice's towelling bathrobe to her chest, surrounded by their daughter's clothes and toys. The clothes even smelled of Alice. A mixture of lightly perfumed floral soap and talcum powder, a scent he associated with youth and innocence.

Louise's eyes were wide open, focused on the photograph of their daughter she kept on her dressing table.

'Hey.' He stooped down beside her and gently touched her shoulder. 'Are you all right?'

She shrank away from him, moving back against the wall. Still clutching the bathrobe, she continued to look at the photograph.

Patrick rose and hesitated, but only for a moment. Squaring his shoulders, he turned his back to her and began to gather up Alice's things. One by one he dropped them into the red bag, and when that was full he dumped it outside their bedroom door. He returned and continued to collect Alice's belongings, tossing them indiscriminately into one of the black sacks.

Louise stiffened. 'What are you doing?'

There was so much anguish in her cry that he found it difficult to ignore her but he carried on gathering and bagging Alice's possessions. 'I know what I'm doing and so do you,' he answered harshly. 'It's like a black hole in here. We have to let in some light.'

Her voice rose precariously. 'We can't just take Alice's stuff and throw it away.'

'No?' he challenged. He stopped gathering Alice's things and looked down at Louise. 'What I do know is that we can't keep them,' he said determinedly.

'Why can't you understand that I still love her, Patrick?' she pleaded.

'You think I don't?' he cried out angrily.

'You'd forget her if you could,' Louise retorted savagely, deliberately and knowingly hurting him.

Silence reigned in the room, thick, blinding and suffocating, while he reeled from the pain she'd inflicted.

Wishing she could take back her words, knowing she'd never be able to, Louise tried to soften her attack by pleading for understanding. 'I'm sorry, Patrick. I'm not ready . . .' Her voice trailed off and she choked on her tears.

He dropped the soft toy he'd been holding into the bag at his feet.

49

'You really do want to forget her,' she whispered so low he couldn't be sure she'd actually repeated the barbed words.

'You know I can't. And I don't want to. Alice, you . . . were – *are* – everything to me. Louise, please,' he appealed to her. 'What can I do?'

Exhausted, she slumped against the wall. 'Let me go.'

He shook his head, refusing to accept that their marriage was over. 'No. You can have anything you want, Louise, but not that.'

'It's not you, Patrick,' she said wearily. 'And it's not even because of you. I left you when she died. That's what happened. I'm simply not here for you. Not really.'

'We still have one another,' he insisted.

'No, we don't,' she contradicted. 'Without Alice I've got nothing.'

He knelt beside her, wrapped her in his arms and held her close. 'All I want is for you to be OK.'

'Please.' She pushed her hands against his chest, forcing him away from her. 'Drive me to the station. Now, Patrick. Right now.'

He went downstairs, sat at the table and sank his head into his hands. He couldn't bear the thought of Louise leaving, but he didn't know how to stop her. A few minutes later she joined him, coat on, bag packed, handbag slung over her shoulder.

Patrick wondered if she'd made the decision to leave before he'd even reached home. He left the chair and reached into his pocket for his car keys. She followed him to the door and he held out his hand. She gave him her bag.

He stepped outside and stowed her bag in the boot of the car. Louise sat in the passenger seat. One look at the expression on her face killed any thoughts he'd had of trying to persuade her to stay. There really didn't seem to be anything more that he could say that would make her change her mind.

He climbed into the driver's seat and turned the ignition.

Patrick and Louise drove in silence along the road that led out of town. Once they left the houses behind them and entered the unlit roads of the countryside, shadows took on monstrous, terrifying shapes that leapt out in front of the car at every corner. Louise found herself shrinking deeper and deeper into her car seat, desperately trying to make herself as small as she could. She was afraid, but she didn't know of what. The winter trees towered black, skeletal and menacing above the car. In the ditches and hedgerows, numerous twin pin-points of light glowed, as nocturnal animals froze, mesmerised and blinded by their headlights.

Patrick glanced occasionally at Louise but she remained withdrawn, silent, as still as a bronze statue. Eventually the silence became unbearable but he didn't dare look at her as he spoke.

'The people in Wake Wood are nice, friendly. I like them, Louise. Maybe if you gave them more time, made a few friends—'

'They just feel sorry for us,' she interrupted bitterly.

'They probably refer to us as "that couple that suffered such a tragedy, losing their only child to a feral dog".'

'No one in Wake Wood knows about Alice,' Patrick countered.

'Men can be so stupid.' She finally looked across at him. 'Of course they all know.'

He waited for her to continue but she retreated back into silence.

'I can't get the colour of her eyes quite right,' Patrick mused, voicing his thoughts, speaking more to himself than to her. 'I can picture her exactly.' He didn't have to explain who 'her' was. 'Her height, her figure, her hair, her mouth, her ears, her nose. But not her eyes. I can recall the expression in them when she was happy and excited. I can even picture them when she was sad – which wasn't often – but not the colour. It's as if I've lost it.'

'That's funny,' Louise murmured. 'I see the exact shade all the time. It's everywhere.'

'I know you're not trying to be cruel,' Patrick began tentatively.

'I didn't mean what I said, Patrick.'

It wasn't much of an apology, but Patrick grasped it.

'That's OK.' He turned the corner and drove around a sharp bend. When the road straightened he reached for her hand. To his astonishment she didn't pull it away. He squeezed it lightly.

The car engine stuttered and cut. Patrick turned the ignition. The engine didn't fire.

'What's the matter?' Louise asked urgently.

'I don't know.' Patrick coasted the car on to the grass

verge that bordered the road and jammed on the hand brake. He turned the ignition key again and again. The engine was dead. He pulled the lever that released the bonnet catch.

'Have you run out of petrol?' Louise suggested.

'No. The tank's almost full.' He took a torch from the back seat, opened the door to get out. Walking around to the front of the car, he lifted the bonnet and looked down at the engine.

Louise opened her door, pulled her jacket closer to her shivering body and joined him.

'I can't see anything wrong.' Patrick shone the torch downwards. 'But then, you know me and mechanics. I don't know what I'm looking at.'

Louise started nervously and drew closer to him.

'What is it?' He peered into the darkness that shrouded the road.

'Didn't you hear it? Listen – it's there when the wind dies,' she whispered.

They both stood stock still. Then he heard it: a weird, unearthly wail. He too shivered. Icicles of fear crawled down his spine.

She saw him tremble. 'Patrick . . .'

'It's an animal,' he declared, trying but failing to sound casual.

'That's like no animal I've ever heard.' She kept her voice low although she had no idea why. As far as she could see into the darkness, they were completely alone.

'Some can make peculiar sounds,' he declared.

'Like what?'

'None I recognise.' Feeling the need to make a noise

in the hope that it would deter the unseen, unknown creature, he slammed the bonnet shut. 'We're not too far from Arthur's place. We'll walk there and get help. He'll know where we can get hold of a mechanic.' He locked the car. She continued to stand frozen beside it as another ghostly, ghastly wail rent the night air.

Feigning a confidence he was far from feeling, he gripped the torch tightly. It was large, solid and would make a reasonable club in the absence of any other weapon. 'We've no choice but to walk, Louise,' he said firmly. He shone the beam ahead of them and set off.

She followed him along the road and up a bank. He shone the torch around in a circle, taking his bearings. 'There's a short cut here, across the fields.' He pulled down a strand of barbed wire and stepped over it. When he was in the field, he continued to hold the wire down with one hand and helped Louise over it.

Their feet sank into the soft ground. Somewhere up ahead of them they heard the raucous noise of a diesel engine. Patrick stopped and looked around again. The lights of a large machine were moving about in a field at the base of a hill about half a mile away.

'Why would anyone be working at this hour at this time of year?' Louise questioned. 'It's not as though they need to get a harvest in. Not in winter.'

'Beats me.' Patrick eyed an old drystone wall topped with barbed wire. 'We can go around that if you like.'

'It'll take too long.' Louise wasn't certain if it was her imagination or not, but the wails seemed to be drawing closer. She stuck her toe in a crack in the stones and levered herself upwards, although it didn't prove as easy as it looked because the wall crumbled beneath her weight. When Patrick followed her, he sent a shower of earth and rocks tumbling in his wake.

Desperately trying to ignore the cries, they left the wall behind them and walked close to one another through a patch of woodland. As they drew nearer to the field they saw an enormous yellow JCB working, its lights blazing as it filled in a hole in the ground.

'That pit looks enormous. What on earth are they burying?' Louise whispered, her voice barely audible above the noise of the engine.

'Could be dead livestock,' Patrick suggested.

'Diseased, you mean? You haven't mentioned anything.'

'There've been none that I've come across.' Patrick deliberately set a course away from the machine – and the direction the wailing seemed to be coming from. They entered another copse of trees. The centre had been cleared and there was a circle of tall, narrow, pointed standing stones.

'I didn't know there were any ancient monuments around here.'

'I read something about one in a history of the area,' he revealed.

'What did it say?'

'Not much, other than it's impossible to gauge the age of these rings of standing stones. Someone once told me that the Victorians were fond of erecting them, so it could be a sort of folly.' Patrick shone the torchlight on them. Offerings of ornaments on leather thongs had been tied to the top of the stone in the centre of the circle.

'They look like grave markers,' Louise observed.

Patrick had thought the same thing but he'd kept his opinion to himself. Anxious to leave the spot, he walked on swiftly.

He scrambled up a steep hillside and tumbled down the other side, falling into a ditch filled with thorn bushes that tore his clothes and hands. He lay, too stunned for a moment to cry out or move.

'Are you all right?' she called urgently.

Hurt, terrified, as another wail echoed through the darkness, he fought the urge to scream. He had to keep strong for Louise. 'Stay where you are,' he ordered when he sensed her drawing near to the edge of the ditch.

'You need a hand.'

'I need you in one piece, not on top of me. It's lethal down here.' He clambered awkwardly from the ditch only for his feet to sink into a quagmire.

'Patrick . . .'

'We'll be fine,' he assured her. He only wished he could believe his own words. 'Take my hand.' He offered it to Louise, who'd remained perched above the ditch on the hill. 'And tread carefully, the ground here is treacherous.'

He shone the torch ahead of her but before she'd walked a step the light dimmed and flickered out.

'Brilliant!' he exclaimed bitterly. 'That's all we need.' His voice rose high, bordering on hysteria.

'Give it a moment for our eyes to adjust and we'll see a little more clearly.' Louise forced herself to concentrate on the practical.

He did as she suggested. The moment she joined him on the other side of the ditch he moved on, setting a brisk pace.

Night had never held any terrors for him before. But the rumble of the JCB working in the distant field, and, above it, the eerie high-pitched wails, had unnerved him as much as they had Louise. The longer they went on, the more ominous they sounded.

Louise was soon breathless from the effort it took to keep up with Patrick. Her sheepskin coat was sodden with the rain it had absorbed and her boots were even worse, soaking wet and caked with mud that squelched with every step she took. Terrified, shivering, she jumped every time the weird cries pierced the air. There were scurries and scuttles in the undergrowth she imagined to be giant rats – or worse. But apparently oblivious to her fears, Patrick plodded determinedly onwards.

After what seemed like hours of walking, they saw a faint glow shining through the trees ahead.

'That's the outside light to Arthur's house. We're nearly there.' Patrick helped her over another barbed-wire fence and they walked up the tarmacked drive. He stood on the doorstep, lifted the metal knocker and brought it down sharply. The sound resounded, echoing and clanging through the house. He waited a minute before knocking again. When there was still no answer, he stepped back and looked around the garden. 'Arthur has to be here. Look, his car is parked in front of the garage.' He reached for his mobile phone. 'I'll try ringing him.'

Feeling distinctly uneasy, Louise couldn't wait to leave. While Patrick dialled, she said, 'I'll check around the back.'

She walked quickly, head down, around the side of Arthur's old stone house. Just before turning the corner, she heard the sound of people chanting. She ducked low behind a wooden fence.

An enormous giant wooden tripod had been erected behind the house. It stood tall and proud, higher than the roof. Ropes had been tied to the top and a long coffin-shaped cage dangled down in the centre between the struts. Inside the cage was a cigar-shaped object that reminded Louise of a cocoon. But it was large enough to take a full-grown adult.

Behind the tripod a bonfire blazed, illuminating a gathering of a hundred people or more crowded into the yard. Louise recognised most of them as townsfolk from Wake Wood. There were so many present she doubted that anyone had been excluded – except herself and Patrick.

As she watched, Arthur picked up bottles of liquid and poured them over the cigar shape inside the cage. He moved back, took an ember from the bonfire and touched the saturated casing.

Flames flared instantly; rising high, they roared into the air. Buckets were passed down a human chain that ended with Arthur. One by one he emptied them over the cocoon, quenching the flames on the dangling burning artefact.

Clouds of white steam rose, obscuring the faces of the crowd, but not before Louise spotted Mary Brogan.

Although she looked through the throng, she couldn't see anyone who resembled Mary's painfully thin niece Deirdre.

Arthur dropped the last bucket. The cage was lowered and the object inside was lifted out and placed on trestles. Arthur picked up an axe. He swung it two-handed high in the air before bringing it crashing down on the cocoon. Blood spurted out in a fountain, drenching the ground, Arthur and those of the crowd standing closest to him.

Louise shuddered. She stuck her fist in her mouth to stop herself from screaming. The blood – the violence brought back memories. Images that floated never far from the surface of her mind rose in heart-rending agony. Alice's face, white in death . . . her eyes closed . . . her small, slim throat torn out, the ugly gaping wound below her chin dark with blood clots . . .

The crowd chanted in deep, low voices. The music they made pounded with a primitive, sonorous rhythm that entered Louise's bloodstream, keeping time with her heartbeat.

An attractive young blonde woman stepped forward. She held out a white towelling bathrobe. The cocoon broke, shattering from the force of an internal pressure.

A hand emerged, fingers waving. It was red, drenched and dripping with blood. Arthur placed his hands either side of the gap in the object, forcing it wide open. Someone came to help him. A minute later a naked man slid out like a fully grown embryo. There was even an umbilical cord that Arthur sliced through with a flash of steel.

Like his arm, the man's entire body was blood-soaked, as though he'd bathed at an abattoir. Working together, Arthur and the blonde woman helped the man to his feet. The woman wrapped the robe around him tenderly, as if dressing a baby. After wiping his face with a cloth, she kissed him.

The crowd gave a collective sigh before applauding. The man and woman turned and faced the witnesses to the strange ceremony. Arthur stood behind them like a priest – or proud father.

The man who'd emerged from the cocoon drifted away with the blonde woman. Two men tipped buckets of water on to the bonfire, adding to the steam in the atmosphere. Another brought a shovel and scraped the mess of the shell the man had emerged from into a pile.

Sensing she was being watched, Louise scanned the crowd. Then she saw Arthur standing slightly to one side of the others, staring right back at her.

She backed into the shadows. When she couldn't see Arthur any longer she turned and fled. Head down, she charged around the side of Arthur's house and ran right into a soft, pliant, warm body.

Stopped in her tracks, she finally let out the scream that had been building inside her since she'd seen the bloody figure of the man emerge from the shell.

Patrick grabbed her arm. 'Louise, it's me. What's the matter?'

'We have to get out of here.' She fought to free herself. As soon as she succeeded she charged past Patrick. He ran after her.

'Louise!'

She heard him but continued to run.

'Louise!'

She headed for the road. There she'd feel safer than she had in the fields. Cars used the road! People would pass and see her. Strangers who'd help her if she flagged them down and asked them to assist her.

Nothing could happen to her on the road – unless the people she stopped had been in Arthur's yard and seen her watching them.

She continued to run and didn't slow down until their cottage came into view.

Dawn was beginning to break, a pale grey line on the horizon as she headed for the back door.

'Louise, you're behaving as though you're demented. Stop and talk to me, will you?' Patrick gasped breathlessly behind her.

She shrugged his hand from her arm. 'I just want to go to bed.' She opened the back door, entered the kitchen, stripped off her sodden coat, boots and jeans. She left her boots to dry on sheets of newspaper. In sweater and underclothes she stepped into the living room.

Mesmerised, she stood stock still.

Sitting watching her from one of the easy chairs at the side of the fireplace, very much at home and as comfortable as if he owned the place, was Arthur.

# Six

Louise shivered from more than cold as Arthur continued to appraise her coolly. The expression on his face reminded her of the dispassionate way she'd seen farmers eye livestock in auction pens.

Terrified, she called out, 'Patrick.' She'd intended to shout, but she barely managed a croak.

It was Arthur who broke the silence. 'Louise.' He was as relaxed as if he were acknowledging her arrival at a garden party.

Louise sensed Patrick moving into the doorway behind her. His presence gave her the impetus she needed to flee. She charged up the stairs. Heart pounding, legs trembling, she sank down on a stair close to the top, out of Arthur's immediate reach. She crouched over, covering as much of her bare legs as she could with her oversized sweater, all the while fighting the fear that crawled down her spine, icy and paralysing.

Patrick glared at his senior partner. 'Arthur, what on earth are you doing here?' he demanded incredulously.

'I just wanted to make sure everything was all right.' Arthur spoke quietly, conversationally, as if he were an invited guest. 'With both of you,' he added.

'What do you mean? Why shouldn't everything be all

right with us?' Patrick's voice rose as his initial surprise was superseded by anger.

'Well, is it all right with you?' Arthur pressed, looking up to where Louise was ensconced on the stairs in sweater and panties.

'Our car broke down in the middle of nowhere. We walked to your place hoping you'd be able to help us. We couldn't raise you . . . But . . .' Patrick's voice rose in indignation when he realised that he was actually offering Arthur an explanation for their behaviour when Arthur was the one who should be making excuses for his unpardonable rudeness in breaking into their cottage. 'What's this, Arthur? Why have you just let yourself in to hang out in our house?'

Arthur smiled sheepishly. 'Sorry, I shouldn't have. Country habits, I suppose. We're used to unlocked doors and treating our neighbours' homes as our own in Wake Wood. I'd forgotten that you haven't had time to become accustomed to our rustic ways. What did you say happened to your car?'

'I told you, it broke down,' Patrick reiterated irritably.

'And you came to my house looking for help. Well, that would make sense.' Arthur glanced up the stairs at Louise, who was watching him intently.

'It makes sense!' Patrick repeated in bewilderment. 'Sense! Nothing makes sense! What the hell's going on here, Arthur?'

Arthur reached for his cane, levered himself out of the easy chair and rose stiffly to his feet. 'All right, I can see you're upset and my presence isn't helping. I'm going.' He moved slowly and awkwardly to the door, leaning heavily on his stick. Then he paused. 'Have I told you what a fine job you're doing here, running the practice, Patrick? I'm so glad you chose to make your home in Wake Wood. I hope you've found solace here. Both of you.' He glanced up at Louise again.

'We're fine,' Patrick asserted, holding the door open to emphasise that he wanted Arthur gone.

Louise looked down at Arthur. She was still shivering but was incapable of making the effort needed to move.

'You're highly thought of here, Patrick. And Louise's work in the pharmacy is very much appreciated by everyone in the town. The two of you are making a wonderful contribution to the daily life of Wake Wood. We couldn't do without you. I couldn't do without you. I'd hate to see you leave. Anyway . . .' Arthur smiled again; a smile that didn't quite reach his eyes. 'I'm just happy that you're both all right.'

'We're fine,' Patrick stated yet again, snapping in a tone that suggested they were anything but.

Arthur walked past Patrick and looked to Louise. 'How about you, Louise? Everything all right with you?'

Louise finally found the strength she needed to rise. She ran on to the landing and fled into the master bedroom without replying. She slammed the door so hard behind her the entire house shook.

Arthur nodded to Patrick, placed his trilby on his head and left without another word.

Exhausted by the trek through waterlogged fields and his sleepless night, Patrick watched Arthur close the door. He waited until he heard Arthur's car drive off before checking and locking all the windows and doors. Only when he was certain that the house was secure did he walk up the stairs and into the bedroom.

Louise lay, curled into the foetal position under the duvet on their king-size bed. Her eyes were shut but he couldn't be certain whether she was sleeping or not. He whispered her name.

'Louise?'

When she didn't stir, he lowered his voice. 'Stay with me, please. We'll leave together.'

He sank down beside her, lifted his feet up on to the mattress and moved her head on to his shoulder.

Just to be physically close to her was enough for that moment. He'd lost Alice. He simply couldn't bear the thought of losing Louise as well.

When Louise woke, the hands on the clock on the bedside cabinet pointed to ten but the light was pale, greyer, colder and softer than usual. The curtains were open. She looked out through the window and saw snow falling, thick and fast, silvering the leaves and branches of the trees next to the house. She left the bed and walked to the window. The snow was sticking and the lawns around the cottage were already carpeted with white. She listened hard.

The house was in silence and she sensed Patrick had gone. There was a yellow Post-it note in the dent in his pillow where his head had lain. She went to the bed, picked it up and read it.

STILL LOVE YOU.

A tear fell from her eye. He still loved her – despite the loss of Alice, and her withdrawal from him and life – he STILL LOVED HER.

The three words burned into her consciousness with the force of a branding iron. If only she were still capable of feeling enough emotion to love him back.

Patrick stood at the side of the road behind a tow truck that had pulled in close to the front of his car. A mechanic was peering beneath the open bonnet of the estate, his toolbox open on the ground at his side.

'Anything obvious?' Patrick asked impatiently, shivering as snowflakes settled inside the collar of his jacket. They melted rapidly, trickling icy water down his neck and into his sweater and shirt.

'From what I can see, it's nothing that looks too bad.' The mechanic poked around in the depths of the engine.

Patrick moved away from the car. The countryside was quiet, unusually so. It was as if the snow had deadened the small sounds such as rustlings in the undergrowth and birdsong. Even the bleating of sheep in a distant field sounded as though it had been muted.

He looked up the hill towards a copse of trees planted just below the summit. A boy was standing there, watching them from a distance. He was dressed in a denim jacket and beige trousers, summer clothes that were far too thin for winter weather. He was stock still, as though rooted to the spot like the trees around him. He saw Patrick looking back at him and waved, swinging his arm wide, from side to side, as if he were signalling or drawing an arc in the air. His movements were wild, extravagant, reminding Patrick of the wind turbines outside the town's limits.

Patrick returned the boy's wave. Seconds later his car engine roared into life. He turned his head to look at the mechanic. His head was still under the bonnet. When Patrick looked back at the field the boy had gone. Patrick scanned the landscape for any sign of him. There was none. It was as though he'd vanished into thin air. He looked carefully at the copse of trees. They were skeletal – surely he'd see the boy if he'd run to them and was hiding among them.

'There you go, Mr Daley. All sorted.' The mechanic slammed the bonnet shut.

'What was wrong with it?' Patrick asked.

'Beats me. I found nothing obvious.' The mechanic shrugged.

'But the car was completely dead,' Patrick insisted.

'Well, it's alive now and ready to go. You can drive off whenever you want.'

'How much do I owe you?' Patrick asked.

The mechanic picked up his toolkit. 'You've moved into the green cottage, haven't you?'

'Yes,' Patrick confirmed.

'I'll drop the bill off the next time I'm passing.'

'Thank you.' Patrick couldn't help feeling that the mechanic thought he was an idiot. No, worse than an idiot – an incompetent who didn't even have the right to own a car because he couldn't get it restarted once it had stalled.

\*

Louise watched the snow settle over the town from her pharmacy window. It had already cloaked the road and houses, covering the grey stones and roof slates, softening the signs of dereliction in the run-down, boarded-up buildings and transforming Wake Wood into a glittering, sparkling fairy-scape. Inevitably, her thoughts turned to Alice. Her daughter had loved the snow. Not that she'd had many opportunities to see or play in it during her short life. But there had been one winter when Alice had been six years old when she, Patrick and Alice had built a snowman in their garden and thrown snowballs at one another in the yard . . .

A couple appeared in a doorway across the road. There was something familiar about them, yet Louise was sure she hadn't been formally introduced to either one. Both were tall, slim, handsome, fair-haired and each was warmly dressed against the weather, her in a sheepskin jacket, him in a thick coat. They were wearing hats and gloves, with scarves wrapped around the lower part of their faces, covering their mouths.

The woman lifted her head and kissed the man's cheek. The gesture was so tender, so loving, it reminded Louise of the strange scene she'd witnessed in Arthur's yard. It was then that she made the connection. She recognised the tall, slim, fair-haired man as the one who'd emerged from the chrysalis covered in blood. And the woman who was with him as the blonde who'd held out the towelling robe and wrapped him in it.

Louise watched them cross the road and walk away along the pavement. They continued to gaze lovingly, almost hungrily at one another. They had no time or attention to spare for anyone else. It was as though they'd just been reunited after a long separation; if they were even aware of their surroundings they ignored them. They were totally and completely engrossed in one another.

Were they the same couple? Or had she dreamed the entire bizarre episode? Now, in cold clear daylight, she simply couldn't be certain. Any more than she could be sure that the peculiar exchange early that morning between Arthur and Patrick had actually taken place in the cottage.

The bell rang on the shop door. Reluctantly she turned from the window to her shop and her customers. An elderly man was browsing the shelves of patent cough medicines. Two teenage girls were trying the lipstick and eyeshadow testers on the sides of their hands, and a middle-aged woman was examining bath products. The woman saw Louise looking at her, smiled and approached, holding a box.

'This shower attachment . . .' she thrust it at Louise, 'will it work on any bath tap?'

Louise checked the box. 'Only if your bath has twin taps. Does your bath have one tap or two?'

'I think it's one big one,' the woman answered doubtfully. 'Do you know, it's really odd, I use the bath every day and now I can't remember. Perhaps I'd better check before I buy.'

'It might be as well to save you from making a mistake.' The bell on the door rang again. Louise glanced up and saw Deirdre walk in. She smiled at the young girl but Deirdre was so engrossed in looking around and examining the goods on the shelves she didn't even see Louise. As Louise watched, Deirdre wandered over to the rack that held sunglasses. She lifted down a pair and tried them on, studying her reflection in the mirror on the stand. She leaned back, eyeing herself from first one angle then another.

Louise couldn't help imagining an older Alice behaving in the same way as Deirdre and the other two girls in the shop. Trying on fashionable accessories, experimenting with clothes and make-up.

As she watched, Deirdre began to shake uncontrollably. The trembling escalated, becoming a full-scale convulsion.

Louise ran to her, but just before she reached the girl Mary Brogan rushed in and pushed her aside.

'There you are, my pet.' Mary hugged her niece, enveloping her tightly in her arms.

'Should I telephone the doctor?' Louise asked anxiously.

'No. There's no need. She'll be fine.' Flustered, Mary guided Deirdre, who was still shaking, around the back of the sunglasses display and into a quiet area between two sets of shelves. 'Look at me, Deirdre.' Mary held Deirdre close, until the girl focused on her. 'You all right, my pet?' Mary murmured.

Calmer, although still trembling, Deirdre smiled. 'I'm going back today. I'm looking forward to it.'

'I know you are, my pet,' Mary replied soothingly.

'I can't wait.'

'This time that we've had together has gone so quickly.' There was an infinite sadness in Mary's voice that struck a chord with Louise. She recognised the same depth of sorrow that beset her whenever she thought of Alice.

Mary opened her bag and lifted out a strange contraption. Roughly woven from rope and twigs, it resembled a sort of necklace with attached bracelets – or neck and hand shackles. It reminded Louise of the enormous but similar wooden structure at the back of Arthur's house that had been constructed to hold the cage that contained the cocoon-type object. Both were rough, rustic and reminiscent of pagan tribal artefacts.

'Here you go, my pet.' The moment Mary placed the rope-and-twig contraption around Deirdre's neck and hooked her niece's hands into the 'bracelets' the girl stopped shaking.

Stunned, Louise shivered as the hairs on the back of her neck rose.

Mary saw Louise watching her and Deirdre and read fear in her eyes. Embarrassed, she took her purse from her bag, removed a banknote and thrust it at Louise. 'For the sunglasses.'

Louise pulled herself together and checked it. 'I'll get your change.'

'Keep it.'

'I couldn't possibly,' Louise demurred. 'Wait, Mary . . .'

'I'll pick it up later.' Desperate to leave, Mary pushed past Louise and shepherded Deirdre out of the door and down the street.

Louise wanted to follow them but the middle-aged woman who'd been examining the bath attachments accosted her again. 'I think I will take this shower attachment, if you don't mind. If it doesn't fit, I can bring it back, can't I?'

'If you haven't used it and the box is intact, yes, of course.' Louise took the box from her and went to the till.

When she was free to look through the window again, the street was devoid of people. There was no sign of Deirdre, Mary Brogan, or the young couple, only the snow, pristine and glistening in the thin watery sunlight.

The rush of customers was short-lived. By lunchtime the shop was empty. There was no doctor's surgery that day, so Louise decided to take advantage of the lull to tidy the shop. While she was restocking the shelves she was startled by a peculiar noise, accompanied by the steady tramping of feet.

She opened the door.

A procession of townsfolk was heading down the main street towards her. A few people in the front row were rattling sticks in hollow bamboo tubes, those behind simply banging sticks together. There was no musical rhythm to the din they were making and the sound that filled the air was discordant, weird, almost primitive in its intensity.

Wondering what the procession was in aid of, Louise walked towards them. No one in the column of people met her eye or appeared to notice her existence. They looked straight through her as though she was invisible.

Every one of them kept their sights fixed straight

ahead as they continued on their way past Louise, the open door of the pharmacy and the shuttered shops that lined the street. She noticed that all the people, men as well as women, wore black feathers in their lapels or affixed to their clothes or hats.

Mary Brogan was the last but one to pass her. Her niece Deirdre brought up the rear.

Mary alone turned to look at Louise as she passed. She gave Louise a wan smile before walking on.

Deirdre slowed her pace. She was wearing the rope-and-stick contraption Mary had strung around her neck and wrists, and the new sunglasses concealed her eyes. She lifted her hands and lowered the glasses as she drew alongside Louise. For the first time Louise noticed the colour of Deirdre's eyes, a startlingly clear brown.

Louise stared back, noting the braces cemented on to Deirdre's teeth and her childish, undeveloped figure. The girl she had placed in her mid to late teens was clearly younger than she'd first thought. No more than twelve or thirteen years old.

Deirdre smiled, displaying the metalwork on her teeth. Her voice was quiet but it cut through Louise like a knife.

'Alice has a lovely voice.'

Devastated, Louise reeled back into the pharmacy window.

'What did you say?'

Deirdre didn't answer. Simply carried on smiling as she followed the rest of the residents of Wake Wood down the street.

Louise closed her eyes. Images whirled through her mind's eye at breakneck speed.

Alice as she had last seen her in her coffin. Her skin a deathly pale grey – the exact same shade as Deirdre's. Her hair unnaturally black in comparison to her face.

The prescription Mary had handed her for Deirdre's Ventolin. A prescription that bore Mary Brogan's Wake Wood address and was more than a year out of date.

The ceremony in Arthur's yard, culminating in the emergence of a fully grown, fully developed man from a womb-like chrysalis. The umbilical cord Arthur had cut with a blade. The man, naked, covered in blood, just like a newborn baby.

The black feathers attached to the clothes of the people marching in the procession. The strange object Mary had fastened around her niece's neck.

*Alice has a lovely voice.*

Alice had been dead and buried for over a year. How would Deirdre know that Alice had a lovely voice unless she were dead too?

How did Deirdre know Alice's name?

The man walking about Wake Wood with the woman he loved, who so obviously loved him too.

Had he returned from the dead? Had Deirdre?

That simply wasn't possible. The dead were dead. Gone for ever from the living. Never to be seen again.

They didn't walk the streets arm in arm. Gaze lovingly . . . longingly at one another. Was she going insane? Had the loss of Alice finally tipped her into madness?

# Seven

Louise returned to her shop after the procession had disappeared from view. It was empty. She looked at the boxes of stock waiting to be put out on the shelves and returned them to the stockroom. The last thing she was capable of was working.

Not wanting to dwell on the question of whether or not she was going mad, exhausted by speculating as to what had prompted Deirdre's comment about Alice's 'lovely voice', Louise decided to pay Mary Brogan a visit. She knew where Mary lived because her town-centre address had been on the prescription Mary had given her.

The more she considered it, the more she thought it strange that Deirdre's prescription should carry Mary Brogan's address. Surely any mother would ensure that her asthmatic daughter would pack more medication than she needed before visiting a relative.

She closed the pharmacy, locked the door and walked to Mary's home. It was a neat terraced house in a street peppered with dilapidated buildings. Most of the doors were boarded up. Mary's was freshly varnished with a polished lion's-head brass door knocker.

There was no answer to her knock. She checked her

surroundings. The street was empty, which wasn't surprising. The procession had been a large one. She hadn't counted heads but she began to wonder if everyone in the town had joined it and, if so, why.

The more she thought about the noise they'd been making and the almost trance-like state of the participants, the less it made any sense. Was it a religious occasion? An anniversary of some kind? Had something traumatic happened in the history of Wake Wood; if so, why was it being celebrated? Was it somehow connected to the offerings tied to the circle of standing stones she and Patrick had stumbled across on their night trek after the car had broken down the night before? Or the strange happenings she'd witnessed in Arthur's yard?

The more Louise mulled over events, the more unanswerable questions she came up with. She left Mary's door and took refuge from the rain that was now melting the snow, sheltering in the porch of a derelict house a few doors down.

Half a damp, bone-chilling hour later she saw Mary Brogan approaching. She was wheeling a bicycle. Given Mary's long flowing skirts and scarves, the bicycle appeared somewhat incongruous. Two bags of shopping filled with the staples of bread, milk and coffee hung from the handlebars. Louise wondered if Mary was wheeling the bike because she was afraid of her clothes getting caught up in the wheels. If so, why even take the bike to the shops?

It was then that Louise realised she was beginning to look for odd and sinister aspects in all her neighbours' movements. Why shouldn't her neighbours march in an unmusical procession down the main street of Wake Wood if they wanted to? Why shouldn't Mary Brogan take a bicycle with her when she shopped? And why shouldn't Arthur visit them at the cottage early in the morning, especially if he was concerned about them? After all, he was Patrick's business partner. And Patrick's ability to do his job was one of Arthur's legitimate concerns.

Louise waited until Mary unlocked her door. When Mary picked up the bags of shopping Louise rushed down the street, in through the open door and into the tiny hall after her. Mary dropped the bags, spun round and tried to close the door against her. But not to be thwarted, Louise forced her way through. Mary retreated. Grabbing Louise's clothes in a futile attempt to steady herself, she fell backwards on to the stairs.

Louise's phone started to ring as she kicked the door shut behind her. She ignored it and loomed over Mary, pinning her down.

'Tell me my daughter's name!' she demanded.

'I don't know,' Mary protested.

Louise grabbed Mary's arms and held her wrists above her head, fast against the tread of one of the stair risers. 'Tell me my daughter's name,' she repeated earnestly.

'I don't know. Truly,' Mary insisted.

'Tell me!' Louise stared into Mary's eyes.

'I don't know.'

There was an honest sincerity in Mary's voice that Louise found difficult to ignore. 'Her name was Alice,' she informed her coldly. 'Now tell me. How did your niece know that?'

'Your phone is ringing,' Mary said, as though Louise couldn't hear it.

'It's not urgent.'

The phone stopped and Louise stepped back. Seeing Mary cower as if she were about to hit her, Louise felt ashamed. Ashamed of breaking into Mary's house the way she had, but more than that, ashamed of threatening Mary in her own home. What was she doing? What had she become? She leaned back weakly against the front door.

When Mary realised she was free to move, she pushed herself off the stairs, rose to her feet and walked into the living room. To Louise's amazement, Mary beckoned her forward.

After a moment's hesitation, Louise followed Mary into her warm, cosy, old-fashioned living room. The carpet and three-piece suite were worn and shabby but spotlessly clean. A fire blazed behind a brass guard in the hearth and the fire irons shone, highly polished, in the light from the flames.

The wooden mantelpiece was covered with knick-knacks, principally small china animals; the sort of cheap ornaments given away as fairground prizes or bought in bargain-priced novelty shops by children with precious pocket money as gifts for their mothers. In pride of place in the centre was a silver-framed photograph of Deirdre. She was wearing a straw hat and smiling as she leaned on a farm gate. Behind her, horses grazed in a field. Louise wondered if the picture had been taken locally, in Wake Wood.

'Sit down.' Mary offered Louise a chair. When Louise took it, Mary sat opposite her and leaned forward. Silence reigned for a full minute. When Mary finally spoke it was obvious she'd chosen her words with care.

'I understand your pain, Louise, but I worry about you. You're putting yourself in serious danger.'

Louise shook her head. 'I saw something last night. Something strange . . . then Deirdre spoke to me about Alice . . . about her having a lovely voice. Alice adored singing. Her teachers said she was talented . . . she sang all the time . . . loved learning new songs . . .' Louise suddenly remembered her reason for visiting Mary. 'I'm looking for an explanation as to why Deirdre mentioned Alice's voice.'

'Put the light on.'

Louise reached out to the side table next to her and switched on a lamp.

'You've suffered a great tragedy with the loss of your daughter,' Mary sympathised. 'But forget what you've seen and heard here. What goes on in Wake Wood is not for everyone.'

'And what does go on in Wake Wood?' Louise demanded.

'Please,' Mary begged, 'you and Patrick should try to make another baby to love.'

'I can't. There were problems.' Louise bit her lip, fighting back the memory. 'The doctors told me that my first would be my last.'

Mary nodded. 'I know how you feel.'

'No, I don't think you do.' Louise watched Mary turn

her head and gaze longingly at the photograph of Deirdre next to the china dogs and cats on the mantel-piece. Realisation dawned. 'Deirdre's not your niece.' It wasn't a question.

Mary refused to meet Louise's eye.

'So please, tell me what's going on,' Louise persisted. 'I won't leave until you tell me the truth.'

Mary left her chair and knelt in front of Louise. She put her arms around her, and pushed her face very close to Louise's. 'You want your daughter back, don't you?'

Louise's voice was thick, clotted with tears. 'Is that really possible?'

'I can't say because I don't know enough about you or about Alice. And that's the truth, Louise.'

'Can anyone in Wake Wood help us?'

'I don't know.'

Louise felt she had no choice but to accept what Mary had told her. Her phone began to ring again. She took it from her pocket and answered it. Patrick's voice echoed down the line.

'Hey, how are you?'

'Fine,' she lied.

'I was hoping you could come out on a job. I need your help.'

Louise was conscious of Mary watching her. 'I can't right now, I'm busy,' she demurred.

'I wouldn't have asked if I could manage without you,' Patrick pressed.

Mary left her chair and went into the hall. She picked up her shopping bags and carried them through to the kitchen, where she began opening cupboard doors and putting away the food she'd bought.

Louise could hear Patrick breathing on the other end of the line, obviously waiting for her to say more. 'You really need me?'

'I do,' Patrick insisted.

'All right, if you really need me, I will,' she agreed reluctantly.

'Thanks. Pick you up outside the pharmacy in ten minutes?' he suggested.

'I'll be there.'

Louise walked into the hall. She watched Mary moving around the kitchen, but although she was certain that Mary was aware of her presence, Mary didn't turn around.

Louise left by the front door. Closing it quietly behind her, she thrust her hands into the pockets of her white coat and walked up the street towards the centre of Wake Wood and the pharmacy.

Patrick pulled his car into the parking bay in front of the shop when he saw Louise watching him from the open doorway. He waited while she locked the door and pulled down the shutters. She pocketed her keys, climbed into the passenger seat and glanced across at him. He nodded to her and drove on, heading straight out of town.

A mile after leaving the last of the houses behind them, Patrick turned left. He bumped along an unmade track for half a mile before reaching a farmhouse that sported a home-made wooden plaque on its front wall.

*O'Shea Farm* had been burned into the wood with a hot poker.

Behind the house was a farmyard hemmed in on all four sides, apart from a narrow access, by a barn and outbuildings. Patrick parked the car to the side of the house, climbed out and opened the back door to get his veterinary instrument case. Louise followed him. A loud bellowing was coming from a building to their right. She followed Patrick inside.

A tough-looking weather-beaten man who could have been any age between forty and sixty was leading a bull out of the bull house towards a pen. The bull was skittish, nervous, snorting and fighting the man's best efforts every step of the way.

'Mick, I'm here,' Patrick announced with a wave of his arm.

'Thanks for coming out at such short notice, Patrick. Much appreciated.' The farmer shouted to a younger version of himself, 'Martin, get the gate open. Sooner we get this devil penned up the safer we'll all be.'

Martin, a square-built, thick-necked young man in his mid-twenties, swung open the iron gate to the pen. Patrick and Louise stood back while the farmer and his son attempted to coax the bellowing animal forward.

'He's creating this fuss because his temperature's shot way up, Patrick. Can you sort him?'

'I can try. But get him into the pen first.' Patrick set his case on the ground, opened it and reached for a syringe.

Mick and Martin O'Shea manoeuvred the bull into the long narrow pen of metal bars the local farmers called a 'cattle crush'. But the bull wasn't happy. It bumped from side to side, holding its ground, refusing to go forward even when Mick and Martin hit its flanks.

'Normally he's as easy to manage as a kitten but he has a bitch of a fever.' Mick was clearly worried and Patrick knew with good reason. A bull like the one he was about to examine could be worth as much as, if not more than, the entire acreage of a hill farm like the O'Sheas'.

'We'll hose him down to cool him off,' Patrick said, 'but first I'll give him a shot to calm him. Louise, can you prep two fifty mils of Tilmicosin? And maybe an anti-inflammatory as well.'

Louise picked up the syringe Patrick had left on top of the instruments in his case. She checked the drug bottles, picked out two and inserted the needle into the casing of the first, drawing up the liquid it held slowly and steadily. When it was empty she reached for the second.

'Move him up into the crush and get the head yoke on so we can hold him firm.' Patrick had to shout to make himself heard above the noise the bull was making.

Mick slammed a stick on the bull's flanks but the creature continued to stand rigid, stiff and obstinate. 'Get up, you,' Mick yelled to no effect. The bull didn't move an inch. Mick looked sideways at Louise. 'Doesn't like her,' he muttered to his son Martin.

Patrick overheard the remark but chose to ignore it. He examined the blood-encrusted bull's muzzle. 'Where's his ring, Mick? Martin?' he shouted.

'Broke it this morning,' Mick revealed. 'Don't know

how. When I saw to him first thing it was lying in pieces in his pen.'

'Come on, hurry up, move him up to that halter,' Patrick ordered.

Mick swung his stick again and Martin reached into the crush to get hold of the bull's massive neck. The animal swung his head, catching Martin's hand sideways and thrusting it tightly and painfully against the metal bar of the pen.

'Watch out, Martin!' Mick shouted too late.

Martin screamed and doubled over in pain. When he managed to extricate his hand it was dripping blood.

The bull continued to low and bang against the bars.

Louise ran to Martin. 'Let me see to that.'

'Quiet, woman!' Mick yelled in irritation as the bull carried on bellowing and kicking. Instead of heading to the top end of the crush where Martin and Mick had been leading it, the beast backed up and started banging the bars, moving from side to side without walking forward.

Mick hit out with his stick and shouted again to no avail. Patrick took the syringe Louise had handed him before she began examining Martin's hand.

'Keep him there, Mick,' Patrick ordered. 'I'll try and sedate him where he is.'

Louise drew Martin aside, away from the pen. 'Where's the nearest water? We'd better disinfect this.'

Patrick leaned in through the bars, pressed the bull's neck and deftly inserted the hypodermic into a vein.

'I'm all right,' Martin protested groggily, going into shock.

'When was your last tetanus shot?' Louise asked Martin, as much to keep him talking as to find out.

'Dad, have I had a tetanus shot?' Martin called out.

At the sound of Martin's voice, the bull lunged forward. Patrick lost control of the syringe and it fell from the bull's flank and hit the floor.

Patrick cried out to Mick, 'This is no good. We have to get him up to the restraint and hold him fast.'

Mick hit the bull again without provoking a reaction from the animal.

'I've had enough of this stupid beast.' Mick climbed the bars of the crush.

'Mick, that's a bad idea,' Patrick called out in alarm, when Mick swung his leg over the side of the crush and prepared to jump down into the pen with the animal.

'Don't go upsetting yourself, Patrick. This is my beast and I know what I'm doing.' Mick swung down into the narrow crush behind the bull and continued to hit the animal's hindquarters in an attempt to move him forward.

'Come out, Mick,' Patrick urged when it was plain that the farmer was having no effect whatsoever on the bull.

Mick ignored Patrick and continued to urge the bull forward.

Patrick turned to Martin. 'Can you get his head collar, now, right away, before you sort your hand?'

Martin ran back towards the bull pen. Alarmed by the wild-eyed, snorting beast that appeared to be staring at her, Louise stepped further back from the crush. She retreated too far and crashed into a stone wall.

The bull continued to stare at her through red-veined and -rimmed glittering eyes.

'Patrick . . .' Louise froze in terror as the bull backed up and reversed down the crush on to Mick.

The animal's massive hindquarters slammed Mick's body against the gate at the far end of the crush. There was a loud and sickening crunch of bone hitting metal as the gate bit into Mick's spine, ribs and pelvis.

Mick screamed. An agonising sound that resounded through the barn.

Galvanised, Louise ran to the bars and joined Patrick in beating the bull over and under the bars, trying to force the beast forward and off Mick.

The bull was still bellowing but the only sound Louise and Patrick could hear was the splintering, crunching and cracking of Mick's bones breaking and shattering. His face turned purple. He gasped for air.

'Go on, move up!' Patrick roared at the bull.

Martin returned with the head collar. 'No . . . Dad . . .' He saw his father pinned against the top gate of the crush and pulled ineffectually at the bull's neck.

Crushed tight against the bars that were biting into his back and legs, Mick whispered to Patrick, 'Get him off me.'

Patrick and Martin banged at the latch on the gate. But it held firm, solid under the pressure the bull was exerting through Mick.

'There's too much weight.' Patrick moved up to the bull's head. He took a line from the side of the pen, looped it around the bull's head and tried to pull the animal forward with all the strength he could muster.

The creature ignored him and continued to stand firm. Patrick screamed at Louise, 'Open the front gate.'

Louise ran forward and opened the gate before darting back close to Patrick. If the animal should take it into his head to run out, there'd be nothing to stop it from charging at any one of them.

The bull still didn't move. She watched in horror as Mick choked and coughed up blood. It ran from his mouth down his chin, dripping on to his chest.

Martin hit the bull again and again, his blows having no more effect than if they'd been flies landing on the beast's back.

Without warning, the bull lurched forward, almost knocking Patrick down. He lost the line he'd looped around the bull's upper lip. Mick slid off the gate on to the floor of the crush pen. His jacket was soaked in blood. He lay face up, half propped on the gate, glued to it by his own blood.

The bull eyed Patrick, who was attempting to retrieve the loop. Then, just as unpredictably as he'd moved forward, he reversed. His hooves trampled over and sank deep into Mick's chest.

Louise lifted her hands to her ears but still she could hear Mick's bones rupturing. Mick coughed again. His lower jaw was soaked in blood. His eyes rolled to the back of his head.

Sensing freedom, the bull snorted and headed at speed down the crush. Louise ducked behind a barred gate and was imprisoned in a small pen set against the wall. She couldn't stop looking at Mick. He lay at the bottom of the crush, no longer human.

Just a smear of bones and tissue covered in blood and gore.

The bull stopped, turned its head and looked at Louise. Only a few feet from his nostrils she struggled to remain still.

Martin knelt beside his father on the floor of the crush. 'Dad,' he whispered. 'Dad, can you hear me? Say something,' he pleaded. 'We'll get help. Just say something. Tell me you're going to be all right.'

Patrick and Louise watched him.

Neither had the courage to tell him that his father was already dead.

# Eight

Rain continued to fall heavily and relentlessly into the farmyard, hammering down into the sticky brown quagmire that coated the cobbles, stirring it and intensifying the peculiar farmyard odour of ammonia and fertiliser that hung, heavy and acidic, in the air.

Martin had insisted on carrying his father's remains into the house and up into his bedroom alone, without assistance from either Patrick or his mother, Peggy, whom he'd ordered to stay indoors. Louise had taken it upon herself to telephone the doctor. He'd arrived within ten minutes of receiving her call and had been ensconced in the farmhouse with Peggy and Arthur ever since. Patrick had had no idea how close Arthur was to the O'Shea family until his partner had driven into the yard a few minutes behind the doctor.

Martin had emerged from the farmhouse after calling his nearest neighbours. With their and Patrick's assistance, he finally succeeded in returning the bull to its pen in the bull house. The beast was mercifully quiet – for the moment. The second dose of tranquilliser Patrick had succeeded in injecting into the animal had worked.

An hour after the event, the only sign of the tragedy

of Mick's death was the smears and smudges of blood and tissue that marred the floor at the top end of the cattle crush.

Despite an invitation from Martin, Patrick and Louise had chosen to remain outside the house. Traumatised, grief-stricken, Mick's death had reminded them of Alice's. Both had been unspeakably horrific and bloody, and both caused by animals.

Patrick felt totally unequal to driving home. He and Louise clung to one another for mutual support, standing just far enough inside the open barn to avoid the rain, their heads resting on one another's shoulders.

'You can't blame yourself for what happened, Patrick.' Arthur had approached so quietly that neither Patrick nor Louise had heard him crossing the yard. 'Mick was a stubborn man. He was the one who climbed into that pen. Martin said you warned him it was a bad idea. You did everything you could to stop him and, afterwards, all you could to save him.'

'Find someone else to run the practice, Arthur.' Patrick's voice was hoarse from emotional exhaustion. 'We're leaving Wake Wood.'

'I'm sorry,' Arthur sympathised. 'This has been such a shock. But let's not talk about it now. Tomorrow will be soon enough.'

'Arthur, we're not staying.' Now that Patrick had made the decision, he couldn't wait to drive away from the town and leave it behind – for ever.

'But you two seemed so happy here,' Arthur protested.

'It's not just Wake Wood. We – Louise and me – we

have a lot on our plate.' Patrick was loath to offer more of an explanation.

'I know, Patrick. But it's not a good idea to do anything in haste,' Arthur advised persuasively. 'I don't know what we'll do without you in the town, but it's you and Louise I'm thinking of.' Momentarily lost for words, Arthur placed his hand reassuringly on Patrick's shoulder before walking across to his car.

Louise lifted her head and watched Arthur. When he reached his car he looked up at the trees that overhung the buildings bordering the farmyard. A night owl swooped low over the roof of the house in its first foray of the evening. Arthur watched it circle twice then fly away. He turned and gazed at Louise.

Arthur and Louise exchanged glances across the yard for what seemed like a long time before Arthur turned on his heel and walked purposefully back towards her and Patrick. When Arthur reached them he closed his eyes for a moment before speaking. It was as though he knew that his words would cause them unbearable pain and he couldn't bring himself to witness the hurt he was about to inflict.

'Tell me about your daughter, Louise.'

Louise stiffened in Patrick's arms. Hot salt tears seared her eyes.

'Now is not the time, Arthur,' Patrick snapped protectively.

'I think now is exactly the time,' Arthur contradicted. 'I believe it's important – very important that we talk about your daughter. And that we talk about her right now.'

'Why?' Patrick demanded.

'Because there are things that need to be said,' Arthur persisted.

'What do you think you're doing? Other than making things even worse for us, if that's possible.' Patrick's anger escalated.

'Arthur, please, just leave us alone—' Louise began.

Arthur interrupted her. 'Look, I can't feel what you feel, Louise,' he said earnestly. 'I can't even pretend to comprehend the depth of agony you're both suffering, but I do have an idea of it. A sense . . . and—'

Patrick cut Arthur short. 'Enough, Arthur! We won't listen to another word.'

'It's true. I don't want you to leave Wake Wood, either of you,' Arthur explained. 'My business has never done as well as it has since you took over. But this isn't about me or Wake Wood and what you can do for the town. It's about you and Louise, Patrick. Well, to be perfectly plain, I simply want to help you in any way that I can.'

'You can't help us, Arthur,' Patrick raged. 'No one can. So stop this right now.'

'Please stop, Arthur,' Louise echoed Patrick's despair.

Arthur heard them and the grief in their voices. But it was their misery that prompted him to persevere with his offer. 'Listen to me, Patrick. Please, listen to me.'

His voice had a soft, hypnotic quality that soothed Patrick's anger and lightened Louise's misery.

'I can bring your daughter back to life for a short time.

So you can see her again, hold her and say goodbye to her properly.'

'That's ridiculous—' Patrick began, but Arthur cut him short.

'But before we even discuss it, Patrick, I want you to ask yourself if bringing Alice back would truly ease your and Louise's anguish and heartache.'

'Alice . . . You know her name?' Louise stared at him.

'Arthur, you're talking absolute nonsense,' Patrick snapped.

'No, it's not nonsense, Patrick,' Arthur contradicted quietly. 'And if you think bringing Alice back will help you and Louise to come to terms with the tragedy of her loss then we should go ahead and make plans.'

Louise wavered on her feet. She placed her hand over her mouth. Patrick tightened his grip on her, holding her close, afraid that she was about to faint.

'That's not funny, Arthur,' Patrick pronounced bitterly.

'No,' Arthur agreed, 'it's not. It's serious. But it can be done. If she's been dead for less than a year, I can bring her back. But I warn you, it will only be for three days. When that time has passed you will have to return her. Most of the people I've helped say that the three extra days spent with their loved ones have been worth the pain of a second separation. But, as I've only ever brought loved ones back for others and never for myself, I can't help you to make that decision. You have to do it yourselves.'

'It's not possible to bring people back from the dead, Arthur,' Patrick declared flatly. 'When someone dies, that's it. The end! Nothingness! They're gone for ever, never to be seen by the living again.'

'No, it isn't, Patrick. And it is possible to bring them back for a last goodbye.' Arthur continued to speak softly but with conviction. 'Ask your wife if you don't believe me. But there's one other thing that you have to ask yourself. Would you want to bring your daughter home, if you knew in advance that you'd have to lose her all over again?'

Hurting more than he would have believed possible, Patrick simply couldn't take any more. 'This is rubbish, Arthur . . .'

Arthur raised his hand as if to silence him. 'All right, Patrick. Have it your way. But I'll ask you to do just one thing before you totally dismiss and deride my offer. Talk to Louise. She knows the truth of what I'm proposing to you.' Arthur finally walked away and left them.

Patrick stood holding Louise for a long time after Arthur went. They heard the engine of his car die away as he headed down the track to the road that led back to town; watched the light in the farmyard fade from light to dark grey as the shadows lengthened and rose from the ground. The owl returned and swooped low, this time catching his prey. He flew off, a wriggling mouse held fast in his beak.

Unseen hands drew the curtains in the farmhouse before lamps were switched on. The wind rustled the treetops. Patrick thought he could hear the sound of a woman's sobs, mingling with the wail of the night breeze, but he couldn't be sure. Reluctant to face the grief of Peggy and Martin O'Shea, when he still hadn't come to terms with the loss of his own daughter, he pushed Louise gently from him.

'We need to go. And we need to talk. But not here, not now. When we get back to the cottage.' He led her across the farmyard to his car, opened the passenger door and helped her inside. They drove back to the cottage in silence. He parked, opened the door, stepped outside and looked at Louise in the light from the interior lamp. She was pale, drawn, her eyes darker than he'd ever seen them before.

He would have given everything he owned to have been able to assuage the pain mirrored in their depths.

'You go on into the house and do whatever you want. I'll make us tea.'

She nodded agreement without looking at him and got out of the car. He locked it and followed her inside. He went straight to the kitchen, filled the kettle and switched it on.

While he waited for the water to boil, he reflected on just how much time he had occupied by concentrating on small practical tasks since Alice's death: making tea, preparing meals, clearing up the kitchen, cleaning the house. Things he had left to Louise and their daily when Alice had been alive because he'd wanted to spend every spare minute with his daughter, teaching her, exploring with her, playing games with her, loving her, seeing the world afresh and anew through her eyes.

How many hours had he whiled away trying to keep

busy in an attempt to distract his thoughts from Alice – and the way she'd died? How many fruitless hours? Because no matter what he did, where he went, or who he was with, he simply couldn't forget her. Nor did he want to.

He poured the tea, placed the cups on a tray and climbed the stairs. He was dreading a confrontation with his wife. But after the peculiar scene with Arthur, he knew that he wouldn't be able to avoid one.

Did Louise really believe that Arthur had the power to bring people in general – and Alice in particular – back to life?

The very idea was preposterous. Should he humour her? She'd been so depressed since Alice's death, if he challenged her, would he precipitate a full-blown nervous breakdown?

Wake Wood was supposed to have been a new beginning for them, but far from escaping from the tragedy of Alice, they'd only succeeded in bringing it with them. And after witnessing Louise's reaction to Mick O'Shea's horrific end, he suspected that she, like him, remembered only the manner of Alice's dying, not the happiness their daughter had brought into their lives before her death. Or the simple joys of the days and nights the three of them had shared.

He rested the bottom of the tray on the bannister, giving him time to compose himself before facing Louise. The door to the guest room was ajar. Patrick watched her moving around inside. She was unpacking Alice's belongings from the black sacks and red bag that he had dumped them into, and was putting Alice's clothes away in drawers and on hangers that she hooked on to the wardrobe rail. And in between sorting their daughter's clothes, she was arranging Alice's stuffed toys, dolls and books on the shelves.

Then he realised: Louise was preparing the room for Alice's return. She actually believed that Alice would soon be with them again! Here in the cottage; in this room, surrounded by her clothes and possessions, just as she'd been in their old home.

He was shaking so much he had to set the tray on the floor and lean against the doorpost for support. She didn't turn around to face him, so he addressed her back.

'Arthur said I should talk to you, Louise. Talk to you about what?' he questioned earnestly. 'What do you know about Wake Wood that I don't?'

If Louise heard him, she ignored him. She simply carried on arranging Alice's clothes and toys.

'Louise, what do you know that I don't?' he asked again, more urgently this time. 'Have you seen something?'

She wiped her eyes on the back of her sleeve and he saw that she was close to tears.

'I need you to tell me what you saw,' he pleaded. 'I have a right to know . . .'

'You don't believe Arthur can bring Alice back,' she reproached.

'No,' he agreed slowly. 'I don't believe him. The dead are dead. The idea that they can return to life is preposterous.'

'Not to me. Not after what I've seen and heard in

Arthur's place and in the town . . . and after Mary Brogan and . . . and D-Deirdre . . .' she stammered into silence.

'What's Mary Brogan got to do with this?'

'I can't . . . I can't explain, Patrick. I just can't. Please, don't ask me to try.'

'Stop this, come on.' He walked into the room and opened his arms to her but instead of going to him as he'd hoped she would, she backed away.

'"Stop this"?' she echoed. 'What am I to stop, Patrick?' She dropped the pile of Alice's T-shirts she'd been holding on to the bed and faced him. 'What do you think I'm doing?'

'I can see what you're doing. You're preparing this room for Alice's return.'

'And you're asking me to stop. You want Alice to return here with nothing prepared for her arrival. No clothes, no room . . .'

'Please, Louise. Be straight with me. How can you possibly believe that Arthur is telling us the truth when he says that he can bring people back from the dead?'

'I believe him because I saw something in Arthur's yard last night. It was like . . .' she faltered.

'Like what?' Patrick demanded when she hesitated.

'It's difficult, impossible to explain. The nearest description I can give is that it was like a birth. Only instead of a baby there was a . . .'

Patrick breathed out slowly. 'I see . . . A birth. And?' he persisted.

'That's it.'

'The birth of what?' When she didn't elaborate he

added, 'How can that possibly be "it"?'

'I believe Arthur, Patrick. I truly believe what he said. I saw what appeared to be a birth. But not of a baby. The birth of a fully grown man.'

Patrick crossed his arms across his chest. 'Someone must have given birth to him. Who was it?'

'Not who – what. He emerged from a casing. Like a cocoon. Arthur cracked the casing and he emerged in a gush – a flood of fluid and blood as if the casing was a disembodied womb.'

'I see.' Patrick hadn't intended to sound sceptical, but he could hear it in his own voice. 'Hasn't it occurred to you that you believe you saw the birth of a fully grown man because you want to believe it? Because somehow you think that it will help us to get Alice back?'

'Maybe,' she replied honestly. 'But it doesn't matter if that's what you think. I know what I saw. And I know what I believe.'

'And you believe Arthur?'

'Yes . . . I do. I believe he can do what he says. That he can bring Alice back to us.'

'I don't understand.'

'Of course you don't,' she murmured.

'Of course,' he mocked caustically.

She turned her back to him.

'I feel dumb and weak and desperate, Louise,' he confessed, 'because, like you, a part of me wants to buy into what Arthur is offering us. I want to believe him. Can you understand that?'

'Yes, I can,' she admitted.

'But you don't just *want* to believe Arthur's fanciful

story – you really believe that he can bring Alice back from the dead.'

'I do,' she asserted strongly.

'You really believe him?' he reiterated incredulously. 'Yes.'

'And you want to try. You want us to go to him and ask him to try to bring Alice back to us?' he checked.

'Yes.' She turned and faced him head-on. 'Yes, that's exactly what I want us to do, because we won't be able to forgive ourselves if we don't try. Neither of us will – not ever – not for the whole of the rest of our lives. Because, just think, Patrick.' Her eyes shone, animated by something he hadn't seen in them since Alice's death – hope. 'We'll be able to see our daughter again, talk to her, hold her, tell her how much we love her . . .'

'And will miss her when she has to return,' he reminded Louise cruelly, recalling Arthur's warning.

'Yes. That too,' she agreed sadly. 'But as Arthur said, most people he's done this for have said that it's been worth it just to say goodbye to their loved ones properly. We never said goodbye to her, Patrick. We never heard her last words. Didn't tell her out that we'd think of her every day . . . every minute. That in losing her we lost everything. We couldn't because by the time we reached her she'd already gone.'

'I know. I was the one who reached her first.' Patrick hated himself for reminding her. He still couldn't bring himself to believe that Arthur could bring people back from the dead. But what he did know was that if he didn't go along with Louise's suggestion that they allow Arthur to try and resurrect Alice, his wife would never forgive him. And after losing Alice he couldn't bear to lose Louise too.

'All right, Louise,' he capitulated. 'We'll go to Arthur and ask him to do this for us – for Alice.' He watched as she continued to fold Alice's clothes, making neat piles, stowing them away in the drawers and cupboards. 'Louise—'

'Yes, Patrick,' she broke in. 'We're going to do this.'

'We'll do it, but I just wish that I could be sure. I wish . . .'

'It will work, Patrick.' She turned and looked deep into his eyes. 'I just want her back with us. Both of us.'

'But even if Arthur can do what he said he can, it isn't going to be that simple, is it? Arthur warned us. And these people, Arthur and the others, here in Wake Wood, they've all been kind to us.'

She met his gaze. 'But if we have to lie, won't it be worth it to get Alice back, even if it will only be for three days?'

'I hope so, Louise,' he murmured. 'I really hope so.'

Louise abandoned her tidying of the guest room. She set the bundles of Alice's clothes that she hadn't stowed away on the bed, along with the remainder of her toys and the bed linen she intended to use to make up Alice's bed.

'You telephone Arthur and invite him over tonight, Patrick. I'll cook.'

Reluctant to invite Arthur without any further discussion, he said, 'Isn't it late for dinner? We can wait until tomorrow.'

'If it's too late for dinner, tell Arthur he's invited for

supper.' She left the room, passed Patrick and the tray he'd abandoned on the floor of the landing, and ran lightly down the stairs.

Patrick waited until he heard her opening the freezer in the kitchen before picking up the tray. The tea had grown cold. His hands shook so much it slopped over the rims of the cups into the saucers as he carried the tray downstairs. He left it on the dining-room table and went into the hall to telephone.

Arthur answered promptly and Patrick pictured his partner, sitting in front of a blazing fire beside the phone in his book-lined snug, a glass of single malt whisky at his elbow, cigar and book in hand.

Arthur was as patient and soft-spoken as usual. He listened attentively while Patrick told him that Louise wanted to go ahead and accept his offer to bring Alice back.

Arthur only answered after he was sure that Patrick had finished speaking. 'And you're quite sure about this, Patrick?' he checked.

'Quite sure,' Patrick lied. He wasn't even sure about inviting Arthur to their cottage that night, let alone Arthur's proposal to raise Alice from the dead. The more he thought about Arthur's proposition, the more bizarre and logic-defying he considered it to be.

'Please, tell Louise she doesn't have to make supper for me.'

'She's already preparing it, Arthur.'

'In that case, thank her and tell her I'll be along shortly.' Arthur hesitated. 'And you, Patrick? How do you really feel about this?'

'It's what Louise wants,' Patrick answered.

'I was asking how *you* feel about this, not Louise.'

Patrick could only repeat what he'd already said. 'It's what Louise wants.'

'I'll see you soon, Patrick.'

'Yes, Arthur.' Patrick was resigned. 'We'll see you soon.'

# Nine

Louise settled on a simple menu of soup, salad and pasta followed by sorbet. While she laid the table, grated cheese, and made the soup and pasta sauce, Patrick poured himself a beer. He took it into the living room, opened the curtains and looked out of the window. The rain had abated and the sky was clear apart from a few light, wispy clouds. A thin sliver of new moon shone down, surrounded by a bevy of stars brighter than he'd ever seen them when they'd lived in the city.

Would Alice have liked living here in this cottage in the country? Would she have settled to rural life and made friends with the young people in the town? Would he have bought a telescope so they could take up stargazing together? Would she have demanded more pets as they had more space and outbuildings to keep them in? Dogs, cats, the pony she'd been nagging for before she'd died . . .

The sound of a car engine put an end to his musings. Headlights glowed, illuminating the garden of the cottage as Arthur's car turned off the main road and swept around the curve of the drive, pulled up and parked behind their estate car.

To Patrick's surprise, Arthur lifted an old-fashioned leather doctor's bag from the boot of his car. Patrick knew it didn't contain Arthur's veterinary instruments. Like him, Arthur owned a modern steel case filled with the latest in equipment.

He unlatched the living-room window, intending to tell Arthur that he'd left the front door open for him, but hesitated when Arthur stood back, looked at the house and then at the sky before solemnly reciting,

> 'There is a web of life, you know,
> That joins all things that breathe and grow.
> But when man gets to meet his mentor
> We're shocked to find we're not the centre.'

Arthur's words were innocuous enough, but the way he said them sent a chill down Patrick's spine. He shuddered, overwhelmed by a dark feeling of foreboding.

Arthur had promised Louise that he would accomplish the impossible. Bring Alice back to life. He should stop the nonsense now, before he, as well as Louise, became totally unhinged by Arthur's promises . . .

'Why didn't you tell me that Arthur had arrived?' Louise reproached as she walked into the room behind him.

He looked at her and caught a glimpse of the young girl he'd fallen in love with, in the ghost of a smile playing at the corners of her mouth and the brightness of her eyes. 'He's only just got here. You go ahead and pour the wine. I'll show him in.'

\*

Louise had laid the table for three. She'd set out her best silver cutlery and porcelain crockery, decorated the table with candles and produced a simple but excellently cooked meal of leek and potato soup, followed by lasagne and salad, accompanied by chilled white Italian wine. But only Arthur ate with any appetite.

The conversation varied from banal observations on the weather to local gossip. By tacit agreement all of them avoided mentioning the tragedy at the O'Shea farm late that afternoon. Both Patrick and Louise found it difficult to concentrate on what Arthur was saying because all they could think of – all they wanted to discuss – was Alice.

Patrick was also on edge because he oscillated between wanting to end the meal quickly along with Louise's false hopes of seeing their daughter alive and well again; and daring Arthur to produce their daughter alive, if only for three days.

Louise was agitated because she couldn't wait another moment to finalise the plans to bring her daughter back from her grave.

After Louise served the sorbet, Patrick poured the last of the wine into their glasses and broached the subject that he'd wanted to since the moment of Arthur's arrival.

'This offer of yours, Arthur,' he began.

'Yes, Patrick?' Arthur looked expectantly at Patrick when he didn't elaborate.

'It's a long way outside of Louise's and my . . .' Patrick searched for the right word and settled on, 'experience.'

Arthur reached down for the bag he'd placed beside his chair and lifted it on to his lap. He opened it and rummaged through the contents. 'Experience is generally overrated, Patrick,' he pronounced with a gravity Patrick found suspect. 'You can never jump in the same river twice, as the fellow said. It's moved on. Heraclitus . . . or was it Heisenberg? I mix up my ancient Greeks. Of course, Heisenberg sounds like a Jew now that I think of it. Must have been Heraclitus—'

'Arthur, you're screwing with us,' Patrick declared flatly.

Arthur smiled. 'Yes, I'm afraid I am . . . I was. But not any more, Patrick. Now, let's get down to serious business.' He removed a peculiar object from the muddle of things in his bag. It was a large, old wooden frame of indeterminate shape, strung with metal bars ornamented by beads. It resembled an abacus but, given the number of metal rods of varying sizes and the myriad of oddly shaped beads, it was like no abacus Patrick or Louise had ever seen.

When Patrick examined the beads closely he realised they were made of drilled bone of varying sizes, dyed different colours. Animal or human bone? Patrick wondered but didn't dare ask. Not with Louise sitting next to him.

Arthur moved his plate aside, laid the object on the table and set his bag on the floor. His demeanour changed as soon as he'd divested himself of his bag. Brisk and professional, he stretched the flats of both his hands over the frame and began his questioning.

'Your daughter's name was Alice?'

Louise confirmed it before Patrick could. 'Alice,' she echoed.

Patrick elaborated. 'Alice Hannah Daley.'

Arthur clicked the beads on the frame and arranged them into position. He appeared to pay special attention to their alignment and colours. 'Did she prefer mornings or evenings?'

'Mornings,' Patrick and Louise answered in unison.

Arthur rearranged the beads and looked at them for a few seconds. 'Was her skin moist or dry?'

'Moist,' Patrick replied.

Arthur continued to work with the beads, sliding them up and down the rods. 'Would she have liked cats, cows or horses best of all?'

'Horses, ponies, definitely ponies. She loved them. She'd only just started riding lessons. She couldn't wait for Saturday mornings to come . . .' Louise realised she was giving far more information than Arthur required and stopped talking.

Arthur clicked more of the beads into position. 'Was her hair thick or lank?'

'It was thick, wasn't it?' Patrick looked to Louise for confirmation.

'Quite thick,' she concurred.

'At what time of the year was she born?' Concentrating on the task in hand, Arthur didn't look up from the frame as he continued to work on it.

'In January . . . the twenty-second.' Louise clenched her fists tightly. It pained her just to say the date.

'That was my next question.' Arthur glanced up at her and smiled before moving more beads. 'And how long has she been in the ground? I need you to be very exact and precise regarding this matter.'

Louise looked at Patrick then pushed back her chair.

'Louise, you all right?' Patrick asked solicitously.

Louise blanched. 'I . . . I'm sorry . . . I can't . . . just can't . . .' Clearly unable to answer any more questions about Alice, Louise left the table and fled from the room.

Patrick rose and followed her to the door. 'Louise?' he called as she entered the kitchen.

She closed the door in his face but he could still hear her sobs.

'Patrick.' Arthur brought him back to the present and immediate. 'How long has your daughter been dead and in the ground? I need an answer and quickly.'

Patrick returned to the table, sank his head in his hands and took a few seconds to answer. When he spoke it was slowly, carefully and deliberately. 'She's been in the ground eleven months, two weeks and two days. She was buried five days after she died.'

Arthur nodded and made a final adjustment to the beads. 'In that case we haven't much time. Just over a week.' He moved his hands away from the beads. As Patrick watched, one seemed to adjust itself, changing place without being manipulated and, in so doing, defying gravity.

Arthur was staring at it but he didn't appear to find the movement in any way odd.

Patrick studied the pattern Arthur had made of the beads. It resembled a mosaic image of a bird. But Arthur frowned as he looked at it, as if he were dissatisfied with the outcome. He continued to flick the bone beads back and forth until a few minutes later he was left with a different image. An abstract picture he appeared happier to accept.

'Now, this is what we can do for you and Louise,' Arthur prophesied. 'Alice will be brought back as soon as we can arrange it, certainly within the next day or two. And when she returns, you will make the most of the time that you'll have with her. Three days.'

'And nights?' Patrick checked.

'Precisely,' Arthur confirmed. 'And after that time she'll have to go back to the woods and into the ground. You'll have to bury her. You and Louise. You do understand? You'll have to cover Alice with earth.' Arthur looked Patrick in the eye. 'Because Alice will just be on loan to you.'

'Will she be normal?'

Patrick turned to see Louise standing in the doorway holding a tray of coffee. She'd moved quietly and neither of the men had heard her return to the room.

'Yes, quite,' Arthur reassured. 'Alice's heart will beat, her lungs will breathe. She'll remember you and the life she had with you. Some of it,' he qualified, 'but she'll also be deceased – although that's something she won't be aware of.' He smiled again. A cold smile that troubled Patrick. 'You'll need to bear that in mind the entire time you're with her.'

Patrick moved the plates on the table, stacking them one on top of the other to make space for Louise to set down the tray of coffee.

Arthur reached for his glass of wine and sipped it

before continuing. 'As Patrick just said, your time with Alice will last for three days and nights, and three days and nights only, during which you must keep Alice within the town perimeter of Wake Wood. That is a physical necessity. An absolute. It cannot be breached or infringed in any way. I cannot stress that strongly enough. Do you both understand? No matter what happens, you cannot take Alice beyond the town boundaries.'

Louise nodded agreement. 'I understand.'

'And when Alice's time is up, the dead will have to return to the dead. There will be no delay, no argument. That is also the rule. It cannot be broken, no matter how much you may want to keep your daughter with you.' Arthur looked from Patrick to Louise. 'You both understand that also?'

'Yes,' they murmured in agreement, Louise watching Patrick as intently as he was watching her.

'Now, for this to work we need a body. And as you're all too aware, we've just had a tragedy in the community. Perhaps we can prevail on the family to sacrifice their corpse to our cause of bringing Alice back to you. But you, Louise, will have to ask Mrs O'Shea and her son for permission to use Mick O'Shea's remains. We cannot do anything unless the family allows us to.'

'Why do we need a body?' Patrick asked.

'You'll see,' Arthur replied enigmatically. 'But first there are some things that you need to understand. The ritual of the return will bind you, both of you, to Wake Wood for ever. This will be hugely to this town's and my own and my business's benefit, but you must also understand that both of you will have to settle here permanently. You will not be able to leave Wake Wood afterwards. Not ever.'

'Never,' Patrick murmured. The word had acquired a new finality.

'Never,' Arthur reiterated emphatically. 'And you, Patrick, will have to serve as Wake Wood's veterinary surgeon until retirement. You'll have to tend to animals without fail whenever you're called, whenever the people of this town need you to minister to their livestock and pets. Needless to say, as I've said already, this suits me very well, but I hope it suits you also.'

'It will have to,' Patrick assented.

'Good. In that case, perhaps we can all get what we want.'

Patrick considered what Arthur had said, but he had a far more burning question to ask before he went into the matter of his and Louise's permanent residence in Wake Wood. 'Arthur, why will we only have Alice for three days?'

'Because when we tap the life force that remains in a fresh cadaver, three days' worth is all that we're given. Perhaps three days mirrors the stages of our existence – birth, life . . . and death. But I don't truly know,' Arthur revealed. 'Three days is a short time, but people who've seized the days as an opportunity to say goodbye to their loved ones have told me afterwards that they're long enough.' He turned from Patrick to Louise. 'Have you understood everything I've said?'

'Yes.' Louise didn't look at Patrick.

'Do we have an agreement, Patrick? Louise?' Arthur demanded.

Patrick looked at Louise. She took a deep breath but he knew that she'd already made her decision and wasn't to be swayed from it.

'Yes, Arthur. I need to hold my baby again,' Louise said feelingly. She reached towards Patrick. He gripped her hand, and stroked her fingers tenderly. He loved Louise with all his heart. He wanted to believe that what Arthur was about to do was possible, for her sake. And – every time he pictured Alice – for his own.

The idea that he could touch and talk to Alice again – tell her how much he loved her, needed her, emphasise how much joy and happiness she'd brought into both his and Louise's lives – was so beguiling he needed it to happen every bit as much as Louise did.

'Yes, Arthur,' Patrick answered firmly. 'We have our agreement.'

Arthur leaned forward and closed his hands around theirs. 'Then, Louise, you will hold your little girl again. I can promise you that much.'

After they'd finished their coffee, Patrick showed Arthur out of the house. He walked with him to his car and returned to the dining room. Louise had already cleared the table and carried the dishes into the kitchen, switched off the light, and was standing in front of the living-room window, watching Arthur drive away.

He went to her, moved behind her and wrapped his arms around her waist. They remained there, still and silent while clouds blotted out the moon and shadows raced across the lawns.

'Patrick,' Louise whispered.

'Yes.'

'What will happen if Arthur and the others find out we've lied to them?'

'I don't know, Louise. It's best not to think about it.'

'It will be all right, won't it?'

'It will have to be.' He moved away from her. 'Come on, it's bedtime. You go up first.'

He checked the house while she went upstairs. When he climbed the stairs there was a light on in the spare room. Louise had finished putting away Alice's clothes and toys and was smoothing the duvet on the newly made bed. The pillows were already plumped up. He recognised the bed linen. It had been Alice's favourite. If the walls had been turquoise, he could have believed himself back in Alice's bedroom in their old house.

Louise looked guiltily at him. 'It's all right, isn't it?'

'It's fine. Just like her old room.'

'I'm hoping she won't see the difference.'

'She shouldn't.'

'Patrick . . .'

He held out his arm to her. 'Come to bed. We have to be up early tomorrow to visit the O'Sheas.'

'Do you think they'll give us Mick's body?'

'I don't know.'

'If they don't . . .'

'Think positive. Hope they do. Come to bed, Louise, please, we're both exhausted,' he pleaded, knowing full well that, bone-weary as they were, neither of them would sleep that night. Not after the things Arthur had told them – and promised.

# Ten

The area in front of the O'Sheas' farmhouse was jammed with cars parked at all angles, blocking one another in. It was obvious that no thought had been given as to how any of the early arrivals were going to drive off if anyone wanted to leave urgently.

Although only two o'clock in the afternoon, the sky was as dark as a winter evening, heavy and black with dense rain clouds. Crows had flocked to the roof of the house and the barn and were perched on the ridge tiles in silent parliament, their ragged feathered silhouettes apt ornaments for a house of mourning.

Patrick, Louise and Arthur left Arthur's car in the lane and picked their way across the muddy path that led up to the front door of the house. All three were soberly and formally dressed in dark suits and white shirts. Both men wore black ties.

'Are you prepared to talk to Mrs O'Shea, Louise? Patrick?' Arthur asked.

Louise swallowed hard but was too choked to answer with more than a nod.

'We are.' Patrick squeezed Louise's hand reassuringly.

'Just ask Mrs O'Shea, Louise,' Arthur advised. 'That's all you can do. Ask her plainly and simply.'

They walked through the open front door into the hall. It was crowded with people from the town, all dressed for a funeral as they were. And every one of them had a drink in their hands. As the three of them moved deeper into the hall, heading for the living room, they were waylaid by an attractive young woman carrying a tray of glasses filled with whiskey. She held it up in front of Louise.

'Hello. We haven't been formally introduced, although I've seen you in the pharmacy. You're Louise Daley, aren't you? I'm Annie. You don't have to take the whiskey.' She thrust the tray closer to Arthur, who was helping himself and Patrick to a drink. 'We also have Baileys if you'd prefer it. The bottle and extra glasses are in the kitchen if you'd like to serve yourself.'

In need of the courage alcohol would give her, Louise took a tumbler from the tray. 'Whiskey is perfect, thank you, Annie.'

'Your husband is the vet, isn't he?' Annie fluttered her eyelashes in Patrick's direction. 'It's great that you're here. I don't just mean here, now, in the O'Sheas',' she gabbled. 'But living here, in Wake Wood.'

Louise followed Annie's line of sight and caught the flirtatious look she was sending Patrick's way. Oblivious to the attention he was receiving from Annie, Patrick was discussing cattle prices with the town's livestock auctioneer.

Embarrassed at being caught out looking at another woman's husband, Annie continued talking at speed. 'It's marvellous to have new people in the town. I was afraid that we were becoming a society of old fogeys. I mean, so many young people leave to find work elsewhere. It's sad to lose them. We were all so excited when Arthur told us you were moving into Wake Wood for good and reopening the old pharmacy. We need all the shops we can get. It's rare to find young people, especially professionals, prepared to live and work in a quiet backwater like this.'

When Louise didn't comment, Annie said, 'Mick's in the bedroom if you'd like to view him. Please excuse me. I'd better make sure everyone has a drink.'

'Of course.' Whiskey in hand, Louise pushed her way through to the stairs. She was aware of the recent trend to follow America in holding 'viewings of the corpse' but if it hadn't been for the request she had to make she wouldn't have dared impose on Mick's widow on so slight an acquaintance.

A light was burning on the landing above her. She drained her glass, left it on a windowsill and walked up the steps. When she reached the first floor, she saw that all the doors were closed except one. She went to it and looked inside.

The room was large and she guessed it was the master bedroom of the farmhouse. It was furnished with a massive old-fashioned oak bedroom suite that gleamed black from the layers of polish that had been applied to it over the years. The bedspread and curtains were gold and crimson tapestry. Beeswax candles had been lit and placed on the mantelpiece of the carved oak hearth surround, on the bedside cabinets and also in front of the mirror on the dressing table. But their light did little to illuminate the room and the overall effect was one of Jacobean gloom.

Mick had been laid out in the centre of the ornately carved, oak-framed bed. He was covered to the chin, but his arms and hands were lying free on top of the bed linen. There was no sign of the wounds he'd suffered or the blood he'd been drenched in, and Louise reflected that whoever had washed, dressed and composed Mick for death had done a masterful job of concealing his massive injuries.

An elderly woman was crouched over Mick's corpse; her back turned to Louise. She was manicuring Mick's nails, scraping the dirt from beneath them and trimming them with nail scissors. Louise watched in silence as the woman carefully and meticulously slipped each sliver of nail clipping into a white envelope.

Sensing she was no longer alone with Mick, the woman turned and faced Louise. Grief was etched deep in the lines around her mouth but her eyes were bright, glittering with unshed tears.

Surmising the woman was Mick's wife, Louise offered her condolences. 'I'm so sorry, Mrs O'Shea. Please accept my deepest sympathies.'

'You were there, in the barn when it happened.' It wasn't a question.

'I was,' Louise admitted.

'You're the vet's wife.'

'Yes, Louise Daley.' Louise offered her hand and Peggy O'Shea took it. She didn't shake it, but she held it for a moment.

'Martin said you cleaned and dressed the injury to his hand.'

'Yes, I did. How is it?'

'It'll mend, in time. There's no real damage done. He'll survive, unlike my poor Mick.' Peggy set the scissors and envelope on the bedside table, moved a straight-backed chair close to the bed and sat down.

Unable to bear the silence, Louise blurted, 'Mrs O'Shea, I really am so sorry. I know how awful the pain is. I really do.'

'I'm sure you do.'

Louise moved a chair away from the wall and sat at the foot of the bed.

Peggy looked down fondly on Mick's corpse and smiled. 'In my mind's eye, he's still the dashing, handsome boy I met all those years ago. And now there he is, all creased up like an old man. It went too fast. Our lives went far too fast,' she echoed despondently.

Louise was suddenly aware of noises in the room, harsh scratching and muted whisperings out of her field of vision that set her teeth on edge. She peered beyond the candlelight into the shadows gathered thickly in the corners of the room. She thought she glimpsed movement but it was difficult to tell in the flickers of the candles.

'Don't look at them,' Peggy warned sharply.

Louise shivered, wondering if she'd heard the old woman correctly.

'It's better not to look at them,' Peggy reiterated.

'Them?' Louise ventured bravely.

'Things that cannot be named. Death excites them, you see. Ignore them. Behave as if you've seen and heard nothing.'

Terrified, trembling, Louise looked back at Mick. Compared to whatever horrors were lurking just out of sight, the corpse appeared strangely reassuring.

Patrick pushed his way into the kitchen and looked around the throng of people for Louise's blonde head. He couldn't see his wife but he noticed that the liberal helpings of whiskey were beginning to have an effect on the mourners crammed into the house. As glasses were emptied and refilled, voices were becoming louder and more animated. To add to the din of conversation a woman was playing traditional Irish airs on a button accordion in the dining parlour and a couple of men, well-oiled by alcohol, had taken it upon themselves to sing an accompaniment.

He only backed out of the kitchen when he was certain that Louise wasn't in the room. He was in the hall when he felt a hand on his shoulder. He turned and found himself looking into Martin O'Shea's eyes. They were sombre, bruised by grief and pain.

'My father was proud of that bull, Patrick,' he slurred. Patrick couldn't tell whether Martin's impeded speech was down to a surfeit of whiskey or grief.

'With good cause, Martin. It's a fine animal,' Patrick complimented.

'And the beast is out there in the bull house now, standing large and fit as life. His temperature came down anyway. As did my father's,' Martin said bitterly. 'He's upstairs laid out cold and stiff for the grave and the bull is alive and well.'

'I'm sorry about what happened to Mick, Martin,'

Patrick said sincerely.

'I know you are, Patrick,' Martin relented.

'If there's anything I can do . . .' Even as he said the words, Patrick knew from bitter experience how useless they were. There was nothing anyone could do to assuage loss on the scale that Martin was experiencing.

'Thank you, Patrick. I know you mean it. You tried to stop Dad from climbing into that pen. But there was no stopping Mick O'Shea once he'd made up his mind to do something.'

'No, there wasn't,' Patrick agreed. 'He was a good man, Martin. And he'll be missed by more than your family in Wake Wood.'

'It's kind of you to say so, Patrick.' Mick looked around the crowded room and acknowledged Arthur, who was signalling to him. 'If you're looking for your missus, Patrick, she's upstairs with my mother in the bedroom. You'd best go in to them.'

'Thank you, I will. I need to pay my respects to your father.' Patrick needed no second prompting. He was anxious to leave the house, the rowdy mourners and all the reminders of Mick's tragic and untimely death.

He climbed the stairs and saw Louise and Peggy O'Shea sitting in silence in the candlelit master bedroom. Both women were gazing at the corpse.

Patrick bowed his head in respect before approaching Peggy. He held out his hand. 'I'm sorry for your loss, Mrs O'Shea.'

'Thank you, Mr Daley.'

'Patrick, please.' After Peggy shook his hand he picked up a chair and sat beside Louise.

Louise took courage from Patrick's presence. She turned to Peggy. 'Our daughter died suddenly last year. Our only child,' she emphasised. 'When she was born things didn't go very well. I'll never have another baby.'

Patrick reached for Louise's hand. The pressure of his fingers on hers spurred her to continue.

'Even though I know this is a time of great sadness and tragedy for you, I want to ask if we can use your husband's remains to help bring back our daughter.'

Peggy glared at Louise. 'You don't know what you're asking.'

'You're right, Mrs O'Shea. I don't know what I'm asking,' Louise conceded. 'But what I do know is that I ache every minute of every day to see my little girl again,' she pleaded.

Arthur entered the room behind them. He lifted his hand to Peggy in acknowledgement but remained behind Patrick and Louise in the shadows that shrouded the doorway.

Peggy looked from Louise to Patrick. 'You two may live in Wake Wood now. But it's not part of you. It's not your home. You're just visiting and, maybe one day, one day soon, you'll move on and go elsewhere. I can't imagine what that's like; moving on, wanting to live in another place, one that's full of strangers. The rest of us, well, we're all born here, rooted here in this land and in the woods. We couldn't survive outside of Wake Wood.'

'Mrs O'Shea,' Patrick interposed. 'Louise and I are happy here in Wake Wood and I promise you we intend to stay here.'

Peggy pursed her lips disapprovingly before she

declared, 'The ritual is not for outsiders. Only those born and bred here, in Wake Wood.'

Arthur stepped forward. 'Not usually, Peggy, but when people want to join us and contribute to the community the way Patrick and Louise have done, we can make exceptions . . .' His voice trailed when she left her chair and confronted him in amazement.

'How can you say that there can be exceptions, Arthur? Patrick's success in running your veterinary practice has blinded you. There's never been an exception in the past. The people wouldn't have stood for it then and they won't stand for it now.'

'Without exceptions the town will never grow, Peggy,' Arthur replied. 'Do you want Wake Wood to wither and die for lack of young people, like so many other small towns in this part of Ireland? Please, Peggy, you know we can't do anything without your permission.'

Peggy took a candle from the bedside cabinet. She stood in front of Patrick and Louise. 'All right, Arthur's had his say. Now stand up for me. Both of you.'

Patrick and Louise obediently rose to their feet. Peggy held the candle very close to Patrick's face and studied him while three full minutes ticked off the bedside clock. Moving the flame even closer, she stared into his eyes for another minute before moving on to Louise and repeating the procedure.

Louise stood unflinchingly as the old woman examined her face, her eyelids, her skin, her hair.

Peggy finally lowered the candle but she continued to stare at Louise for a long time before turning back and replacing the candle on the cabinet. 'No, Arthur. It's not right,' she declared finally. 'The ritual is for people born and bred in Wake Wood only. There can be no exceptions. Certainly not for incomers who haven't even lived out a full year in the town.'

'Peggy, haven't you listened to a word we've said to you?' Arthur pressed.

'I listened,' she snapped.

'Louise has explained to you about her daughter?' Arthur checked.

'She did.'

'Then how can you say the ritual's not for them?'

'Because it's the truth,' Peggy insisted stubbornly. 'It's not for them.'

'You must have a reason for saying that. What is it?' Arthur questioned.

'There's a reason, a good reason, but I can't see what it is, so I can't explain it.' Peggy returned to her chair. 'I can only say that Patrick and Louise aren't right and I won't give them Mick's body. That's my last word on the matter.'

Arthur moved close to Peggy and laid his hand on her arm. 'Peggy, they have to ask. Everyone who begs the return of a loved one has to ask, we both know that. But I can see that now is too soon for you. It's not a good time. You're upset.'

'Of course I'm upset, Arthur. My Mick is dead,' Peggy retorted. 'But there's something else. Something I don't like about them,' she reiterated.

'They have to ask,' Arthur repeated. 'But as you know, you have to be amenable. It's the only way that the ceremony of the return can continue. Don't you want to see Mick again yourself, Peggy? I thought that you'd have wanted to spend those last days with him.'

Peggy's eyes rounded in alarm and her voice rose in anger. 'Surely you wouldn't deny me Mick's return, Arthur. That's my right as a resident of Wake Wood. The last three days with my loved one so I can say goodbye, properly.'

Arthur shrugged. 'Patrick and Louise need your help, Peggy.'

'I see. That's the way it is.' She looked from Arthur to Louise and Patrick.

'That's the way it's always been, Peggy,' Arthur pointed out calmly. 'A life to bring back a life. You know that.'

'And you'd blackmail me over this?'

'Blackmail's an ugly word, Peggy. I'm merely pointing out that Patrick and Louise feel the same way about seeing their daughter again as you do about seeing Mick. Everyone here in Wake Wood has a right to a last goodbye. What's it to be, Peggy?'

'Seems you're not giving me much choice, Arthur,' Peggy answered ungraciously. She turned to Louise. 'All right, you can have Mick's corpse. But I don't mind telling you, I still don't like it. It's not right. I can't tell you why.' She shook her head. 'I can only say it isn't. And mark my words, no good will come of it.'

Subdued by Arthur's intimidation of Peggy O'Shea, Patrick and Louise made their way back down the stairs, through the hall, where the wake was in full, noisy swing, and pushed their way to the front door.

Martin was holding it open for guests who were leaving. Patrick shook his hand.

'Thank you for coming. It was good of you to pay your respects.' Martin spoke automatically. Patrick had heard Martin repeating the phrase to every departing guest as he'd walked down the stairs.

Louise held out her hand. To her surprise, Martin didn't shake it. Instead he hugged her and kissed her cheek.

'Goodbye, Martin. Take care of yourself and look after your hand,' she murmured.

'I will, Louise. And thank you.'

Arthur joined them and Louise allowed him to usher her out of the door. The three of them walked down the lane to Arthur's car. The light was poor and it wasn't easy to negotiate the pools of mud. Arthur didn't say anything until they were all safely closeted in the car, and even then he glanced around for potential eavesdroppers.

'Now listen to me,' Arthur said solemnly when he was sure he couldn't be overheard. 'Now listen to me.'

Just like in the barn, Arthur's voice had taken on a mesmerising quality. 'You will need to produce a relic of Alice for the ritual.'

'A what?' Patrick asked in bewilderment.

Louise thought she understood. 'Something like her favourite teddy bear? I've kept everything that belonged to our daughter. Her toys, her clothes, all her books and drawings. Just tell me what you want, Arthur, and I'll find something suitable.'

'The relic needs to be more directly connected to Alice

than one of her possessions,' he said decisively. 'A lock of her hair would normally do, but we're very close to the time limit when we can bring her back. So it needs to be something far more personal.'

'A pillowcase or pyjamas that haven't been washed since she died?' Patrick suggested.

Arthur stroked his chin thoughtfully. 'Eyelashes often adhere to the inside of a death mask. Still, the more I consider it, the more I don't think eyelashes or even eyebrows would suffice in this case. And speaking of a death mask – I don't suppose you had one made?'

Stunned by the suggestion, Patrick muttered, 'No, it never occurred to us at the time.'

'Some people keep children's baby teeth.' Arthur was trying to be helpful. 'That would probably work.'

'We didn't keep any,' Louise revealed.

'I see.' Arthur jammed his car keys into the ignition. 'Well, whatever you provide, it must be personal to Alice. Very personal in a corporal, physical way. I hope you understand.'

'We do, but we need time to think of something,' Patrick pleaded.

'Not too much time, Patrick. That's the one thing that's in desperately short supply. Whatever you find, you will have to deliver it to me tomorrow evening at sunset. I'll have everything arranged by then. If we decide to go ahead at that point, tomorrow night your daughter will sleep under your roof. You have my word on that.' Arthur turned the key and drove slowly down the track towards the main road.

# Eleven

The clouds burst and rain began to fall when Arthur drove Patrick and Louise from the O'Shea farmhouse to their cottage. Large drops thundered down on the roof of the car, making conversation impossible. Louise wasn't sorry. Preoccupied with Arthur's demand for a 'relic' of Alice, she was racking her brains, trying to think of something they could use.

By the time Arthur dropped them off at their door, the winter chill had iced the rain to sleet. They didn't invite Arthur in. He drove off quickly and they went into their living room.

'The relic,' Patrick began.

'Yes?' Louise looked expectantly at him.

'I have an idea where we can get one.'

She listened in silence while Patrick outlined his suggestion.

'Yes,' she answered briefly when he had finished speaking.

'Yes,' he repeated, shocked by her reaction. 'No argument, no protest, just "yes"?'

'It's a ghastly, horrible prospect and I would argue with you if I could think of a single alternative, but I can't.'

128

'What we're about to do will be illegal as well as ghastly, Louise. If we're caught we could be imprisoned—'

'I know,' she cut him short.

'Yet you still want to go ahead?'

'We have no choice, Patrick. Not if we want to see Alice again.'

'You're right.'

She made an effort to concentrate on the practical. 'We'd better change out of these clothes.'

'Given the weather, into something warm and waterproof,' he advised.

They went upstairs, hung their funeral clothes away and donned thermals, flannel shirts, thick sweaters, slacks and boots. While Louise piled their warmest waterproof coats, gardening gloves and her handbag into the car, Patrick went to the garage. He switched on the light and left the door open. Louise sat in the passenger seat and watched him pack a holdall with tools he picked out from his wall racks. When he'd finished gathering what he wanted, he zipped up the bag and carried it to the boot of the car. After depositing it inside he returned to the garage, brought out a spade and pickaxe and tossed them alongside the holdall. He switched off the light inside the garage, locked the door and proceeded to check all the doors and windows on the cottage.

After he'd disappeared around the side of the house, Louise pulled down the sun visor above her seat and hit the car's interior light. She'd taped the last photograph that had been taken of Alice to the back of the visor.

She ran her fingers over the contours of Alice's face, so beautiful and so heartbreakingly familiar. Slowly, lingeringly and lovingly she traced the smile on her daughter's lips with her forefinger. What had Alice been smiling about? She recalled taking the photograph in the garden of their old home. She remembered that they'd both been laughing beforehand but, try as she may, she couldn't recall why. Had they been playing a game? How could she have forgotten?

She started when she heard Patrick's approaching footsteps and immediately flipped up the visor. Keys in hand, Patrick shut the boot before sitting in the driver's seat.

'What's the time?'

She checked her watch. 'Nearly ten o'clock.'

'We should reach there in about three to four hours, depending on traffic. Hopefully there'll be no one about at that time in the morning.' He switched off the interior light, turned the key in the ignition, reversed the car and set off down the drive.

For the first time since they'd moved to Wake Wood they headed directly out of town into the network of narrow lanes that led – eventually – to the motorway. A silent hour and a half later they reached the six-lane thoroughfare. Patrick flicked through the channels on the car radio until he found one that played innocuous background music.

Louise settled back and tried to pretend that the drive was no different from any other she and Patrick had taken. But she couldn't prevent a sick sour feeling of foreboding rising from the pit of her stomach. Her imagination went into overdrive. She tried to picture Alice in her coffin – not as she'd been when they'd buried her, but as she'd be after months in the earth. How long did it take a child's body to decay? She hadn't asked at the time, but now she wondered if the coffin they'd chosen was airtight. If it was, would that have delayed decomposition? Would Alice's face still be recognisable? Would she be able to bear to look on her again?

What seemed like half a lifetime later, Patrick turned off at an exit and entered a 1930s-built suburb of the city centre. After the rural surroundings of Wake Wood, even at night the built-up area appeared strange, almost alien. The lights were too bright, the neon signs gratingly garish, the streets dirtier than Louise remembered from the time they'd lived there. She'd never felt at home in Wake Wood. And now she felt like a stranger here. Would she ever find a place she could truly call home again?

It was then that she remembered the promise Arthur had elicited from Patrick. Alice's return would bind them to Wake Wood for the rest of their lives. They could never leave the town afterwards. She'd wanted to ask Arthur what would happen if they tried but she'd lacked the courage.

She dared to look at Patrick but he was staring straight ahead, concentrating on the road. She couldn't believe they were even contemplating what they were about to do. But, as she'd told Patrick, she simply couldn't think of an alternative.

They reached the deserted city centre and turned west. They passed tower blocks of social housing, pubs, a solitary church, a supermarket, off-licence and a bingo hall, before turning down a side street bordered on one side by an Edwardian terrace of houses long given over to multiple occupation and, on the other, the railings of the cemetery where they'd buried Alice.

Patrick slowed the car to walking pace. Behind the railings, uniform rows of gleaming wet marble headstones stretched as far as they could see. He finally parked on a grass verge some distance from the locked gates and as close to the railings as he could get. He switched off the engine and the windscreen wipers fell silent. Rain was still sheeting down from the skies in a heavy, unrelenting downpour that gleamed blue-white, like icicles, in the light of the street lamps.

Louise sensed Patrick looking at her. His voice was eerie, disembodied by the darkness. 'We don't have to do this.'

'Yes, we do.' It wasn't that she was simply contradicting him. They had no option but to carry out the plan they'd made in order to bring back Alice. The danger of discovery they faced in the cemetery was very real. But she was prepared to risk everything she had, even her life, in order to see, touch and hold her daughter again. She made an effort to empty her mind of everything other than the task in hand.

She couldn't predict with any certainty what was going to happen with Arthur or with the ceremony of Alice's return. She only knew that now she and Patrick had made the decision to proceed and set the chain of events in motion, they would have to continue and see it through. Risking the outcome, whatever it brought them – and Alice.

'It's foul out there. You should wait in here. I'll be as quick as I can.' Without waiting for her to reply, Patrick left the car and stepped out into the rain. She heard him open the boot. He lifted out the shovel and pickaxe and pitched them over the railings. The bag and torch followed, but he leaned over the rails and deposited them more carefully on the ground.

She watched him step up on to the bonnet of the car and jump over the metal fence into the cemetery. When he landed, he picked up and switched on his torch, pointing it away from himself and the road and into the cemetery. She glanced at the car door. Patrick had parked too close to the rails for her to open her own door, so she took her handbag and slid across the seat to his.

Patrick looked round when he heard her click the car door closed. He turned up the collar of his jacket against the rain and came to the railings when he saw her climb on to the bonnet of the car, as he'd done. Extending his hand, he helped her jump down on to the cemetery side.

'Are you sure you want to come with me?' he asked.

'We made this decision together. I want to help.' She picked herself and the shovel up from the ground and followed Patrick along a path between the headstones. Ten minutes later they were in front of the white marble angel they'd chosen because of its resemblance to their daughter.

Patrick shone the torch on to Alice's name and dates

and the pair stood for a moment, rain streaming down their faces, remembering their lives as they had been before Alice had been taken from them.

The angel was heavy. It took their combined strength to lift it and its plinth from the plot and set it aside on the path. When they finished, Patrick handed Louise the torch and raised the pickaxe over the ground that held their daughter's coffin.

'Ready?' he whispered.

'Ready,' she answered softly. She propped the light on the ground behind the headstone in front of Alice's grave and prepared to wield the shovel.

Rain had already soaked through their clothes, weighing them down and dampening and chafing their skin before they'd even started digging. The ground was wet, sloppy. Earth had turned to soft liquid mud that oozed into their boots, permeated their trouser legs, and slimed beneath their coat sleeves. It irritated and rubbed but they worked on steadily, gasping in cold gulps of air as they shivered and froze.

The cemetery was quiet, still, and Louise was very aware of the noise Patrick was making every time he hit the earth with his pick. It was easier for her to work quietly. All she had to do was slide the spade into the earth and pile it out beside the grave.

When they heard a car engine Patrick hissed, 'Stop!'

Louise switched off the torch and they flung themselves flat on the swampy ground between the grave markers until the car headlights moved on and all sounds of the engine died away.

Patrick waited for silence to reign once more among

the tombstones before reaching for his pick and returning to the hole. Louise continued to shovel out the sodden clods of earth he loosened, adding them to the pyramid she was building to the side of the grave.

Louise's spade hit Alice's coffin before Patrick's pick. When she heard the dull *clunk* of steel on wood, she tensed and looked across at Patrick. His eyes were enigmatic, glittering pools in the light from the torch.

'I need the bag,' Patrick whispered. He was standing waist deep in the hole they'd made, covered in mud from head to foot.

Louise was closer to the bag than him. She stretched out and pulled it towards her. After unzipping it she lifted the torch on to the side and studied the contents.

'There's a small axe somewhere in there,' Patrick prompted.

She found it and handed it to him before moving away from the hole to give him more room to work.

Patrick lifted the axe high above his head and struck a blow. The blade bounced off the highly polished oak. It was then she remembered that they'd opted for the highest-quality coffin because neither of them could bear the thought of cheap wood rotting beneath Alice, leaving her to lie in the dirt.

Patrick followed the first blow with another, and another. Louise closed her eyes and winced after every one. The noise he was making echoed around them so loudly she was sure it could be heard in the bedrooms of the houses across the road.

Mouth dry, heart pounding, skin crawling with fear, she stared at the darkened windows, expecting curtains to move or a light to be switched on at any moment.

Apparently oblivious to the din he was making, Patrick continued to strike the wooden coffin lid. He only stopped chopping when he heard the wood splinter.

Crouching low, he inserted the blade of the axe into the gash he'd made in the surface, pushing and twisting, exerting pressure to widen the aperture until it was large enough for him to insert his hand.

He leaned back and wiped his face, rubbing more dirt on to it than he removed.

'Here.' He handed the axe back to Louise.

She took it and returned it to the bag.

Patrick kneeled down on the coffin in the bottom of the grave and felt around inside the hole he'd made with his right hand. The torch flickered and the shadows thickened.

'I can't see what I'm doing down here. Move the light closer,' he ordered Louise, emotion making him brusque.

She lay on the ground, leaned over and shifted the torch to the edge of the grave. She blanched when, through the hole Patrick had made in the coffin lid, she caught a glimpse of Alice's shroud clinging to her decomposing remains. She closed her eyes tightly against the sight of blackened skin and pale bones. But it was too late. The image was already imprinted on her memory, as was the deterioration in the coffin lining she remembered as white satin trimmed with lace. It was now green with mildew and, after Patrick's rooting around, stained by brown slimed earth. The thought of the daughter she'd loved and cared for every single moment of her life since her birth, lying in the ground in such filth, horrified and sickened her.

Nauseous, trembling, she crawled behind a neighbouring tombstone and retched.

Patrick climbed out and followed her. 'Louise . . .'

Ashamed and disgusted by her reaction and of their desecration of their daughter's grave, Louise couldn't bear to look at Patrick.

'Louise,' Patrick repeated, urgently. 'I can't do this alone. I need your help.'

She mumbled, 'Sorry.'

He touched her shoulder. 'Think of Alice.'

She pulled herself together and crawled back to the side of the hole. Picking up the torch, she waited until Patrick had climbed into the grave again before shining the light down on the coffin and its macabre contents.

Fresh wooden splinters were strewn around the oak box, all mixed in with the rain and mud, and she couldn't help thinking that now the coffin had been breached her daughter's body would decay all the quicker. The words the minister had spoken at the service echoed through her mind.

*Ashes to ashes . . . dust to dust . . .*

She turned aside but it was useless. The sight of the hole, the coffin and its contents had seared into her memory and she knew the images would haunt not only her nightmares but her waking moments from that time on.

'The bag.' Patrick held out his hand.

She passed it to him.

He took it from her, opened it wider and moved her hand that was holding the torch so the beam illuminated the contents.

He searched through it until he found a pair of garden secateurs. Angling the torch again so it shone down on the coffin at the bottom of the hole, he said, 'Try to keep it steady there,' before stooping down over the damaged lid.

Breathing heavily, desperately trying to think of what Patrick was about to do as 'necessary', Louise watched as he inserted his right hand back inside Alice's coffin. He rooted around in the muddy, waterlogged remains for a few minutes before pulling what was left of Alice's right arm through the gap he'd made. It was pale against the mud, skeletally thin. Louise had to suppress an urge to lean down and stroke it.

Holding the arm up outside the coffin, Patrick passed Alice's fingers into his left hand. Something was wound around them. It glittered silver in the torch-light when Patrick removed it and slipped it into his pocket. Then Louise remembered. She'd placed the silver chain she'd bought Alice for her birthday in her daughter's hands before the undertaker had closed the coffin.

Patrick separated and splayed Alice's fingers. He gripped the little finger tightly, picked up the secateurs with his right hand and, taking his time, placed the blades either side at the base where it joined her palm. He exerted pressure on the secateurs and snapped, freeing the slender bone that still had skin, flesh and nail attached to it.

He released Alice's hand, and it and the length of arm he'd exposed slithered back inside the coffin. He felt in his back trouser pocket and removed a sample bag. He dropped Alice's finger into it and offered it to Louise. She stared at him in horror.

'Take it,' he ordered.

She reluctantly took it from him, went to her handbag, opened it and laid the bag gently inside.

When she turned back, she saw that Patrick had climbed out of the hole and was busy with the spade, filling in Alice's grave. She knelt down beside the earth she'd piled up and helped him to push the mud back on to the splintered coffin.

All the time they worked, she felt that it was Alice and not the angel who was watching them, and all the while Alice's voice echoed through her mind.

*Mum? Dad? Are you both mad?*

Was she? Was Patrick?

Had they both been driven insane by the loss of their daughter?

Were they crazy to believe Arthur? Would they really be able to hold Alice again tomorrow night? Not the rotting, decomposing Alice buried in the grave they'd just despoiled. But the smiling, living, breathing child they had both loved.

When all the earth had been returned to the grave, Patrick scraped as much of the mud from the path as he could. He shone the light around Alice's plot.

'Too much mud – someone might get suspicious. Take that flower pot to the standpipe and fill it with water. We'll wash down this whole area.'

Louise did as he asked. When it was as clean as they could make it without brushes, they dragged the angel and its plinth back on to Alice's grave.

Patrick stared at it. 'No one would ever guess we'd been here,' he murmured.

'Except us, Patrick. We know and we'll never forget it,' she said sadly.

He lifted up the pick and shovel. 'All we can do is hope that Arthur keeps his promise and that this will have been worth it.'

She retrieved the bag and her handbag and followed him back towards the railings.

# Twelve

Patrick and Louise were emotionally and physically drained by the time they drove back into Wake Wood. When they turned up the drive to the cottage, Louise noticed a faint streak of a lighter shade of grey lining the eastern horizon that suggested dawn was breaking somewhere above the rain clouds.

Patrick parked the car, turned off the engine and slumped over the steering wheel. Louise switched on the interior light and glanced at her watch. 'In one and a half hours I'll have to open the pharmacy.'

'No, you won't.' Patrick sat up and rubbed his eyes. 'It's more important you sleep for a couple of hours. If people find the shop locked they'll return later if they want something. I only hope no animal is hurt or falls seriously sick today. I'm barely capable of rational thought, let alone operating or doctoring.'

She glanced down at their filthy clothes. 'Before we make any decisions about today, the first thing we both need to do is shower and change.'

'And give the car a good clean,' Patrick added ruefully; the interior light illuminated seats and a car interior coated in a layer of mud as thick as that on their boots and coats. 'If you take first shower,

I'll tackle the car. I can't get any dirtier than I am now.'

Louise clutched her handbag close to her chest. 'Do you think—'

'There's no point in discussing what's going to happen. Not now, Louise.' Patrick spoke harshly, cutting her short.

It was then Louise realised that he'd had as many, if not more, misgivings than she had about their desecration of their daughter's grave.

'We'll find out one way or another tonight,' Patrick said in a softer tone.

Louise knew it was the closest she would get to an apology. She glanced at her handbag. She couldn't stop thinking about the contents of the sample bag inside it. She longed to ask Patrick if he was as terrified of a negative outcome of the 'return ceremony' as she was. Especially when she recalled the lie they'd told Arthur. But she simply couldn't bring herself to phrase the question. There were so many imponderables that could affect the outcome.

Patrick was right. At nightfall they would find out the truth – or not – of Arthur's promises. And if he really did return Alice to them, despite their lie, then all the trauma and horror of the night would have been worth it. Wouldn't it?

Patrick finished cleaning the car, stripped off his filthy clothes in the porch off the kitchen and went upstairs to shower. Clean and dry, he went into the master bedroom to dress. He'd assumed Louise was downstairs but as he was about to go down the stairs he noticed the door of the guest room was open a little. He pushed it wider. Louise was standing in the middle of the room, looking around.

He gazed at the shelves full of toys and books. 'It might be a different room in a different house, but it's as if Alice had never left,' he murmured. 'You've arranged all her things just as she had them on the morning of her ninth birthday.'

'Do you really think the room looks the same as Alice's in the old house?' she asked.

'Exactly,' he murmured.

Louise went to the wardrobe, opened it and lifted out one of Alice's dresses. 'Do you think Alice's clothes will still fit her—'

He interrupted her. 'I don't know, Louise.'

'There are so many things I should have asked Arthur and didn't think to. Will she—'

'I don't know any more than you do about what's going to happen tonight, Louise.' He opened his arms to her and she went to him. 'But one thing I do know is that this is going to be a very long day. For both of us.'

Patrick was right. That day was the longest Louise had experienced in her life. Restless, unable to sleep or relax, she cleaned the shower and bathroom, put on a load of washing and opened the pharmacy, all before nine o'clock. Customers wandered in and out, most browsing, few buying. She served pills, potions, medicines and cosmetics, answered questions automatically without really thinking about what she was saying, all the while watching minutes tick past longer than hours.

During the slack times when no one demanded her attention, she stared out of the window at the rain-sodden street, preoccupied with thoughts of the night ahead. She'd given the sample bag containing Alice's finger to Patrick. She hadn't asked what he intended to do with it until it was needed.

And . . . in the meantime, all she could do was wait and wonder.

'Do you realise it's finally stopped raining?' Patrick commented when they left their car and walked across the windswept yard at the back of Arthur's house.

Too emotional to risk answering, Louise nodded.

'The sky's clear. We'll be able to see the moon and stars tonight.' He wrapped his arm around her shoulders and gave her a brief hug.

They weren't alone. Half the residents of the town were already in the yard, and behind them more people were parking their cars or walking across the fields towards the back of Arthur's house.

The strange contraption Louise had seen the night their car had broken down dominated the skyline as it had then, rising high above the roof of the house. Again, Louise noted its similarity in shape and structure, albeit of a very different size, to the rope-and-twig object Mary Brogan had placed around Deirdre's neck when she'd convulsed.

A tractor was parked in the yard next to the metal cage that hung from a central point in the high wooden frame. Arthur stood alongside it, feeding an enormous bonfire that had been built in the exact centre of the yard. He waved Patrick and Louise over as soon as he caught sight of them. The heat grew more intense the closer they drew to the flames.

'Watch out.' Arthur pointed to a yellow JCB lurching its way out of the barn. Mick O'Shea's body lay inert in the shovel. Ben and Tommy, the two farmer brothers who'd watched Patrick perform a Caesarean on their cow a few days before, stopped the JCB but left the engine running. They jumped down from the cab, lifted Mick's body from the shovel and hauled it up inside the metal cage, fastening it into a metal harness that hung inside the cage.

Working together, they secured the corpse with metal chains, wrapping them around Mick's neck, limbs and chest. When they'd finished, they closed the cage and attached it to a power drive at the back of the tractor.

Arthur checked every inch of Ben and Tommy's handiwork meticulously before turning to Patrick and Louise. He held out his hands to them and the assembled townsfolk.

'You're all very welcome here, especially Patrick and Louise, Wake Wood's newest permanent residents.'

Louise's attention was drawn to a table behind Arthur. It held an array of archaic-looking surgical and medical instruments resembling nothing she'd seen before. She glanced at Patrick, intending to show them to him, but his attention was fixed on the tractor.

Something whipped through the air above them and the tractor engine exploded into life. It belched out a dark, foul-smelling cloud of diesel smoke that engulfed Louise and provoked a fit of coughing.

When the smoke cleared, she saw that the drive at the back of the tractor was spinning, tightening the chains wrapped around Mick's body. The group of townsfolk drew closer to Arthur, Patrick and Louise. She recognised Martin and Mrs O'Shea among many of her customers. Both of the O'Sheas were watching her and Patrick intently. Mary Brogan left the mass of people, approached Louise and hugged her in a gesture of solidarity and friendship.

Arthur waved to attract the tractor driver's attention. When he was sure the man was looking at him, Arthur rotated his finger, signalling that he should increase the revs on the engine. The man pressed down the accelerator and the air was filled with the sound of bones cracking, snapping and shattering. Mick's limbs and torso shuddered as his skeleton splintered, jerking his corpse in a parody of the way he'd moved in life.

Mesmerised, Patrick and Louise watched Mick's corpse break and crumble before their eyes.

'In times past they did that' – Arthur indicated Mick's swaying body locked in its peculiar dance of death – 'with a lump hammer. Hard work and messy for those who had to carry it out.' He turned to the driver and shouted, 'That will do.'

The driver cut the engine.

'Patrick, lend a hand,' Arthur ordered.

Arthur took a couple of the peculiar surgical instruments from the table and led Patrick around to the back of the mangled corpse hanging limply in the chains and harness inside the cage. Slicing Mick's jacket open, Arthur exposed his buckled thorax and made an incision along the line of Mick's backbone. Held taut by the chains, Mick's vertebrae extruded through the cut, protruding one by one, each in turn as Arthur opened the flaps of skin.

Arthur exchanged the blade he was wielding for a tool that resembled long-handled wire cutters. He slipped the head inside the incision he'd made in the corpse and fitted it carefully around the spinal cord, but stopped short of severing it.

'Do the honours and cut it, will you, Patrick?'

Patrick took the instrument and squeezed the handles together. The spinal cord snapped and fell back in two separate halves.

'It's time to produce the relic.' Arthur waited expectantly.

Patrick took the sample bag containing Alice's finger from his pocket and handed it to Arthur, who opened it and examined the contents. 'That will suffice. Well done, Patrick.'

Louise approached the men.

'You both all right?' Arthur asked solicitously. He waited for Louise to signal assent before reaching into the cage and prising open Mick's jaw. He placed Alice's finger below the tongue in the corpse's mouth, and closed it. Pulling Louise close, he murmured, 'Stay with me.'

Pushing her in front of the blazing bonfire, he raised his voice and declaimed upwards to the night sky. The moon had risen, a bright yellow waxing segment surrounded by a litter of twinkling stars, that seemed to grow brighter by the minute.

'On the wild wind ye fly, 'tween this world and the
    next.
From that twilight realm ye see
O'er your perch, the trials of the living . . . and the
    wake of the dead.'

A vast flock of enormous ravens flew in from the woods and circled above the yard, once . . . twice . . . three times . . . flapping their wings so hard Louise and Patrick could feel the breeze they spawned. Their harsh, guttural cawing vied for supremacy with the spitting and cracking of green wood on the bonfire.

Arthur raised his voice further so he could be heard above the noise of the birds. He appealed to the assembled crowd as well as to the sky. Conversant with the ritual, knowing what to expect, people reached for their neighbours' hands. Holding them, they surged forward in a single line as Arthur spoke.

'Help us now call Alice. We bring her here three days to say her farewells, and afterwards return. Go to the trees, lie among the roots. Go to the trees, lie among the roots . . .'

The townsfolk joined in Arthur's chant after Arthur spoke Alice's name.

'Take these hands, ALICE!' Arthur shouted.

'Take these hands, ALICE!' the assembly echoed.

Patrick and Louise found themselves crying out their

daughter's name willingly for the first time since her death.

'Take these bones, ALICE . . .' Arthur continued.

'Take these bones, ALICE.'

Above them the ravens continued to swoop and wheel. Their wings beat ever more furiously, until they whirled and stirred the air with all the strength of a high wind. The electric lights on the outside of Arthur's barn and house flickered and dimmed. Unseen hands moved in the darkness and poured liquid fuel on the bonfire. It flared instantly, the flames rising high and illuminating the upturned faces of the crowd gathered before Arthur in the yard.

'Take this heart . . . ALICE!'

'Take this heart . . . ALICE!'

'And ALICE!' Arthur looked to the crowd for support. 'Take these eyes . . .'

'Take these eyes . . . ALICE.'

Dark blood flooded from beneath the eyelids of Mick's corpse. Seconds later, rivulets of blood ran in steady streams from his ears, nose and mouth. It was a foul and ghastly sight, but Louise simply couldn't stop staring, charting the slow disintegration of the body as it reverted to its base composition of liquid, tissue and chemicals.

Finally, Arthur broke the spell that was holding everyone in the yard in thrall. 'Take him down,' he shouted to Ben and Tom.

The two men lowered the cage, extricated Mick's corpse still held fast in the harness, and manoeuvred it until it rested on iron trestles. When it was finally lying flat and firm, they unbuttoned the front of Mick's jacket and shirt. After they'd prepared the corpse for the next stage of the ritual, they retreated behind Arthur.

Arthur picked up a wedge-shaped tool from the table and a large mallet. He stepped forward, placed the wedge on Mick's chest, and with three deafening, ringing blows split open Mick's sternum, laying the interior of his chest and lungs bare.

Louise took a deep breath of cold night air and steeled herself against the horror of what Arthur was doing to what had been the living, breathing body of a man she had met and known.

Arthur again gazed up at the sky. 'Now we need living blood.'

Patrick drew alongside him but Arthur looked past him to Louise.

'Female blood would be better.'

Louise joined the two men and held out her hand to her husband. 'Cut me, Patrick.'

Arthur positioned Louise's hand over Mick's open chest and passed Patrick a scalpel. Patrick hesitated and looked into Louise's eyes. Reading Patrick's reluctance, Louise took the scalpel from his hand and sliced deep into her palm. Her blood dripped slowly at first, then gushed into Mick's open chest cavity.

'Enough!' Arthur declared.

Mary Brogan left the crowd again and handed Louise a clean towel that she helped her wrap around the wound.

'The fuel,' Arthur demanded.

Arthur's prompt galvanised Ben. Like an altar boy

obeying a priest, he bowed to Arthur's command, picked up a can and liberally doused Mick's body in tractor diesel. Arthur watched Ben drain the container. When it was empty, Arthur waved him back and yanked a flaming length of wood from the bonfire.

'Step back, away to a safe distance, all of you,' Arthur ordered.

He waited until the tide of people had receded to the edge of the yard before dropping the torch on to Mick's body. It flared instantly, bathing the corpse in a searing bright blue flame that dazzled the eyes of the crowd, temporarily blinding them.

Mick's body jerked and writhed. Expanding from within the open chest cavity, it grew ever larger and darker, swelling in shape and size, straining the constraints of the harness that held it fast.

Overhead, the ravens screeched and fled the heat of the flames in a single massive movement. Their raucous cries faded as they flew back and disappeared over the woods.

The crowd swayed, shaking as though they'd all been caught up in a violent gusting hurricane.

Arthur turned his head skywards again and declaimed to the stars.

'Feel now the power of transformation course through your true selves . . . and look away, avert your gaze . . .'

The crowd moved as one, turning their backs on the fearful flaming and squirming remains of Mick's body.

Louise, Patrick and Arthur began to vibrate, heave, shake and tremble along with the rest of the crowd.

Louise looked at Patrick and saw trickles of blood seeping from his ears and nose. Then she turned to the crowd and realised that they were all bleeding. She smelled the iron tang of her own blood, strong in her nostrils, felt it dripping down from her nose, over her mouth and down her chin.

Arthur raised his hands to demand attention. The crowd fell silent, waiting for him to speak again.

'Now, all present here, join me again to bring Alice back among us.'

The blue flames that had engulfed the corpse moments before now flickered low and became a dull greenish glow.

Arthur looked wordlessly to Tom. The man knew what Arthur wanted him to do. Tom ran to pick up a fire extinguisher, returned to the corpse and doused the last remnants of the fire.

Clouds of steam rose hissing, white and billowing in the air. Arthur studied the table of instruments for a moment before picking up a gnarled ancient-looking tool with a long thin blade forged from black metal.

Tom retreated and Arthur approached the steaming husk that had been Mick O'Shea.

'The harness,' Arthur shouted.

Ben, Tom and two other men pulled on thick leather gloves, went to the trestle and forced open the metal harness.

Mick's body lay unrecognisable before the crowd. It was burnished hard and brown, transformed into a thick bronze eggshell-like cocoon.

Arthur hit the top of the cocoon with the instrument.

The shell cracked open, splintered, shattered and broke. A small piece of the outer casing fell to the ground and a sluggish stream of sticky blood-streaked coagulating liquid trickled out. It dripped from the edge of the trestle, covering the shell fragments on the ground.

Arthur rattled the tool around the aperture, enlarging it. When he'd finished, he plunged his arm inside to the elbow. He moved it around for a minute. When he finally withdrew his hand, he was holding a pulsating umbilical cord that dripped blood. He pulled it up, high in the air so everyone could see it, then, using his instrument, he cut through it. The crowd cried out.

Discarding the cord, Arthur turned his attention to the burned remains of Mick's head and shoulder girdle. He attacked them slowly and methodically with his instrument. Every cut and thrust he made on Mick's body shattered more pieces of the shell and released yet more glutinous, gelatinous bloodstained fluid.

Patrick and Louise continued to watch, stunned, speechless – awestruck by the spectacle unfolding before their eyes.

Arthur looked around. Anticipating his need, the men who'd helped him throughout the ceremony joined him at the trestle and assisted him in tearing pieces from the shell.

When they'd made a wide enough gap, Arthur inserted both his arms inside the cocoon to the elbows. He pulled back smoothly, drawing out the head and shoulders of a young girl.

He turned to Louise and smiled. 'Here she comes.'

Louise's eyes filled with tears. Through a mist she

watched Alice slide out into Arthur's arms. Her daughter was covered with broken pieces of charred shell, viscera and blood. Her eyes – Alice's wonderful dark eyes that she thought she'd never see again – were wide open.

Alice looked directly at Louise and murmured, 'Mum.'

Sobbing, Louise ran forward and enveloped her daughter in her arms. She was barely aware of the applause from the crowd.

Patrick moved alongside them. He took the towel someone handed him and wrapped Alice in it. Throwing his arms around his wife and daughter, he turned gratefully to Arthur.

'No need for words, Patrick. One look at the three of you together says it all.' Arthur reached out to the young girl. 'Welcome to Wake Wood, Alice.'

# Thirteen

Patrick drove them to the cottage. Louise sat in the back cradling Alice, who seemed very tired and sleepy, but wonderfully, blissfully alive.

While Patrick parked the car, Louise carried Alice upstairs into the bathroom. She stripped the blood-stained towel from her daughter and knelt beside the bath after Alice climbed in. Holding the shower head in one hand, Louise gently sponged and rinsed Alice down with the other. The residue of blood, ash and slime washed away easily, leaving Alice's skin white, clean, smooth and blemish-free.

Patrick followed them upstairs. Scarcely daring to believe what he was seeing, he leaned against the doorpost and watched his wife bathe their daughter.

'Just look at your hair, Alice. It's so long.' Louise finished soaping Alice's hair and combed through the length with her fingers. 'And your nails.' She sponged Alice's hands, paying special attention to her fingers. Every one of them was whole and unmarked, but that didn't stop her from re-examining the little finger on her daughter's right hand – the one Patrick had severed and taken from the grave.

Alice smiled at Louise sleepily through half-closed eyes. 'Mum, I had the strangest dream.'

'It's over now, sweetie. You're home safe and sound. Nothing can hurt you here.' Louise continued to shower Alice until clean, unstained water spiralled down the plughole. 'As soon as we've got you dry, it will be bedtime. And this time, I promise, you'll have the sweetest, not strangest, dreams.'

'Here.' Patrick lifted a bath towel from the heated rail. He handed it to Louise, who enveloped Alice in its folds before carrying her through into the room she'd prepared.

Patrick stood back while Louise towelled Alice dry, dressed her in clean pyjamas and tucked her into bed. Alice fell asleep before Louise even began to tell her a story but, unwilling to leave their daughter, Louise lay beside her. She lay looking at Alice for a long while but eventually her eyelids grew heavier and heavier and then she too slept, leaving Patrick to keep watch over both of them.

Exhausted as he was, Patrick simply couldn't stop looking at Alice, and even when he did manage to turn aside in the early hours he found it impossible to close his eyes. He simply had to keep glancing back at Alice to reassure himself that she was really there – with them in the cottage.

Dawn found him standing in front of the window of the guest bedroom watching the sun rise over the eastern horizon into a storybook illustration of a beautiful clear blue sky. The room was drenched in a marvellous golden light. Birdsong filled the air and in the distance he could hear cattle lowing and sheep bleating. It was a perfect pastoral scene and he wondered why he and Louise had decided to live in the city after they'd qualified. If they'd moved to Wake Wood before Alice's birth they'd have opened their eyes every morning to views like this one. And maybe – just maybe – there would have been no dog and their lives . . . and Alice's . . . would have been different.

He turned his head and gazed lovingly at his wife and daughter, still lying curled together, side by side, on the bed. Louise's arm was flung high, curving around Alice's head as though she were trying to protect their daughter, even in sleep.

He tiptoed out of the room and went into the bathroom. He showered, dressed in his own bedroom and, happier than he'd been in over a year, made his way downstairs to prepare a breakfast feast for his family.

Patrick was so busy cracking eggs and flipping pancakes that he didn't hear Louise enter the kitchen. He remained unaware of her presence until she moved behind him and slipped her arms around his waist. He grasped her hands, revelling in the feel of her body pressed against his back.

'Where's Alice?' he asked.

'Getting dressed upstairs in her room,' Louise answered.

The door opened behind them and Alice walked in.

'Good morning, honey.' Patrick turned around and beamed at her.

'Hey, sweetie.' Louise dropped a kiss on top of Alice's head. 'Did you sleep well?'

Alice thought for a moment, as though trying to decide. 'I think so.'

Louise poured herself a cup of coffee. 'Guess what – Dad's made pancakes for us.'

'Oh.' Alice looked around at the kitchen. There was uncertainty and something else – something they couldn't quite decipher in the expression on her face.

Patrick glanced at Louise uneasily.

'This house seems strange, different somehow,' Alice commented.

'Well, it is . . . a little,' Louise swiftly improvised. 'We came here to take a break, a kind of holiday.'

'I must have slept the whole way.' Alice left the kitchen, went into the hall and looked around before entering the living room.

Louise turned anxiously to Patrick. 'Do you think she's all right?'

'There's one sure way to find out.' Patrick opened the back door, disappeared and returned with two super-sized water guns. He filled them at the tap and handed both to Louise.

She smiled. 'You're right.' Then she shouted, 'Alice. War games! Us against Dad!'

Ten minutes later the three of them were racing around the garden. Louise and Alice were spraying Patrick with cold water, soaking him, his hair and his shirt, and he was laughing louder than either of them. When the guns had been emptied, Patrick rummaged in the shed and found a football. Alice jumped up and down with excitement when she saw it and threw herself enthusiastically into the game.

As she charged around with the ball, kicking, dribbling and blocking Louise's moves, Patrick and Louise exchanged glances and read one another's thoughts. How could they have thought their daughter was in any way different?

She was perfect, exactly as she had been . . . before . . .

Relieved, they joined her in fighting over and kicking the ball. It was just like old times. Alice hadn't changed, hadn't changed at all.

The only thing that had was their love for her. If anything, it was even stronger than they remembered.

When finally she tired of football, Alice demanded an afternoon game of hide-and-seek in the woods because she wanted to explore them. Patrick drove them all a short distance down the road to a thicket of woodland that had become one of his favourite places. He often took ten minutes out of his day to walk there between farm visits and, when his schedule allowed, he ate his lunchtime sandwiches there as well.

After he parked the car Louise volunteered to be 'it'. She stood behind a tree, closed her eyes and started counting to a hundred. Loath to be separated from Alice for a moment of the precious time they'd been granted to spend together, Louise opened her eyes at fifty. Patrick and Alice were already out of sight. She continued to count while she walked in the direction she thought she'd heard them take. When she reached a hundred she called out, 'Ready or not, I'm coming to find you.'

She could hear the noise of the wind turbines, loud and discordant, as she travelled deeper into the woods. The whirring felt unnaturally loud because of the stillness of the air and Louise shivered, suddenly apprehensive, as if someone were watching her. She raised her head and looked around. 'Where are you, guys?' she shouted at the top of her voice.

Picking up on the alarm in Louise's voice, Patrick stuck his foot out from behind a tree. Louise saw it, sneaked around behind him and pounced.

He pretended to be surprised but he could see that he hadn't fooled her. 'You got me, fair and square.' He kissed her, grabbed her hand and they walked on together.

Louise shouted, 'Alice, I'm coming to get you. Your father's already my prisoner and we're going to capture you.'

They searched, splitting up after ten minutes had ticked by and they'd failed to catch a glimpse of Alice, but they took care to keep one another in sight. Gradually their shouts became more insistent and panic-stricken. Louise saw the muscles tense in Patrick's jaw and she knew he was thinking the same as her. Had they found Alice again only to lose her?

At that moment, realisation cut into her deeply and agonisingly with all the force of a knife. They would lose Alice again anyway in two more days and nights.

'There she is.' Relieved, Patrick charged over winter's dead leaves into a clearing. Alice was standing immobile, staring up at something caught in the branches of a tree high above her. When Patrick and Louise drew close they saw it was a dead crow strung upside down, its claws bound tightly together, wings flapping open as the wind stirred the body and ruffled its feathers.

Louise rushed to Alice's side, reaching her just after Patrick. 'Alice, are you all right, sweetie?'

Alice didn't look away from the dead bird. 'What's it doing up there?'

'I don't know.' Patrick caught Alice's hand. 'Maybe someone put it there to ward off other birds.'

'Why?'

'That I can't answer, honey,' he murmured.

Alice continued to stare at it.

'Let's go, sweetie,' Louise prompted, pulling Alice gently towards her.

Alice tugged her hand free from Patrick's and felt the edge of her jacket. 'Look what I found, here in my pocket.' She held up the silver chain Louise had given her on her birthday.

The silver chain that had been buried with her in her coffin. Louise looked at Patrick and he smiled knowingly. She realised he must have slipped it into Alice's pocket when they'd been playing football.

'Do you remember when you got it?' Louise questioned.

'You gave it to me . . .' Alice frowned with the effort of trying to remember. 'Some time. I can't quite remember when.'

'It's beautiful, like its owner.' Patrick took it from Alice's hand and fastened it around her neck. He tenderly kissed the crown of her head. 'Come on. I'm hungry. Time to go home.'

They turned and trekked down the path towards the road where Patrick had parked the car. In the distance, the arms of the tallest wind turbine turned slowly in the evening light, the noise it made grating and hostile.

Arthur's words echoed unbidden through Louise's mind.

*I can bring her back. But I warn you, it will only be for three days. When that time has passed you will have to return her. Most of the people I've helped say that the three extra days spent with their loved ones have been worth the pain of a second separation. But, as I've only ever brought loved ones back for others and never for myself, I can't help you to make that decision. You have to do it yourselves.*

She also remembered Patrick's sceptical comment.

*It's not possible to bring people back from the dead, Arthur. When someone dies, that's it. The end! Nothingness!*

Had Patrick known how much his declaration had hurt her? How she couldn't bear the thought of Alice dissolving into nothingness after all their daughter had meant to them and all she'd been?

And Arthur's final warning.

*No, it isn't, Patrick. And it is possible to bring them back for a last goodbye. Ask your wife if you don't believe me. But there's one other thing that you have to ask yourself. Would you want to bring your daughter home, if you knew in advance that you'd have to lose her all over again?*

The one thing that Louise was sure of already was that she wasn't prepared to lose Alice again after finding her a second time. Not without putting up a fight to keep her close and with them for ever.

And if that meant disregarding Arthur and his warnings, so be it.

They all climbed into Patrick's car. Because Alice and Patrick were silent, Louise found herself talking too much, too quickly, too brightly, saying the first things that came into her mind. Talking about what she could make for tea, about the games they could play afterwards in the garden, the stories Alice might like at bedtime.

Patrick started the car and edged off the verge on to the road. Alice leaned forward from the back seat and moved close to Louise.

'Mum?'

'Yes, sweetie?' Louise reached back and stroked Alice's cheek with her forefinger.

'Did you hear music last night?'

'What's that?' Louise turned around and looked at her daughter.

'Did you hear music last night when you were asleep?'

'If I was asleep I wouldn't have heard anything,' Louise replied logically. 'What kind of music?'

'Voices singing my name.'

Louise's blood ran cold. She glanced across at Patrick, who appeared to be concentrating on driving. 'No, I didn't hear anything.'

'I did,' Alice said matter-of-factly.

Without warning Patrick slammed on the brakes. Ahead of them, three cars were parked in a lay-by. Half a dozen men were standing in a circle at the entrance to an abandoned building on their right. The ground at the men's feet was stained with blood.

'Stay in the car,' Patrick ordered Louise and Alice. He wrenched open his car door and shouted to the men, 'What's going on here?'

One of the men cried out, 'Quick! Scarper! It's the vet.'

Two men ran off. Patrick strode up to the other four and looked down at the ground. Two dogs lay in the dirt. Both were battered, torn and bleeding from dozens of wounds, bites and puncture marks.

'Proud of yourselves? Forcing dumb animals to fight to the death for your amusement?' Patrick questioned scathingly. Disgusted with the men, he crouched down and examined the dogs.

The remaining men shuffled their feet in embarrassment, turning their faces away from Patrick's judgemental eye.

'This dog's dead,' Patrick pronounced bitterly to no one in particular. 'You'd better bury it. This one's alive but needs treatment. Get me a blanket or something I can carry him in . . . Fast!' he emphasised when no one moved.

One man scurried off to one of the parked cars.

'Whose dog is this?' Patrick demanded forcefully, finally looking up at the men.

'The owner's gone. He left him for dead,' a young boy volunteered.

Patrick stroked the dog's muzzle tenderly. 'It's OK, boy; you're all right with me. I'll see to you.'

The man returned from his car with an old coat. He handed it to Patrick, who laid it on the ground. Patrick eased the dog on to the coat, wrapped the animal in it and scooped it into his arms. Returning to the estate car, he laid it in the back and settled it down before climbing into the driving seat.

Alice turned and leaned over the back of the estate. The dog was lying flat, whimpering in pain. She reached down.

Patrick saw her move in the rear-view mirror. 'Alice, don't touch him,' he shouted. 'He's injured and frightened and could bite.'

'It's all right, Dad.' Alice stroked the dog's head and it fell silent. 'He'll be fine now. He knows I'm not going to hurt him.'

Louise took a deep breath. Weak with relief, she gazed at Alice. 'You have Dad's touch with animals, sweetie,' she complimented.

'I do.' Alice continued to pet the dog. 'And Dad and me will soon have him better. Won't we, Dad?'

When they reached home Louise headed for the kitchen so that she could start making a meal. Patrick carried the dog into the outbuilding he'd converted into a surgery. Alice followed and watched him sedate the dog before cleaning and disinfecting his bites and wounds. When the sedation took hold and the dog fell unconscious, Patrick began to stitch his injuries.

'Dad?' Alice drew closer, watching him work on the animal.

'Mmm, yes, honey?' Patrick concentrated on drawing two pieces of badly torn skin together.

'Can I do it?'

Surprised, Patrick looked down at her. 'If you want to. But you'll need to put on surgical gloves. They're in that box.' He pointed to the shelf where he kept the disposable items he used every day, such as paper sheets, tissues and antiseptic wipes.

Alice took a pair of latex gloves from the box, pulled them on and joined Patrick. He handed her the implement he'd been using.

'Now hold it like I did . . . that's right. And pull it tight.' He watched as Alice carefully tugged the suture and closed the wound he'd been stitching. 'Now push the needle through again, just here.'

Alice did as he asked and inserted the tip of the curved needle neatly through the lips of the wound. She frowned in concentration but no emotion registered on her face, either in her eyes or her mouth, as she carried on closing the dog's injuries.

'People shouldn't hurt animals, should they?' she asked after she'd finished the second suture.

'No, they shouldn't,' Patrick agreed warily, wondering what she was going to say next.

'And animals shouldn't hurt people either.'

Patrick hesitated before replying, uncertain what, if anything, she remembered about the dog that had attacked her. 'It's not the same,' he ventured. 'Because animals can't think logically the way we do, they don't mean to hurt people in the same way that people mean to hurt them.'

'Oh. Do you really think so?'

Patrick took the needle from her. 'You're doing very well, but I'll finish this last one. It's awkward.'

The door opened behind them and Arthur walked in. 'I heard there was a bit of trouble, Patrick.'

'You could say that,' Patrick concurred quietly, looking at Alice before giving Arthur a warning glance.

Alice continued to stroke the dog's head while Patrick worked. 'Dad, can we keep him?' she asked suddenly.

'I don't see why not.' Patrick looked up and saw Arthur watching both of them.

'Mum said we could,' Alice added.

'Oh, she did, did she?' Patrick smiled.

Alice stripped off her gloves and dropped them into the bin at Patrick's feet. 'I've decided to call him Howie.'

'Howie,' Arthur repeated. 'It's a good name for a dog. I like it.'

'I'm going to see Mum and help her make dinner.' Alice left and closed the door behind her.

Arthur leaned against the wall and crossed his arms. 'Patrick, it will be only three days. Don't make it hard to say goodbye,' he warned.

Patrick looked up from the dog. 'I don't need a reminder, Arthur.'

'Just don't forget it, that's all.'

'I can't and I won't, Arthur, not for an instant.' Patrick looked back at the dog and carried on stitching.

# Fourteen

'How's Howie?' Alice asked when Patrick returned to the living room after checking on the dog.

'He'll be stiff and limp on three legs for a while but he'll be up and about in the morning, thanks to your brilliant doctoring, honey.' Patrick sat on the sofa and looked down at his veterinary case on the coffee table. He'd brought it in from the surgery so he could clean his instruments.

They'd finished supper two hours ago. Louise had cooked Alice's favourite, macaroni cheese followed by chocolate ice-cream sundaes. After she'd cleared the dishes, Louise had made hot chocolate topped with marshmallows and cream for Alice and coffee for them. Patrick had stoked the fire and it blazed cheerfully in the hearth. The curtains had been pulled and, although there was a cold wind blowing outside, the atmosphere inside was warm and cosy.

Patrick picked up a scalpel but he was more intent on watching Louise and Alice than polishing the tarnish from his tools. Louise was trimming their daughter's fringe. It was a normal, everyday scene that in the days before Alice's death he would have accepted without a second thought. Now he wanted to savour every moment and imprint every word Alice uttered and every movement she made, no matter how small, on to his memory.

The way his daughter was sitting bolt upright, back straight, hands relaxed in her lap on the low stool. So much taller than she'd been a year ago. Her dark brown eyes shining as she glanced curiously around the room, studying every object in turn.

'Mum?' Alice began.

Louise ran her fingers through Alice's thick hair, combing it back away from her face. 'Yes, sweetie,' she murmured.

'This place feels strange. If we're really here for a holiday, why do we have so many clothes with us? The wardrobe and drawers in my room are full. You seem to have brought everything I own.'

Patrick felt the need to reply. 'Because everyone needs clean clothes, honey. If we only had one or two sets, Mum would be spending every day washing to make sure we had something clean to put on the next day.'

'But you're working, Dad,' Alice pointed out. 'That's peculiar when we're taking a break, isn't it?'

Patrick tried and failed to think of a suitable reply. Louise came to his rescue by changing the subject. She made a final snip at Alice's fringe. 'There, all done, sweetie, and very beautiful. I think it's sleepy time now, don't you?'

'How about a story?' Alice begged.

'"How about a story?"' Louise repeated teasingly.

'Please . . .' Alice coaxed.

Louise capitulated. 'You can have one, but only after you're tucked up in bed.'

Patrick grabbed Alice and kissed her cheek as she ran out through the door. He followed his wife and daughter when they climbed the stairs.

Alice ran into her bedroom and jumped up and down on the bed. Louise caught her mid-jump, pulled back the duvet and settled her under the covers before sitting next to her.

'Story?' Alice's eyes seemed even larger than usual as she looked up at Louise.

Louise hugged her daughter, loving every minute of what had been their bedtime ritual every night of Alice's short life. 'Once upon a time, there was a little tearaway called Alice—'

Alice interrupted her. 'No, not Alice – called Louise,' she contradicted.

Patrick remained in the doorway, watching them, unwilling to leave the scene that was so familiar – and so emotional. Tears welled in his eyes. He looked away lest Louise see them.

'So this is going to be about me, is it?' Louise asked Alice.

'Yes, it is.' Alice nodded enthusiastically.

'All right,' Louise conceded. 'Once upon a time there was a little tearaway called Louise. And she lived with her brothers and sisters—'

'And their sheepdog,' Alice interceded.

Patrick smiled as Alice recounted word for word the opening of the story Louise had told her so many times.

'And their sheepdog,' Louise added, answering

Patrick's smile with one of her own. 'And they all lived together in a big house on the side of a hill overlooking the city . . .' Louise faltered when Patrick slipped out of the room, but a tug on her sleeve from Alice prompted her to continue.

'. . . The house had a field and an orchard and every year the trees in the orchard would be laden with more fruit than they could pick and . . .' Louise saw Alice's eyelids droop and dropped her voice to whisper, '. . . eat.'

Alice's eyes finally closed.

Louise switched off the bedside light. Patrick returned with a quilt and pillows. He set them down on the floor and made a makeshift bed beside Alice's bed. Louise snuggled down next to him, settling where she could still see Alice's face and watch her breathe.

When Louise woke with a start the room was in pitch darkness. She had no sense of time or how long she'd been asleep. Disorientated, she only knew that she was uncomfortable. She'd fallen asleep in her clothes and they were bunched up around her waist, bulky and chafing. Moving slowly and quietly, trying not to disturb Patrick, she began to undress under the quilt.

Her subterfuge didn't work. Patrick felt her move, nuzzled her back and embraced her. He slipped his hand low, into the waistband of her jeans and into her panties. She gripped his fingers, kissed his cheek and whispered in his ear.

'Not here – outside.' She rose to her feet and stole out of the bedroom.

Patrick picked up the quilts and pillows and crept out of the room behind her. He pulled the door to without clicking the lock. Louise waited until he'd spread the quilts and pillows before wrapping her hands around his neck and tugging him down on to the landing floor. They kissed and began to slowly undress and caress one another with a tenderness that had been absent from their lovemaking since the morning Alice had died.

Engrossed in the pleasure they were giving and receiving, neither of them noticed the door to Alice's bedroom swing wide and remain open.

And even if they had, they might have assumed that there was simply a draught blowing through the house from the open bathroom window.

Patrick woke and opened his eyes wide. Louise was lying, eyes closed, beneath the quilt next to him on the landing directly outside Alice's door. Moonlight streamed in as bright as daylight through the skylight above them, silvering the walls, bedclothes, Louise's face and blonde hair. He looked up and jumped.

Alice was standing over them, her eyes wide, unblinking.

Patrick sat up and stared at his daughter for a few seconds, wondering if she was sleepwalking.

Louise opened her eyes, saw Alice and, even before she was fully awake, reached out instinctively to her. 'What's wrong, sweetie?'

'I heard music again,' Alice murmured. 'People singing my name, over and over again. Didn't you hear it?'

'No, there's no music, Alice. You must have had a dream,' Patrick reassured her.

'As Dad says, there is no music, sweetie. Come on, back to bed for you.' Louise scooped Alice up and carried her back into her bedroom. She tucked her in and curled up beside her on the bed. She lay there holding Alice until Alice's eyes had closed again and her breathing steadied to the soft regular rhythm of sleep.

Louise waited while ten minutes ticked past on the alarm clock on the bedside cabinet before creeping off Alice's bed and out through the door. The landing was empty. Patrick had taken the quilt and pillows and retreated to their bedroom. Tired, she stumbled into their room and joined him in the bed, leaving the door open lest Alice wake again.

She was unaware that the moment Alice had heard her walk away, she'd opened her eyes wide again and was staring blankly up at the ceiling.

Alice left her bed before the sun rose in the sky. She showered, dressed and went down the stairs to the kitchen. She searched through the cupboards until she found a roll of black plastic bin bags. She took it and returned to her room. Ripping off a sack, she opened it and went around the room, picking out toys from the shelves and clothes from the wardrobe and drawers that she then dropped into the bag one by one.

When the sack was full, she tied the top in a knot and carried it out of her room to the top of the stairs and dropped it to the floor. She knelt beside it and studied the outside, tracing the outlines of the contents through the thin layer of plastic with her finger.

Choosing a spot near the bottom of the bag, she ripped a small hole in the plastic and burrowed her fingers inside. Slowly, she pulled a doll out of the hole she'd made, first tugging out the head, then the shoulders; next came the arms and torso and finally the legs.

She looked at the doll for a few minutes before grabbing it by the arm and carrying it back into her bedroom.

A knocking at the front door brought her running back out on to the landing. She picked up the bulging bin bag and dragged it down the stairs, bumping it on every step. Dropping it in the hall, she reached up and unlocked the front door.

Peggy O'Shea was standing outside, holding a paper carrier bag. 'Hello, Alice. How are you today?' Peggy asked brightly.

'Fine, thank you for asking,' Alice replied politely.

'I've brought some home-made bread for you and your parents.' Peggy held out the carrier bag. Alice looked at it but made no attempt to take it from Peggy.

'You probably prefer shop-bought bread, don't you?' Peggy fished.

'Do you want to speak to my dad?' Alice ignored Peggy's comment.

'No.' The smile Peggy gave Alice was forced, artificial. 'I want to speak to you, Alice.'

'Me?' Alice looked at the old woman in surprise.

'Yes, you,' Peggy answered. 'I wondered if you'd like

to visit our farm and ride our pony. He needs the exercise and a little bird told me that you like ponies better than all other animals.'

Louise had disappeared into the bathroom. Patrick could hear her electric toothbrush whirring. He was stretched out in bed, enjoying the morning's peaceful time before he had to get up, when he heard Alice talking to someone at the door. He charged out of bed and ran protectively down the stairs, zipping up his flies and buttoning on yesterday's shirt as he went.

Alice turned to him when he reached the hall and said, 'Dad, I'm going pony riding.'

Patrick went to the front door and leaned against the doorpost.

'Good morning, Patrick.' Peggy handed over the bag that contained the loaf of bread. 'I brought some home-made bread for you and your wife,' she explained.

'Very kind of you, thank you, Mrs O'Shea.' Recalling Peggy's reluctance to give them her husband's corpse, Patrick couldn't help wondering if the old woman had an ulterior motive for visiting them.

'Peggy, please,' she corrected him. 'I heard that Alice liked ponies . . . Arthur mentioned it in passing,' she added when Patrick frowned quizzically at her. 'So I wondered if she'd like to come up to the farm and ride ours. He could certainly do with the exercise now that all the children in our family have outgrown him.'

'Thank you for the invitation,' Patrick replied, 'but as you can see, we've slept in late this morning.'

'No matter.' Peggy offered Alice her hand. 'Alice

wants to ride our pony and, as I said, it needs the exercise. I'll take Alice with me now and drop her back here later.'

Patrick pulled Alice aside before she had a chance to take Peggy's hand. Speaking too low for Peggy to hear, he murmured, 'I thought you were going to help me to look after Howie today?'

'Howie'll be fine with you,' Alice said dismissively. 'I want to go riding.' She stepped out of the door.

'No, wait,' he said in a louder voice. He caught her arm and pulled her back. 'You can't just go off somewhere, Alice.' Patrick eyed Peggy; the last thing he wanted to do was insult her after she'd given him and Louise her husband's body, but their time with Alice was so precious and short, he didn't want to share it with anyone other than Louise. 'I'm sorry. We've already made plans for today.'

'Then perhaps Alice can go riding up at our farm another time?' Peggy O'Shea suggested.

'No, Dad! I want to go now,' Alice's voice rose precariously.

'Alice, calm down.' Patrick made an effort to keep his voice low in an attempt to defuse the tension that was building between him and his daughter.

'I'm very calm,' Alice protested in a voice that was anything but.

Louise ran lightly down the stairs and joined them. As soon as Alice saw her she shouted, 'Mum, I've been invited to go pony riding and Dad won't let me.'

Sensing trouble between father and daughter, Louise hesitated, uncertain how to react.

Given Patrick's reluctance to accept her invitation, Peggy modified it. 'Why don't you all come to the farm?'

'After breakfast,' Louise qualified. 'Alice, we'll eat first, all right?' She glanced at Patrick, who was staring at the bin bag of clothes and toys Alice had dumped in the hall.

'See you all later, then. I'll get the pony tacked up and ready.' Peggy turned, waved goodbye and walked down the drive to where she'd parked her car.

'Breakfast, sweetie. What do you want? Cereals, pancakes, eggs, beans . . .' Slipping her hand around Alice's shoulders, Louise ushered her into the kitchen.

'We have to go soon, so I'll just have cereal this morning. It will be quicker to prepare and eat,' Alice said, when Patrick opened the fridge and lifted out a box of eggs.

'You sure, sweetie?'

'Just cereal,' Alice repeated in a voice that Louise knew from past experience would brook no argument.

Patrick replaced the eggs, made coffee, took orange juice from the fridge and set out cups and glasses. Louise laid three bowls, milk and sugar on the table and they all filled their bowls and began to eat.

Alice dawdled over her meal and although Patrick held back from challenging her, he was sure that she was being deliberately provocative and awkward.

'You're still wearing yesterday's clothes. I'm already showered and dressed so I'm all set to go to the farm. You're not,' Alice informed Patrick when he looked pointedly at the food she'd scarcely touched in her bowl.

'Then I'd better get ready, hadn't I?' Patrick handed Louise his empty bowl and left the kitchen. Louise rinsed the bowl under the tap along with hers and stacked them in the dishwasher.

'Finish your cereal, sweetie. I'll get ready and hurry Daddy.' Louise ruffled Alice's hair before following Patrick upstairs.

As soon as she was alone, Alice ate quickly. When she'd finished her cereal, she carried the bowl to the sink and left it there. The loaf of bread Peggy O'Shea had given them stood on the table. She picked it up, turned to the stairs and shouted, 'Are you ready?'

She waited a few minutes. When there was no reply from either of her parents, she took the bread knife from the knife block, placed the loaf on the breadboard and very slowly and precisely began to cut the bread.

'Anyone want a slice of home-made bread?' she shouted after she'd cut the first thin slice. When she didn't receive a reply, she started to cut another slice. Just like the first, it was uniformly thin.

Then she began to cut another . . . and another . . . and another.

Patrick left the bathroom wearing only a towel wrapped around his waist, to find Louise in the bedroom waiting for him to finish.

'Is Peggy snooping on us or trying to be nice?' Louise asked him as she stripped off and stepped into the shower cubicle.

'Could be both,' he suggested.

'I thought that after everything we've been through,

the people here would have the tact and the sense to leave us alone with Alice.'

'Speaking of Alice, where is she?' he asked.

'I left her finishing her breakfast in the kitchen.' Louise closed the cubicle door and turned on the shower. Patrick had almost finished dressing by the time she returned to the bedroom, damp and scented with moisturising cream and soap.

'Did you see the bag of things Alice filled to throw away?' Patrick flicked through his wardrobe, picked out a clean shirt and buttoned it on.

'Yes, I saw it,' Louise confirmed. 'What about it?'

'They were all the things you'd put in her room. Why did she clear them out?'

'Perhaps she's grown out of a lot of her toys. She's certainly grown out of some of her clothes,' Louise observed.

'Haven't you wondered how that's possible . . . ?'

'Ssh.' Louise went to the open door and listened.

'You think she's eavesdropping on us?' Patrick checked.

'Just making sure she won't overhear us talking about her.' Louise opened the wardrobe door and took out a pair of jeans, a shirt and a sweater.

'Mum? Dad?'

They both fell silent when Alice's voice wafted up the stairs. 'I'm bored waiting. Are you two nearly ready to go?'

'On our way.' Patrick pulled on his last sock, left the bedroom and went downstairs. He walked into the kitchen and saw the loaf of bread on the breadboard sliced neatly and uniformly from one end to the other, apart from one crust that was thicker than the rest.

Alice looked at him, raised the bread knife and cut into it.

'Careful, honey,' he warned when she brought the knife down perilously close to her finger. The moment he spoke, the knife slipped.

'Alice.' He ran towards her in alarm.

'It's fine, Dad.' She studied the gash on her finger. Her skin was sliced through to the bone. She squeezed the edges but no blood came.

'Let me look at it,' Patrick demanded.

She hid both her hands behind her back. 'No, Dad. I said it's nothing.' The belligerence of earlier had returned to her voice. 'Is Mum ready? If she is, can we go to the farm right now? This minute. I can't wait to see the pony.'

'Not before I see your finger,' Patrick persisted.

'And I said it's all right, Dad. There's Mum.' Alice slipped past him into the hall when Louise walked down the stairs. 'Come on, Mum. Let's go.' She opened the front door and ran out on to the drive ahead of them.

Patrick went to the breadboard and checked the bread and the knife, searching for signs of blood.

Louise glanced in from the hall as she put her shoes on. 'You all right, Patrick?' she asked anxiously.

'Yes. Fine,' he murmured absently.

'Alice is waiting.'

'I know.' He turned and smiled at her. 'I'm with you.'

They left the house, locked the door and followed Alice out to the car.

# Fifteen

Irrespective of Peggy O'Shea's motives in inviting them, the last place Louise wanted to visit was the O'Shea farm. Asleep or awake, Mick O'Shea's bloody and tragic death haunted her and she had to steel herself to return to the place where she'd witnessed his violent end. It also wasn't easy when she considered that if Mick hadn't died when he did and Peggy hadn't given Arthur permission to use his body, she and Patrick wouldn't have Alice.

Seeing her shiver when she got out of the car, Patrick took her hand. 'It'll be all right. Alice will ride the pony for half an hour or so and then we'll go.'

'Perhaps Peggy O'Shea is only trying to be kind,' she commented, wishing she could believe it, 'but I don't want to stay any longer than that.'

'Think about what you want to do afterwards?'

'Go back to the cottage and spend the rest of the day together. Like we did yesterday,' she suggested.

'I'd like that.'

She smiled at him. 'It was a good day, wasn't it?'

He squeezed her hand reassuringly. 'The best.'

Peggy was waiting for them in the farmyard with a beautiful grey pony. As she'd promised, the pony was already bridled and saddled. Fearless when it came to horses, Alice ran across to him and stroked his muzzle. Peggy picked her up and hoisted her into the saddle before taking hold of the lunge rein she'd attached to the pony's bridle.

'Now ride him, Alice. That's it exactly,' she complimented when Alice dug her heels into the pony's flanks just as she'd been taught on her first riding lesson. 'There's no way that he can charge off with you because I have him safe on the end of this rein. That's it, darling, well done,' she sang out when Alice kicked him gently again, 'keep him awake and moving.'

'This is fun,' Alice shouted to Patrick and Louise when she began her second circuit on the rein.

'Would you like to pop over a jump?' Peggy asked Alice after she'd been riding for a few minutes.

Alice didn't hesitate. 'Yes, I'd like that,' she shouted back.

'Is she ready for a jump?' Louise asked anxiously. 'She's only had two lessons.'

'She'll be fine,' Peggy said to Louise, 'just look at her. The way she's sitting in that saddle. She's a natural. There aren't many young girls who take to riding the way Alice has after only a few lessons.'

Patrick and Louise looked on nervously as Peggy led the pony down to a low jump at the end of the yard. The pony cleared it easily and Alice continued to sit firm and secure in the saddle. She waved triumphantly to Louise and Patrick and smiled broadly until the pony turned and she was facing away from her parents.

Her expression changed instantly and dramatically

from animated to deadpan the moment her face was out of her parents' line of vision.

She glanced down at Peggy and realised that the old woman was watching her intently and had noticed the change.

'Are you feeling all right, Alice?' Peggy asked.

'Why?' Alice demanded. 'You hoping I'm not?'

'Just asking, darling,' Peggy replied, struggling to keep her voice light and even. 'Just asking.'

Alice was loath to leave the pony after her ride and insisted on accompanying him back to his stable. Peggy helped her to remove his saddle and the tack. Then she showed Alice how to use the dandy brush and curry comb. Alice set about grooming the animal with enthusiasm. Louise and Patrick stood outside the stall and watched their daughter work on the pony through the open door.

Louise felt distinctly uneasy and worried in Peggy's company, although she couldn't quantify her feelings. Peggy was being kind to all of them and especially nice to Alice. Perhaps that was it. She was being overly suspicious of the motives behind Peggy's invitation and generosity.

Then, when she considered the situation, she realised that, given Mick's recent death, Peggy was suffering too. Bereavement and loss affect different people in different ways. It was possible that the old woman's benevolence towards Alice was simply her way of expressing her own grief.

Martin O'Shea came out of the farmhouse and joined

them in the stable. He leaned on the side of the stall and watched Alice for a few minutes. 'You're doing a grand job there of grooming him, Alice, but you'd better hurry up. I have tea and sandwiches waiting inside in the kitchen. Come on in and enjoy them in the warm.'

'Alice, are you ready?' Louise prompted when Alice totally ignored Martin and carried on brushing the pony.

Peggy walked out of the tack room and joined them. 'The sandwiches won't spoil, and Martin can always make fresh tea. Let Alice finish up here. I'll bring her inside when she's done.'

Louise stood helplessly, unable to think of a single excuse to give Martin as to why she and Patrick should refuse his offer of tea.

'Coming, Patrick? Louise?' Martin stood by the door, obviously waiting for them to join him.

Pressurised, Louise felt she had no choice other than to turn her back on Alice and follow the two men into the farmhouse.

Peggy waited until she and Alice were alone in the stable before joining Alice in the stall.

'Alice,' she began, excitement making her breathless. 'There's a game I want us to play together.'

'What kind of game?' Alice looked up at her.

'That's enough grooming for now. Set the brush and comb back on the shelf and come with me outside. We'll start the game when we've sat down. You'll like it, I promise you.' Peggy led the way out of the stable to a partially roofed open area at the side of the building that wasn't overlooked by any of the windows in the farmhouse.

Covered in wood chippings, the site was dominated by a large circular chopping block and axe. Piles of logs stood behind it, neatly stacked and stored under a tin roof to shelter them from the worst of the rain before they were needed to feed the wood-burning stove in the kitchen.

Peggy sat on the block and indicated that Alice should sit beside her. A fresh breeze whipped across the yard, ruffling their hair and the tops of the trees that had been planted around the farm.

'What's the game?' Alice repeated curiously.

'It's a quiz. I'll ask you questions and you give me the answers. I'll keep the score.' Peggy lifted out a bag she'd hidden among the logs that were waiting to be cut. She opened it and drew out a wooden frame with bone beads on wooden bars.

It was similar to the one Arthur had brought to Patrick and Louise's cottage, but without the metal bars, of a more bizarre shape and, if anything, even more ancient.

'What's that?' Alice asked.

'Just something I use when I play this game,' Peggy answered. As Arthur had done when he'd talked to Louise and Patrick about bringing Alice back, Peggy began flicking and clicking the beads, moving them up and down the wooden bars.

'Now, Alice Daley,' Peggy began, 'what's your name?'

Alice giggled. 'That's a tough question. I pass.'

Peggy forced a laugh. 'Right! I see the way it's going to be with you. Lots of jokes.' She fell serious. 'Now tell me, when you close your eyes when you're tired, do you see more yellow or brown?'

Alice giggled again. 'I see a big red enormous shape like a huge spinning doorknob.'

Peggy clicked more beads into place. 'Alice, if you were hungry right now and you had to choose between something salty or sweet, which would it be?'

'If I was hungry I'd get a great big burger and fries and lots of extra little salt containers and a strawberry milkshake. And then, when you weren't looking, I'd open all the salt packets and tip them into the milkshake, then trick you into drinking it.'

Peggy continued to watch Alice carefully. Her hair blew into her eyes as the wind started to pick up around them. She brushed it aside.

'Let me see your hand, Alice.' Peggy held out hers in preparation to take Alice's. Alice hesitated before holding it out. Peggy examined the ends of Alice's fingers, particularly her cuticles and fingernails. After she released the hand, she flicked some more beads around. 'The date of your birth. What would that be?'

'The twenty-second of January.'

'And the year?'

Alice's only reply was to blow a very loud raspberry.

Peggy smiled. 'I think I know anyway. A little bird told me.'

'The same little bird who told you that I like ponies?' Alice asked.

'It might be.' Peggy carried on clicking the beads.

'Although if you don't become more cooperative—'

'Cooperative?' Alice interrupted as if she didn't know the meaning of the word.

'That means that if you don't answer more of my questions honestly and correctly, I doubt you'll be riding that pony again anytime soon.'

'Hmm, I can't remember,' Alice mused. 'Is that what they call bribery or blackmail?'

Peggy froze. She gazed at Alice, who was scuffing the dirt on the ground with her feet and studying the marks she was making.

Peggy looked down at the coffin shape Alice had sketched out with the toe of her shoe. She thought back to the ceremony of the return. The other people Arthur had brought back. Even children . . . Deirdre . . . they had all been so calm. So compliant. Yet Alice was different. She couldn't have said quite how, other than what she had told Arthur when he had asked for Mick's corpse.

Something was wrong. Wrong with Patrick and Louise. But most of all wrong with Alice. Her eyes rounded in fear and she began to shake. 'Alice,' she blurted nervously, 'are you a normal little girl?'

Alice slowly raised her eyes and stared at Peggy. 'Now, why would you ask me a question like that?'

Peggy deliberately looked away and stared at the trees that were now being buffeted wildly in the wind that had picked up speed.

'Why won't you look at me?' Alice demanded.

'Because I've seen enough of you.' Peggy's voice was hoarse with fear that she could no longer disguise.

*

Martin poured boiling water into the teapot and carried it over to the scrubbed-down pine table in the kitchen where Louise and Patrick were sitting. He covered the pot with a home-knitted tea cosy and pushed a large plate of sandwiches towards Louise.

'Go on, Louise, have another one. You too, Patrick. They're going to go to waste if you don't eat them.' Martin poured fresh tea into their cups.

'Thank you.' Patrick took a sandwich.

Louise spooned sugar into her tea then, deciding that she couldn't sit still another minute, pushed her chair back from the table. 'I really think I should check on Alice. She's not used to being with strangers.'

Patrick dropped his sandwich on to his plate. 'Good idea. It's time we found her, if only to make sure she's not wearing out your mother with her chatter, Martin.'

'My mother's used to children's chatter and Alice will be happy enough with her,' Martin countered. 'So there's really no need to disturb yourselves. Drink your tea and eat the sandwiches. My mother will be bringing Alice in any minute now.' He glanced out of the window at the stable, but he knew that his mother would have taken Alice around the corner of the building into a comparatively private area where they couldn't be seen from the house.

Then he caught a glimpse of Peggy moving into his line of vision. 'In fact, there's my mother now, so they've already left the stable,' he said to Patrick. 'Look, she's crossing the yard.' He helped himself to another sandwich.

'If you don't mind, I'll still go out and meet them.'

Without waiting for Martin to reply, Louise opened the kitchen door and ran down the steps into the yard. Alice rose to her feet when Louise came into sight but she didn't look at Louise – she was facing and staring at Peggy O'Shea.

'Is everything all right, sweetie?' Louise asked Alice in concern.

'I don't like that woman,' Alice declared, pointing to Peggy, who was backing away from her while apparently studying a point way above Alice's head.

Patrick, coming out of the farmhouse, turned to Peggy. 'What's happening here, Peggy?'

Louise crouched down in front of Alice to make sure she wasn't hurt in any way before turning on Peggy. 'What have you done to our daughter?'

'She's not right.' Peggy spoke vehemently without looking at any of them. Her voice was high-pitched, insistent. 'You've got to take her back, now!' Peggy demanded. 'At once. You dare not wait a moment longer. She has to go back to the woods. Now!'

Alice walked away from Peggy, Patrick and Louise. Quickening her pace, she rushed out of the yard and into the lane that led from the farm to the main road.

Patrick called out after her, 'Alice. Please, honey, stop. Wait for me.' But she ignored him and kept on walking.

Peggy watched Alice for a moment. 'Take her to the woods and return her. Now! I was right all along. I should never have allowed Arthur to talk me into giving you Mick's corpse. You don't belong here. None of you. Especially Alice.' Deliberately turning her back on Patrick and Louise, she went into the house and closed the door firmly and noisily behind her.

'What are we going to do?' Louise begged Patrick when she heard the door slam behind Peggy and the key turn in the lock.

'First of all, get Alice and make sure she's safe.' Patrick raised his voice and shouted down the lane, 'Alice . . . wait for me.'

'Let's leave here, Patrick,' Louise pleaded.

'What . . . ?' Patrick turned to her in confusion. 'You mean O'Shea's farm?'

'Yes, the farm,' she said impatiently. 'And Wake Wood. Right now, right this minute. Alice is different. You heard Peggy O'Shea say, "She's not right, you've got to take her back," the same as me. We don't know if their rules apply in Alice's case and nor do they, because we've done it differently from what they're used to.'

'Louise . . .' Patrick faltered in bewilderment as he tried to think clearly.

'Do you *want* to send Alice back?' she demanded. 'This is her second day. Tomorrow they'll come to the cottage and try and make us do just that.' Louise hated inflicting pain on him but she felt she had no choice.

Patrick suddenly realised that Louise had asked the question he hadn't thought about or even wanted to consider since Alice's return. 'Of course I don't want to send Alice back,' he retorted seriously. 'Yesterday and today . . . they were wonderful . . . so special . . .'

'As every day could be for us as a family from now on, provided we keep Alice with us,' Louise pleaded.

He thought rapidly. 'You're right. We should leave here right now, right this minute,' he said decisively. 'We won't go home. We'll leave everything and start again somewhere else. Somewhere far from here. Go and fetch the car. I'll run after Alice. You can pick us up on the main road.' He handed her the car keys.

Louise took them and hurried off.

Patrick raced after Alice but he didn't catch up with her until she was nearing the main road. 'Hey, honey,' he shouted, 'be careful, that's not a lane but a busy road. You have to watch out for traffic.'

Alice stopped and looked around when she reached the bottom of the lane that opened on to the thoroughfare, but the noise of the nearby wind turbines was so loud it drowned out Patrick's warning shouts.

'Hey, Alice.' Patrick continued to run after her until he was only six feet from her. 'Do you mind if I come and talk to you? Mum's just behind me. She's going to pick us up in the car and we're going to take a trip together.'

When Alice backed away Patrick halted. 'What's the matter, honey?'

Alice stared at him.

'Did Mrs O'Shea say something to frighten you?' Patrick persevered. 'I'm sorry if she did, honey. If you talk to me about it, I might be able to help you understand and make it better.'

Alice finally spoke and when she did, Patrick felt as though his heart had been pierced by an icicle. 'Dad, am I dead?'

Dumbfounded, Patrick was unable to reply for a few

seconds. 'Well . . .' he began tentatively. 'You don't seem very dead to me, honey.'

The wind turbines continued to turn, making it difficult for either of them to hear what the other was saying.

Patrick reached out and caught Alice's hand. Together they walked slowly past the turbines and around a bend to the narrow bridge that marked the boundary of Wake Wood.

Patrick looked down at Alice and caught sight of the edge of the sign, WELCOME TO WAKE WOOD. Arthur's warning about keeping Alice within the confines of the town came to mind. But he also recalled what Louise had said.

*We don't know if their rules apply in Alice's case and nor do they, because we've done it differently from what they're used to.*

He didn't stop Alice from walking resolutely past the sign.

She took a few more steps then stumbled. When she fell she didn't attempt to rise. Then she whimpered.

Unable to bear the thought of her in pain, he hesitated. 'Alice . . . wait . . .'

She turned to face him. His warning shout had been too late.

'Alice . . .' Patrick cried when he saw Alice's skin split and open on her hands. Blood dripped from her finger. It was the same spot he'd seen her cut herself with the bread knife.

She looked up into his eyes, held out her arms to him and cried out, 'Dad!'

Before he could pick her up she began screaming uncontrollably. He watched in horror as her skin continued to split, crumple and shrivel, exposing enormous circles of raw wounded flesh that bled copiously. Within seconds the same devastating, appalling wounds that the dog had inflicted on her face and neck had opened. The wounds that had killed her.

Her screams escalated and she writhed in agony, shrieking, 'Dad! . . . Dad!'

Patrick hadn't felt so impotent or so useless since the morning she'd died. He ran to her and swept her up into his arms. He raced back past the sign, only stopping when he was once more safely inside the boundary of Wake Wood.

Alice was gasping for air. He knelt on the grass holding her close to him, willing life into her just as he'd attempted to do on the day she'd died.

He tried to study her injuries with a professional eye. Frantically tried to exert pressure on her wounds to halt the bleeding, but it was hopeless. As soon as he pressed down on one injury, another opened up close by.

'I'm so sorry, honey.' Tears fell from his eyes on to her poor, small, broken, bleeding body. 'So, so sorry . . .'

Louise drove their car around the bend. Seeing him leaning over Alice on the grass verge, she applied the brakes and screeched to a halt. She reversed next to him and ran from the car.

'Alice!' She joined Patrick and stooped over Alice's body. Too shocked to cry or assist Patrick, she sat back helplessly on her heels and watched Alice's pain.

'Is it my imagination? Are her injuries fading?'

Patrick whispered after a few minutes, scarcely daring to hope.

A car slowed as it drew alongside them.

Louise and Patrick looked up to see a grinning Martin O'Shea watching all three of them. The look of blatant contempt in Martin's eyes sent a cold chill of absolute terror rippling down Patrick's spine.

# Sixteen

Patrick leaned over Alice in an attempt to shield her from Martin O'Shea's sight. But the expression on Martin's face suggested that he'd already seen all he wanted to. Martin parried Patrick's steady gaze before accelerating hard and driving off down the road.

Patrick waited until the road was clear before lifting Alice gently from the verge and carrying her to the back of the estate car. He laid her down on the bench seat in the back and climbed in beside her, cradling her head on his lap. In less than a minute most of the wounds and blemishes on Alice's body had faded, leaving her skin clear and perfect.

'What happened?' Louise knew her question was superfluous as soon as she'd asked it. Given Arthur's warning that Alice would still be 'deceased', as he'd put it, coupled with his insistence that they keep Alice within the confines of Wake Wood, she knew exactly why Alice's injuries had returned. Alice had walked past the town's boundaries and her body had begun to disintegrate; just as it had begun to recover as soon as Patrick had carried her back within the limits of Wake Wood.

Alice was in thrall to Wake Wood and could never

leave the place. Not if she wanted to stay alive and breathing. But it wasn't only Alice who was bound to the town. Louise and Patrick were. Because there was no way that they could abandon their daughter . . . and when they gave Alice up . . . what then?

Arthur had extracted a promise from Patrick that they'd stay in the town and Patrick would continue to work there as a vet. In view of that, could she and Patrick ever leave Wake Wood? Would they be able to, should they want to flee the place and the people?

Patrick cut in on her thoughts. 'You drive, Louise. Reverse the car here and go back.' Patrick shut the car door, closing himself and Alice in.

Louise sat in the driver's seat and turned to him. 'Go back where, Patrick?' she asked in confusion.

'Where else but the cottage?' Patrick answered despondently. 'There's nowhere else that we can go.'

Louise turned the car around and drove quickly back into the town. Occasionally she raised her eyes to the rear-view mirror and glanced at the back seat. Alice was curled like a kitten on Patrick's lap, her eyes open, the skin on her face and neck now totally blemish-free.

She was making shapes with her fingers and, holding them up, partially covering her eyes. The small, achingly familiar childish gesture brought a lump to Louise's throat. How could she have forgotten how much Alice had enjoyed forming shadow animals on the wall? Even making up stories about the strange beasts she'd created.

She looked at Patrick absently stroking Alice's forehead with his free hand. She could see from his expression that he was stricken with remorse and guilt for trying to take Alice outside the town limits and subjecting her to so much agonising pain.

'Dad,' Alice said suddenly. 'Do you remember that big fierce dog that bit me?'

'Yes.' Patrick was so choked by emotion he could barely get out the single word.

'What happened to him?'

Patrick tried to answer her but no words came. When he failed, Alice answered for him.

'You put him down, didn't you, Dad?'

'Yes, I did,' he admitted.

'Then you killed him?' If there was condemnation in her voice, neither Louise nor Patrick picked up on it.

'Yes, I did,' Patrick confessed.

'That's all right then.' Alice settled back on his lap.

Louise continued to drive towards the cottage, but every time she looked at Patrick and Alice in the back of the car she was conscious of time ticking inexorably on. It was nearly the end of their second precious day with Alice. Only one more to go and she knew . . . just knew . . . that when the moment came – as it must – she would no more be able to give Alice up than she would be able to stop breathing.

After a supper of scrambled eggs and ham on toast, Alice went into the garden to play with Howie, who was limping, just as Patrick had prophesied, but up on his feet. Patrick busied himself clearing the table and stacking the dishes in the dishwasher but, unwilling to allow Alice out of her sight, Louise remained in front of the window in the living room, watching her daughter coax the dog around the garden. When Howie tired of walking and lay down on the grass, Alice played 'tug' with him; putting a stick in his mouth, she pulled the other end. Louise couldn't decide who was enjoying the game more, Alice or the dog.

The clatter from the kitchen ceased. Patrick stole up behind her and kissed the back of her neck.

'We're trapped here in Wake Wood, aren't we?' she murmured.

When he didn't answer her she turned her head and looked up at him. 'We're here for ever, we can never escape.'

Her only answer was his continued silence.

'How will we bear it?' She didn't have to explain what.

'We'll bear it, Louise, because we have to,' he said. 'What other choice do we have?'

When twilight fell and the shadows lengthened beneath the trees, Louise left the window and went into the garden with Patrick to call Alice and bring her inside.

'It's getting cold and dark – time for bed, sweetie.'

Alice came without argument. She gave Howie one last pat before Patrick herded him into the outbuilding next to his surgery where he housed the pens and beds for the sick animals he treated.

Louise chased Alice upstairs, but underlying the fun, familiar ritual of bedtime was the ever-present thought of just how short a time was left to them. When Patrick came in from outside, she allowed him to take over because she was almost blinded by tears.

They both put Alice to bed. Louise told Alice a story until her eyes closed. She lay beside her for ten more minutes, then, believing her daughter to be asleep, Louise tucked the duvet around her, straightened her pillow and stroked her hair. Alice turned sleepily and opened one eye.

'This is our house now, isn't it, Mum?'

'Yes, sweetie,' Louise whispered.

'Then we live here all the time?'

'We do,' Patrick confirmed.

Alice closed her eyes again and giggled.

'Is something funny, sweetie?' Louise asked.

'I was thinking of Howie. Animals are funny, aren't they?'

'They certainly can be, honey,' Patrick agreed.

Alice's giggles became high-pitched. Louise turned back at the door to see her in the throes of convulsions, just like the ones she'd witnessed Deirdre having in the pharmacy. She rushed back to Alice's bedside but by the time she reached her, they'd passed. Once more Alice appeared sound asleep and quiet.

Patrick was still in the doorway and she saw the pain that was crippling her mirrored in his eyes. He opened his arms and she went to him, clinging to him as if she were a shipwreck victim embracing a spar of driftwood.

Unwilling to abandon Alice alone upstairs, Patrick and Louise left the door of her room ajar and went into their bedroom. By tacit agreement they also left their door open so they could hear Alice's shallow breathing. Patrick sat on the end of the bed and leaned forward, head in hands, sunk deep in thought.

Louise sat in a chair she'd pulled up to the window. The curtains were closed and she tried to empty her mind of painful thoughts and remember only the happy times with Alice. But no matter how hard she tried to concentrate on the past, she couldn't block out the thought that tomorrow would be their last day with Alice. Not just for now but for ever.

Every time she recalled a happy time, the bleak, transient nature of the present intruded – bleak because she couldn't forget for an instant that the situation would last only a few more hours. Alice couldn't stay with them beyond the allotted time – and, as for the future, she simply couldn't bring herself to dwell on the prospect of a life without her daughter.

After experiencing it, just the thought of returning to that despairing time of grief and depression after Alice's death was untenable. She'd rather return with Alice to wherever her child was going. Could death really be that dreadful? Even more so than the living nightmare she'd experienced before Arthur had returned Alice to them?

Louise moved restlessly on the chair. Sleep was out of the question. Her mind was awash with images of Alice: Alice asleep . . . Alice awake . . . Alice racing around . . . Alice sitting, reading by firelight . . . Alice quiet and thoughtful. But the pictures that dominated her mind were those of her daughter's dying, broken and bleeding body after the dog had attacked her, and her decomposing corpse in her coffin.

She closed her eyes tightly and tried to banish the tragic scenes. But then the question of the mechanics of the 'return to the woods' that Arthur had spoken of raised its ugly head. When Mary Brogan had talked about Deirdre she'd said 'they' – meaning Deirdre and others like her – 'returned willingly'. Had Mary meant to the earth in the woods?

Did Arthur seriously expect her to dig a grave and lay Alice in the ground a second time, the only difference being that this time Alice would be aware and awake and alive?

And after she'd laid Alice down in the earth – would Arthur actually expect her to cover her own child's body with dirt?

Losing track of time, she sat and pondered, imagining the event without coming to any clear conclusions. The shadows thickened, the room dimmed then darkened as night fell outside the closed curtains. And still she and Patrick continued to sit in despairing silence, seeking answers to imponderable questions while trying to face up to the second loss of their only child.

When it was too dark to see across the room Louise heard a strange noise. It appeared to be coming from downstairs. Instantly alert, she strained her ears and thought she could hear the muffled sound of movement. She looked out on to the landing. She could see the reassuring shape of the pine bannister, a streak of light in the blackness, the square frames of the flower prints on the wall, a beam of moonlight lightening the carpet below the skylight.

All appeared still and quiet apart from Alice's soft regular breathing. Then she heard another noise, different this time. Metal scraping against metal. Could it be a key turning in a lock?

'Did you hear something?' she asked Patrick urgently.

Patrick, who'd been as still as a bronze statue since he'd sat on the bed, lifted his head and looked at her. 'No. Did you hear a noise?' he asked blankly.

'I think so. I'll check on Alice.' Louise tiptoed to Alice's room and pushed the door a fraction wider. Alice was lying exactly as she'd been when Louise had left. Her head sunk into her pillow, the duvet pulled to her chin, her eyes closed, her mouth relaxed in a sleepy smile.

Louise retreated. When she reached the landing she heard the noise again, the unmistakeable sound of a key being turned in a lock.

She looked into their room and hissed, 'Patrick!'

He picked up on the panic in her voice and rose to his feet. Padding softly out of their bedroom, he joined her at the top of the stairs. They stood side by side, glancing into one another's eyes, listening hard as they looked down into the hall.

Detecting movement in the shadows below them, Patrick lifted his finger to his lips and began to descend slowly and silently in sock-clad feet. Louise followed. They both hung back at the foot of the stairs.

The door to the living room was wide open. The fire

had burned low and the room was in darkness. Then, as their eyes adjusted to the low level of light, black silhouettes gradually began to take on human dimensions in the gloom. They saw them moving in the dim glow emanating from the ashes that still smouldered in the hearth. The first things Louise could make out were the ragged outlines of the clusters of black feathers that they all wore on their lapels or shoulders.

Then she recognised the intruders as their neighbours. The farm hands Tommy and Ben were there, as were Peggy and Martin O'Shea and Mary Brogan. And, standing in the centre of the throng like a godfather surrounded by his henchmen, Arthur.

Without warning they began to make the same unmelodious, primitive sound that they had when they'd marched down the main street in procession with Deirdre. Rattling wooden sticks in bamboo and hitting the sticks together.

Arthur waved his upturned hand at Louise and Patrick. They returned his stare.

Peggy stepped forward and faced Louise and Patrick. 'Put Alice back in the ground where she belongs. Now!' she hissed above the racket that her neighbours were making. 'There's no time to lose. You have to do it now!'

Patrick shrank back from the vehemence in her voice. Louise touched his shoulder. The gesture gave him the courage he needed to face down their neighbours' demand.

'Alice is upstairs in bed and she's staying there.' He spoke quietly but firmly, conscious that the racket they were making had probably woken his daughter.

'My mother's right. You have to do it now!' Martin added his plea to Peggy's.

'Three days,' Patrick said. 'We were promised three days with Alice. We've only had two. We have one whole day left to spend with our daughter. And we're not giving up a single second of that precious time. Not for any one of you.'

'Something's not right with Alice. You dare not delay another hour, let alone twenty-four,' Peggy warned.

'Arthur,' Patrick addressed his partner. 'You promised us three days. Why have you all come here now, in the middle of the night like this?'

Arthur stepped up alongside Peggy and raised his hand. The people around him stopped hitting, drumming and rattling their sticks and bamboo. 'We're here, Patrick, because we had to talk to you urgently about Alice,' he explained.

'Why couldn't you have waited until morning?' Patrick demanded. 'We still have the whole of our last day with Alice.'

'You tried to take Alice out of Wake Wood,' Arthur challenged.

'Wait a minute. We had no choice but to try. She . . .' Patrick pointed accusingly at Peggy. 'She frightened Alice. Absolutely terrified her. Tried to get Alice away from us. It was very cruel of her.'

'It was necessary. I knew something was wrong. I sensed it and I had to find out exactly what it was.' Peggy robustly defended her actions.

'I'm disappointed in you, Patrick. You too, Louise,' Arthur admonished. 'I've protected you. Spoken up for you when no one else would, because of the contribution you've made to the town. But you have to obey the rules of Wake Wood. I thought I'd made that absolutely clear to both of you when I first explained the ceremony of the return.'

'Take Alice to the woods. Put her in the earth. Do it now, straight away,' Ben boomed in his deep voice.

Sensing a presence behind her, Louise turned and saw a flash of white. Alice, in white pyjamas, was standing at the head of the stairs above them, listening to every word that was being said.

'You have to put Alice back in the ground now so we can all be safe,' Tommy shouted.

'Forgo your last day.' Peggy stepped forward alongside Arthur. 'Forgo the time you have left and return Alice to the woods.'

'You're wrong. All of you . . .' Louise's voice rose hysterically. She turned, charged back up the stairs and, ignoring the impassive, blank expression on her daughter's face, scooped her into her arms and hugged her. Alice didn't respond to her embrace but Louise was too distraught to notice.

'Louise,' Arthur interrupted. 'Much as I like both of you and am grateful to Patrick for what he's done for Wake Wood and myself, taking over the veterinary business, you'd better bring Alice down to us now. We're all here. Every one of us who was at the return ceremony, and we're ready and prepared to do what's necessary. We can start the feather walk right now, from here.'

Louise tightened her grip on Alice and turned her

back on them. 'You're not taking Alice from this house. Not now. Not yet. I won't allow you to.'

'We're here because we want you to do this, Louise,' Arthur persisted. 'We're asking you. Not telling you, but you should listen to us.'

'You're not taking my baby!' Louise's emotion was raw, agonising to witness.

Alice spoke for the first time, her voice faint, heavy with sleep. 'Mum . . .'

Louise retreated to the landing and headed for the safety of her and Patrick's bedroom.

'Why are they all here, Mum?' Alice murmured.

Louise carried Alice inside and slammed the door behind them.

Patrick backed up the stairs, still facing the visitors, preparing to do whatever was necessary to protect his family.

Arthur walked up to Patrick and confronted him. Patrick held out his arms. He gripped the bannister tightly with one hand and laid the flat of his hand against the wall on the other, blocking Arthur's path.

'Three days, Arthur,' Patrick reiterated. 'You're not taking our daughter one minute before we've had the full three days you promised us.'

'Please, Patrick, see reason,' Arthur pleaded.

'I'll fight you. Every one of you, if I have to,' Patrick threatened. 'Do you understand?' He squared up to Arthur.

Arthur stood his ground. 'We came here to talk, Patrick, to reason with you and ask you to take action, not to fight. There are people here who believe something serious is amiss with Alice . . . something's not gone according to the plan. Have you seen any signs of that in Alice?'

'No. Not at all.' Patrick continued to stare tight-lipped at Arthur.

'All right,' Arthur conceded. 'But you have to tell me if you observe anything unexpected or beyond what we've discussed. Do you understand? Anything that seems in the slightest out of the ordinary.'

'"Out of the ordinary",' Patrick mocked. 'As if this entire situation isn't out of the ordinary, Arthur. It's so out of the ordinary I refused to believe a word you said when you told me what you could do. Even though Louise did.'

'You know what I mean, Patrick. No one knows Alice better than you and Louise. I mean odd, out of the ordinary for your daughter—'

'Alice is fine,' Patrick broke in defiantly. 'She's our little girl and she's fine. Just as she was.'

'Yes, she's fine for the moment,' Arthur agreed. 'And she's here for one more day. But tread carefully until you return her to the woods, Patrick. I mean it.' Arthur signalled to his neighbours.

The first of the uninvited visitors left the living room, crossed the hall and opened the front door. One by one the townsfolk left, melting into the darkness outside as quietly as they'd arrived.

The only sound that signalled their leaving was the harsh click of the lock on the front door when the last of them shut it behind him after they'd all passed through.

Afraid his legs were about to give way, Patrick sank down abruptly on the stairs. Above him he could hear Louise singing softly to Alice.

*One more day*. Arthur's words cut through him like a knife. Only one more day and then . . .

# Seventeen

After their neighbours left the cottage Patrick felt drained. Barely capable of thought. He was beset by a sense of foreboding. A premonition that something catastrophic was about to happen. He felt the need to check every downstairs room. Leaving the stairs, he went into the kitchen and bolted and locked the back door. He took the key from the lock and hung it in the key cabinet in the hall.

After securing the front door and fastening the chain, he made sure every window was firmly fastened. Then he began to check all the appliances, the boiler, the stove, the electrical sockets.

Was he making something out of nothing? Was his feeling of unease simply attributable to his neighbours' nocturnal and undeniably threatening visit, coupled with his anger and impotence in the face of Alice's impending 'return'?

For the first time he questioned the decision that he and Louise had made. Would it have been better if they'd turned down Arthur's offer? Seeing Alice again had been a marvellous, wonderful miracle; so much so, he didn't even want to imagine letting her go a second time.

Would it have been easier for him – and especially for Louise – to have come to terms with the loss of Alice if they'd never allowed Arthur to summon her back?

He couldn't decide. Especially as Alice was sleeping upstairs. She was here, in this house with him, and he wanted to protect her. But he couldn't and wouldn't be able to care for her after tomorrow night! It was a father's duty to protect his child and he'd failed. Failed dismally! He'd failed her when the dog had killed her and he was about to fail her again by giving in to Arthur and their neighbours' demands that he put her back in the ground.

He returned to the hall, intending to go upstairs, but stopped in his tracks when he caught a glimpse of a figure in the hall mirror.

Had someone stayed behind?

Someone dressed in white? He shrank back against the wall. He couldn't recall any of his neighbours wearing that colour.

He stared into the mirror until his eyes burned. There was someone standing in the middle of the living room. He was sure of it. A young girl with dark shoulder-length hair. Her back was turned to him.

Summoning his courage, he stepped closer. The figure turned. He felt the blood drain from his face. It was Alice in her white pyjamas.

Steeling himself, he walked into the living room and switched on the light.

The lamps illuminated an empty room. There was no one there.

He turned around twice, checked behind every piece

of furniture until there was no doubt. The only person in the room was him.

He searched every downstairs room again before climbing the stairs and opening the door to his bedroom. Louise was sitting, propped up by pillows on the bed beside Alice, who was sleeping soundly.

'I thought she'd be safer in with us after what happened,' Louise whispered, raising her finger to her lips after she'd spoken.

He nodded to show he'd understood, went to the window and pulled aside one of the curtains. Their visitors hadn't left the garden. They were standing grouped around Arthur on the lawn. Every one of them was looking up at him and he sensed they'd been holding a silent vigil while watching him move around the house.

He left the curtains slightly open and pulled up a chair. Terrified for Alice and Louise, conscious that he could do little against so many, he sat and stared at his neighbours. If they weren't going to sleep that night neither would he.

The rays of the rising sun woke Patrick at daybreak. The trees around the house stood black, skeletal and windblown, etched like woodcuts against the dawn light. He left his chair and stood in front of the window. The lawn was bereft of people and silvered by frost. It glittered hard and cold. He presumed his neighbours had ended their watch some time during the night while he'd slept.

He left the chair and went to the bed. Alice and

Louise were lying side by side, entwined and curled together like kittens in a basket. An oddly peaceful scene after the trauma of the night. He looked around, wondering if his ears were deceiving him. He went to the door and returned to the bed.

There was no doubt in his mind – the closer he drew to Alice, the more audible the voices became. The sound of singing – children singing, very softly and quietly – singing out Alice's name, 'Alice . . . Alice . . . Alice . . .'

He gazed at his daughter, but his loving glance was tempered with horror when he noticed the congealed blood on her hands and the dirt beneath her fingernails.

He didn't want to think how her hands had got into such a state. He stared at her face, tracing every line, imprinting it on his memory. She was his daughter and he loved her. Nothing else mattered. How could it?

The voices persisted, softly whispering and singing. He ignored them and lay on the bed beside Alice, wrapping his arm around both her and Louise. He closed his eyes and concentrated on the sound of their breathing. It was a lullaby he never wanted to end.

When Patrick next woke, the light was stronger and the sun higher in the sky. He reached out and touched Louise, then realised Alice was no longer lying between them. Panic-stricken, he sat up and looked around. When he saw that their daughter wasn't in the room with them he left and checked her bedroom. It too was empty. He ran downstairs and grabbed the back-door key from the cabinet in the hall.

To his relief he found Alice in the kitchen. She'd already showered and dressed, her damp hair was neatly brushed back away from her face and she smelled of soap and toothpaste. She was rummaging around in the freezer, searching through the drawers.

'Hi, Dad,' she greeted him brightly. 'I'm thinking of cooking sausages for all of us for breakfast.'

He smiled. 'Great idea, but make sure you ask Mum to help you.'

She frowned at him.

'You know how Mum worries about hot stoves.' When she didn't say anything, he continued, 'Thanks, honey. We'll all enjoy eating them.' He hesitated when he saw a black feather on the kitchen counter. He picked it up, unlocked the outside door and scanned the immediate area. There was no sign of anyone or any more feathers. He threw the black feather into a bush in disgust and headed for his surgery. He hadn't reached the door when he heard a frantic knocking. He looked back at the house. Louise was banging the window of the dining room.

Her cry was muffled by the double glazing but the look of horror on her face was obvious. 'Patrick!'

He turned to see what she was pointing at and reeled back as though he'd been punched. Fixed to the door of the garden shed by half a dozen nails was the bloodied furry pelt of Howie. There was no mistaking the distinctive markings on what had been the dog's coat. Something was lying on the flower bed beneath it. He stepped closer. It was the dog's lifeless corpse; a lump of freshly skinned, raw, bloodied flesh, with huge eyes that appeared abnormally round and staring without their lids.

He turned and looked back at the house. Alice was walking out of the kitchen door. Louise had left by the front door and was shouting at her as she came around the house.

'Alice, stay in the house, sweetie. Whatever you do, don't come out into the garden. Stay indoors. Just for a little while.'

'What, Mum?' Alice turned to Louise as if she hadn't heard a word she'd said.

'Please, baby. Stay inside,' Louise pleaded. 'Promise me that you'll stay inside and don't look out of the window. Don't argue with me, sweetie. Just do it.'

'All right, if you want me to, Mum.' Alice returned to the kitchen.

Louise waited until Alice was back in the house, then closed the door on her before running across the garden towards Patrick. She took one look at the dog's skinned carcass, clapped her hand over her mouth and began to retch.

Too angry and devastated to offer Louise either help or comfort, Patrick swung the door on the shed wide so he wouldn't have to touch the pelt, took a spade and a pair of gardening gloves from inside and began to dig a hole next to the animal's body.

'I don't understand,' Louise whispered hoarsely when she could finally speak again. 'Why would Arthur and the others do this to a defenceless animal?' She fought back tears as she watched Patrick enlarge the hole until it was big enough to take the dog.

His eyes darkened as he stopped digging and looked at her. 'Can we be sure that it was Arthur and the others?'

Louise stared at him in disbelief as the importance of his words sank in. 'What are you saying?'

Patrick's only answer was to resume digging, fast and furiously. He drew in quick shallow breaths of air but didn't slacken his pace for an instant. It was as though he were trying to erase the horrific scene by sheer physical exertion.

When the hole was large and deep enough, he wrapped the skinned dog's carcass in a tarpaulin and lowered the bundle into the bottom. Only then did he remove the torn and bloodied pelt from the shed door and drop it on top of the dog. He pulled off his gloves, now soaked and steeped in the dog's blood, and tossed them dank and dripping into the hole, before picking up the spade and piling earth back into the grave. He continued to work quickly, perspiration running down his brow on to his cheeks.

Louise watched in silence. She expected him to say something, but when he didn't she couldn't find the courage to prompt him. When Patrick had shovelled the last of the earth into the hole, he returned the spade to the shed. Avoiding meeting her eye, he left her and started walking towards the house.

'Patrick?' She followed him. 'Please, tell me, what are you suggesting? If you don't think Arthur and the others killed Howie, you must suspect someone else of doing it. Patrick, please, talk to me . . .'

Patrick went into the kitchen. Alice was standing by

the cooker staring blankly into space. She didn't turn around or look at Patrick and Louise but murmured, 'I'm daydreaming.'

Patrick went to her. He took a deep breath and said, 'Show me your hands, Alice.'

Louise moved close to them and took his arm. 'Patrick, what are you doing? You can't be suggesting . . . you can't . . .' She leaned against the worktop for support.

'Why do you want to see my hands, Dad? Is it a game?' Alice asked.

'Yes, honey, it's a game,' Patrick answered.

Alice closed her eyes and held out her hands; then suddenly changed her mind before Patrick had a chance to look at them. She thrust them behind her back.

'Alice, let me see your hands,' Patrick reiterated irritably.

'Dad, what exactly is this for?' she demanded.

Patrick softened his voice. 'Just do as I ask, honey.' He continued to watch her.

The expression on Alice's face became impassive, her eyes cold, but after only a moment's hesitation she held out her hands to him and turned them over so her palms were uppermost.

Both Louise and Patrick had to brace themselves to look at them. They needn't have concerned themselves. Alice's hands were pink, shiny and spotlessly clean.

Alice cooked the sausages she'd taken from the freezer. Patrick made and buttered toast, Louise sliced tomatoes and laid the table. She wasn't hungry and, after burying the dog, she doubted that Patrick would be, but they sat at the table alongside Alice and forced themselves to eat.

Alice piled sausages, toast and tomatoes on to her plate, reached for the bottle of ketchup, upended it and squeezed a blob next to the sausages. She cut up her toast, dipped it into the sauce, set down her knife and fork and announced, 'I don't want to eat now. I was hungry when I got up but I'm not any more.'

'Try and eat something please, sweetie,' Louise coaxed. It was one of the phrases she'd used before Alice had died: 'Try and eat something, please'; 'You have to keep up your strength'; 'You need nourishment'; 'You're a growing girl'.

She saw Patrick looking at her and realised there was no earthly reason why Alice should eat. She had no need to keep up her strength and she wasn't a growing girl. Not any more, nor would she be ever again.

'You piled all that food on your plate, Alice,' Patrick admonished. 'The least you can do is eat one sausage.'

Alice sat back in her chair and looked at him from under her eyelids. 'I don't want to.'

Not wanting to witness an argument between father and daughter, Louise was glad when they were interrupted by a knock at the door.

'I'll go.' She walked through the hall and opened the front door. Mary Brogan was standing on the doorstep.

Louise's first thought was for Alice. Panic-stricken, she found herself dumbstruck.

'It's all right, Louise,' Mary said softly. 'I'm here to help, not take Alice,' she added as though she'd read Louise's thoughts.

'Where are my manners? Please, come in, Mary.' Louise stepped back to make room for Mary to enter. The last thing she wanted was to sit and talk to Mary or invite her into the strained atmosphere in the dining room. But she did want to avoid a visit like the one they'd had the night before. And she felt she had no choice but to be polite.

Patrick saw Mary through the open door to the dining room and rose to his feet. His first thought, like Louise's, was to protect Alice. He decided the best way to do that would be to get her out of sight. 'As you're not hungry you can go and play in your room, Alice, while we talk to Mrs Brogan.'

'Do I have to?' Alice whined.

'Yes, you do,' Patrick answered firmly. 'Go on. We won't be long, and then we'll go out for a walk or do whatever you want.'

'Play football and hide-and-seek like we did the other day?' Alice suggested.

'If that's what you really want, honey, then that's what we'll do,' Patrick acquiesced.

Louise led Mary into the dining room. When Alice passed them in the hall, Mary smiled and greeted her.

'Hello, Alice. I'm Mary Brogan.'

'Hi,' Alice replied unenthusiastically.

'Nice to meet you. Are you excited about going back?'

Patrick answered for Alice. 'Yes, I think she is.'

Alice looked confused for a moment, then climbed the stairs. When she reached the top she called down, 'Have you seen Howie anywhere, Dad? I couldn't find him this morning.'

Patrick fought to keep control of his emotions. 'No, I haven't seen him,' he answered in a tense voice.

'See you later, Alice,' Mary called out.

The sound of Alice's bedroom door slamming shut resounded down the stairs.

Mary took the chair Patrick offered her, sat down and looked at Louise. 'I'm here for a reason.'

'Like last night?' Patrick couldn't resist the gibe but Mary managed to ignore it.

'As you know, this is Alice's last day. Tonight there'll be a procession, a "feather walk" as we call it, but just a short one because Alice is so young. You've already seen one, Louise,' she reminded her. 'You were in the street when Deirdre's feather walk went through the town.'

'You saw a procession?' Patrick asked Louise in surprise. 'You knew about these "feather walks"?'

'Yes,' Louise murmured.

'You never said anything to me about them,' he protested.

'Only because I wasn't sure what I'd seen at the time,' she explained. 'I didn't understand the significance of the walk or the black feathers until I saw people wearing them again last night.'

'On today's walk you'll both have to be strong for Alice,' Mary said emphatically. 'But she'll want to go back herself. You won't have to persuade her.' She opened her bag and removed three sticks joined by woven roots. It was an identical contraption to the one she'd placed around Deirdre's neck when Deirdre had succumbed to a fit in the pharmacy. 'This is something for Alice to wear around her neck. We call it a clutch. If she becomes agitated, put it around her neck like a necklace and slip her wrists into these loops. You'll find that it comforts her.' She placed it on the table.

'Thank you,' Louise said politely.

'You can fasten the loops about her wrists, in front or behind her back, it doesn't matter which way you do it.' Mary demonstrated how the sticks could be twisted into a crude form of handcuffs.

Louise took a deep breath and steeled herself. 'Mary, if you don't mind, I need to have a word with Patrick about all this. In private,' she added.

'Of course,' Mary said. 'I quite understand. This is not an easy time for either of you.'

'Please, stay here, help yourself to coffee,' Louise offered politely. 'We won't be long.'

Louise went into the hall. Patrick followed and closed the door behind him.

As soon as they were alone, Louise grabbed his hand. 'Patrick, I'm not ready to give up Alice,' she pleaded urgently. 'Please, don't ask me to because I can't . . .'

Patrick wrapped his arms around her and held her tight.

She thought rapidly. 'We can run . . . we can go away . . . we can take your car . . . we have to . . .'

'So Alice can scream in pain and collapse like she did yesterday when all her wounds opened up the moment she left the confines of the town?' Patrick reminded her.

'Maybe it will be different today,' Louise gabbled. 'Maybe that was just something that happened yesterday. Maybe it will work today . . .' If willpower alone could get them out of Wake Wood, Louise felt she could summon enough for all three of them.

Patrick stepped back from her and leaned against the wall. 'This isn't easy for me to say or admit, Louise. But things aren't right with Alice. You do know that, don't you?'

She gazed at him wordlessly.

'You do know that, don't you?' he repeated.

'Yes, I know,' she conceded miserably.

Patrick's phone rang.

He ignored it. It eventually stopped ringing, only to start again almost immediately.

'You know better than me what people are like when their animals are sick. It won't stop ringing until you switch it off or answer it,' Louise advised.

Patrick wrapped his arm around her shoulders, took the call and listened for a moment, then said, 'I can come tomorrow . . . No, I can't . . . How high did you say his temperature is? . . . OK . . . OK . . . All right, twenty minutes. I'll be there.'

Louise broke free. 'No! Please, Patrick, not today. You can't leave Alice and me, not today of all days.'

'I have to go,' he declared reluctantly.

'Please . . .'

'I have to,' he insisted. 'If I don't, they'll be back here again with their black feathers and demands that we return Alice instantly to the woods and the earth, just like last night. Do you want that?'

Too overwrought to speak, she shook her head. Her tears fell to the floor.

'Louise?'

She turned her back on him and opened the door to the dining room.

'I won't be long,' he called after her.

'You'll be as long as it takes.' She took a moment to wipe her eyes and pull herself together before returning to Mary.

Mary noticed Louise's tears. 'Is everything all right?' she asked sympathetically.

'Patrick's been called out,' Louise informed her briefly.

'I see. I'm sorry. Hopefully he won't be too long.' Mary rose from her chair. 'It's time I was going, but I'll be back for you before midnight and we'll all join the procession to the woods. The whole town will be there for you, Alice and Patrick.'

Louise didn't trust herself to comment. 'I'll see you out.'

'How are you really, Louise?' Mary enquired earnestly. 'Are you in good heart?'

'I'm fine,' Louise lied.

Mary hugged her and left. Louise watched her pick up her bicycle and wheel it down the drive.

Louise returned to the house and closed the door. When she looked up she saw Alice watching her from the top of the stairs. She forced a smile. 'Want to play a game, Alice? Any game, your choice.'

Alice glared back at her. 'When's the baby coming?'

# Eighteen

The O'Sheas' farmyard was dark and deserted. Black clouds had blown in suddenly and heavily, transforming midday to twilight. The shadowy outlines of farm machinery parked on the fringes of the yard had adopted strangely prehistoric dinosaur-like silhouettes. The chickens, ducks and geese were silent, safely locked away in the poultry houses secure from marauding foxes. Even the dogs were quiet and sleeping in the barn after a morning spent out in the fields with the sheep and the cattle.

A solitary light burned at the entrance to the cow house. Inside, the animals were restless, lowing noisily, flicking their tails and shuffling and stamping their hooves. Martin O'Shea leaned against a pillar at the entrance. Conscious of his animals' disquiet, he was alert, watchful, eyeing the cows in between glancing apprehensively towards the gate of the bull pen.

Patrick was taking his time over examining the prize bull and Martin wasn't sure whether that was a good or a bad thing. The beast had looked in bad shape to him but a good vet could work miracles, or so Arthur always said. And he and his late father had always believed everything Arthur said, with good cause. The vet had looked after all their animals and well, since Martin had been a small boy.

And Arthur had brought Patrick into Wake Wood and trusted him to carry on his good work.

When the gate swung open, Martin stepped forward, immediately preparing himself for what he suspected was going to be expensive news. A vet's services didn't come cheap, especially when an animal was in as bad a way as the bull appeared to be.

Patrick stood framed in the doorway, his gloved hands and overalls saturated with bright red blood.

'He's a mess, Martin,' Patrick declared flatly. 'I've never seen an animal as bad that's still breathing. When and how did this happen to him?'

'I have no idea. His fever was up when I last checked him, that's when I went into the house to phone you. When I came back here I found him like he is now. And that's all I know,' Martin replied defensively. 'What's he got?'

Patrick met Martin's eye. 'It's not an illness, Martin. Someone or something did this to him.'

'Someone . . . you mean deliberately attacked and hurt him!'

'That's exactly what I mean,' Patrick confirmed.

'Well, don't look at me,' Martin countered pre-emptively. 'I think the world of that bull, even after what he did to my dad. He's an animal and animals can't think. Not like us. They don't know what they're doing and can't be held responsible when they hurt people. Can they?'

'No, they can't.' Patrick left the gate open, returned to

the bull pen and gazed down at the bull. The creature lay on his side, gasping for breath. The pool of blood beneath and around the beast was inches deep and more was pumping from his wounds every second. Wide gashes on his head and neck exposed the white of the skull and spinal bones in places. But even worse than the head and neck injuries was the sight of one of the animal's eyes lying on the floor beside his empty eye socket. It had been viciously and inexpertly gouged out.

Martin moved reluctantly into the doorway of the pen, nauseated by the sight that greeted him. He could barely bring himself to look at the wreckage of what had been his father's prize animal.

Patrick crouched down beside the bull. He'd spotted something glittering on the ground, floating in the blood. He picked it out with his gloved fingers and held it up. It was a silver chain. He recognised it as Alice's. The one Louise had given her on her birthday. The same one he'd taken from Alice's grave, washed, disinfected and cleaned and hidden in Alice's coat pocket, for her to find later, when they'd played football in the garden on the first day after her return to them.

Patrick studied it for a moment, then blanched as his suspicions hardened. He looked back at the bull, evaluating its injuries and considering how they might have been made. Surely not . . .

'Did you drop something?'

Patrick started. 'Sorry, Martin, I heard you speak but I was miles away. What did you say?' He pocketed the bloodstained chain.

'I asked if you'd dropped something,' Martin repeated.

'I was minding my daughter's neck chain for her. It fell out of my pocket,' Patrick lied.

Martin looked at the bull. 'You'll be wanting some hot water, Patrick, so you can tend to him. I'll get a couple of buckets from the kitchen.'

The bull heard Martin's voice, recognised it and moved his head so he could look up at him with his one remaining eye. Martin saw the beast move and fought back tears.

Patrick knew that Martin would be embarrassed by sympathy so he pretended not to notice his distress, although he was in danger of being overcome by emotion himself. He patted and smoothed the bull's flanks before glancing back at Martin and shaking his head. 'I won't need any hot water, Martin.'

'There's nothing you can do for him?' Martin didn't want to believe it.

'All I can do for him now is put him out of his misery,' Patrick said quietly.

Martin squared his shoulders, stared at the ailing bull for a moment, then looked away. 'Fair enough, Patrick. At least you came out to see to him, so you gave him every chance. Injection, is it?'

Patrick opened his bag and prepped a hypodermic. He hesitated after he'd drawn the contents of a phial into the syringe, then checked the notes on the back of the bottle of solution he'd used to fill the needle.

'He's too big for this. It won't have any effect on a beast his weight.' Patrick capped the hypodermic. He returned to his bag and removed a small bolt-type gun. 'They call this a humane killer. It will be quick,' he explained.

'And painless?' Martin asked hopefully.

'After what he's already been through, as painless as I can make it,' Patrick promised. He looked around the shed at the rest of the cattle, aware that they were all watching his every move. He primed the gun, rose to his feet and walked deliberately to the bull's head. He pressed the device to the animal's forehead and fired.

The noise of the shot ricocheted around the shed, driving the cattle further back into their pens in fright. They moved even more restlessly, mooing and lowing noisily. The bull went into a seizure. Its legs thrashed wildly in its death throes, drumming the concrete floor and splashing the walls and gate of the pen with blood.

Martin O'Shea had closed his eyes. He didn't see Patrick slip the hypodermic syringe into his pocket.

The world whirled crazily around Louise. She felt as though she were standing in the centre of a roundabout that was rotating wildly out of control. The only constant was Alice, standing stock still on the landing.

Louise lost all sense of time and self as she continued to stare up at her daughter. The searing, contemptuous glare in Alice's eyes went beyond anger. It was disdainful, dismissive, and ferocious in its intensity. Louise burned under that steady gaze until Alice broke the spell by turning her back, flouncing to her room and shutting herself in with a loud bang of the door.

Only then did Louise take a deep breath. She felt

giddy, nauseous, as if she'd run a marathon. Could it be . . . was it possible that she was really pregnant? After all that the doctors had said?

She hurried through to the kitchen, picked up her keys and went outside to the old dairy that Patrick had paid a builder to convert into a stockroom for her pharmacy.

Hands trembling, she unlocked the door, burst inside and switched on the light. She searched frantically along the steel shelving units until she found the box she was looking for. She lifted it down to the floor and, taking one of the metal box-rippers she kept on the end of every shelf, tore it open.

Her fingers reacted clumsily. They felt as though they'd swollen to double their normal size but somehow she managed to tear open the flaps on the box. She removed one of the pregnancy testing kits it contained. Taking it, she left, locked the stockroom door, charged across the garden back to the house and upstairs to the bathroom. She closed the door, fumbled with her zip, pulled down her jeans and panties and dived on to the toilet.

Her hands were still shaking when she fought to tear apart the cellophane that sealed the box. She extracted the litmus stick, thrust it beneath her, urinated on it, leaned forward and closed her eyes, counting off the seconds twice over until she was absolutely certain she'd passed the three-minute mark.

She opened her eyes, lifted the stick out from under her and stared at it. The result was unmistakeable. A definite pregnant '3+ weeks'. She placed the stick carefully on the shelf beside her as if it was her most precious possession, rose from the toilet, pulled up her panties and jeans, fastened the zip and flushed the cistern.

Her gynaecologist had been so definite when she'd examined her after Alice's birth. The diagnosis brutal. Her uterus had been so badly damaged when Alice had been born that there wouldn't be any more children. Not for her and Patrick. There couldn't be. When she'd broached the subject of IVF the consultant had discounted it, insisting she'd never conceive another child.

The doctor had tried to be kind, telling her, as gently as she knew how, the only chance she and Patrick had of increasing the size of their family lay in adoption or surrogacy.

The diagnosis had been a difficult one for both her and Patrick to come to terms with because from the time they'd first discussed marriage they'd planned to have a large family. Yet, somehow, a miracle had happened and now she was carrying another child.

She ran a sink full of water, plunged in her hands, soaped them and rinsed them off. Another baby to love, another child for their family. Her and Patrick's baby! She could actually think of babies again. Tiny, soft, warm, pink bodies smelling of baby lotion and talcum powder. Minute clothes, bassinets, toys, baby smiles and giggles.

She picked up the pregnancy test again between her thumb and forefinger, read and reread it. All her training as a pharmacist told her the results were definite and positive, yet she still had difficulty believing it.

She closed her eyes. It was all she and Patrick had hoped for and more. She couldn't wait to tell him, to see the expression on his face. She unlocked the door and left the bathroom, her mind still reeling from the thought. A baby! Another baby! Hers and Patrick's!

Then she remembered Alice. This was their last day on this earth with her. She hated herself even as the thought formulated in her mind, but she knew that this news would make her and Patrick's parting from their daughter a little easier to bear. No baby could ever replace Alice. Nothing and no one could, but it was another life . . . it would add another dimension to their family.

She looked out of the landing window at the trees waving their skeletal winter branches. Spring would soon come, bursting with new life. Head swimming giddily, needing air, she walked downstairs, opened the front door and went outside to the flower beds. The reassuring signs she'd craved to see were all there. The tips of spring bulbs, daffodils, crocuses and tulips pushing up through the soil; the camellia and azalea bushes heavy with buds, the small green shoots that would soon grow into clumps of perennial geraniums.

She moved her hands protectively over her abdomen and turned to the house. The smile died on her lips when she saw Alice standing in her bedroom window, staring down at Louise through cold, dead eyes.

Beset by remorse and regret, her heart went out to her daughter. Alice had been her and Patrick's entire world. She couldn't even begin to imagine how much pain Alice was feeling at this moment at the prospect of another child entering their lives. A child who'd arrive long after Alice had left them – for ever.

For ever – and go where? She froze in terror at the immense finality of the black unknown that was death.

She had to talk to Alice, convince her that she and Patrick hadn't set out to deliberately conceive a baby. That, no matter what, the new arrival would never replace her or take the love they had reserved solely for her. Alice had to know that she would always be their first, their darling; nothing and no one could take the space she had occupied in their lives and their hearts.

Louise returned to the house and entered through the kitchen. She heard it as soon as she closed the door. The sound of discordant music; childish voices rasping horribly out of tune, accompanied by monotone instruments; it seemed to be emanating from upstairs.

The noise was terrifying, yet somehow she was drawn to it. Unable to leave because the love she bore for her daughter was greater than her fear. Shaking, shivering, ice cold, she followed the sound. It grew louder and louder, increasing in volume until it deafened her when she reached the top of the stairs.

A wave of nausea washed over her. Faint, she reached out to the door handle of Alice's bedroom.

The instant she touched it, the singing stopped momentarily, only to be replaced by a myriad of noisy, jabbering voices. Summoning her courage, she pressed down on the handle and pushed the door open.

The voices quietened to the sound of just one little girl crying out, whining pitifully. Then it stopped.

'Alice?' she ventured tentatively. She looked into the room. Seeing no one, she peered behind the door. The room was empty. She stepped inside, looked beneath the bed, behind the curtains and opened the wardrobe door to reassure herself that no one was hiding in there.

Wondering if she were locked in an all-too-realistic nightmare, she turned around. Alice was standing on the landing behind her, swinging one of her old dolls from her right hand.

'Mum?' Her voice was soft, whingeing, insincere.

Louise retreated, hitting a wall and painfully bruising her spine. 'Alice,' she murmured. She needed to get a grip on her emotions. It was ridiculous to be afraid of her own daughter. She forced a smile. 'What is it, sweetie?'

'When's the baby coming?'

'Not for months,' Louise answered. 'I didn't even realise I was pregnant until you told me.'

'You didn't?' There was disbelief as well as reproach in Alice's question.

'I really didn't, sweetie.'

'But it's true.'

'Yes, it is.' Louise tried not to sound too glad. It wasn't difficult. Despite her best efforts to remain calm, Alice was frightening her.

Alice moved closer towards Louise but she didn't seem to take a step. It was almost as though she were gliding across the floor of the landing.

Terrified, unable to move back any further, Louise slipped sideways, slithering along the wall.

'You and Dad don't want me any more,' Alice pronounced bitterly.

'That's not true, Alice. Dad and I love you very much. You're everything to us. Our entire world, sweetie,' Louise protested.

'No, you're lying. You don't love me or want me. Not any more.' Alice threw the doll at Louise. It hit her cheekbone. Hard!

Louise reeled more from the shock of Alice's anger directed at her than the force of the impact. 'Alice . . .'

Alice moved closer and Louise continued to slide away from her until Alice began to convulse.

Seeing her daughter in pain, Louise's maternal instincts held sway, quelling both her misgivings and her terror. She went to Alice and wrapped her arms around her, holding her tight as if she could will her daughter to stop shaking and her teeth to stop chattering.

She continued to hold Alice for a few minutes after she'd quietened. Remembering all the other times when she'd comforted Alice, after all her childhood illnesses; her coughs and colds and sore throats; her temperatures, rashes and toddler temper tantrums.

She was catapulted harshly back to the present when Alice struggled to escape her arms. Releasing her daughter, Louise rose clumsily to her feet.

She tripped on something hard that was lying on the rug and reached out to the wall to steady herself. She looked down and saw an abacus-type instrument similar to the one Arthur had used the night he'd come to supper – the night he'd told her and Patrick that he could bring Alice back from the dead.

Louise couldn't help feeling that she'd seen the identical instrument somewhere before. And not that long ago. Then she recalled Peggy O'Shea holding one just like it when she'd been walking away from Alice in the O'Sheas' farmyard.

'You're not telling the truth when you say that you and Dad love me, Mum,' Alice admonished, seeing Louise looking at the object on the floor.

'Yes, I am, sweetie. And now it's your turn to tell the truth, Alice.' Louise picked up the instrument and held it up. 'Where did you get this?'

Alice turned aside, gathered her doll from the floor and waved it in front of Louise's eyes. 'It's always been mine.'

'Not your doll, this . . . thing.' Louise pushed the abacus towards Alice so there could be no mistake. When Alice didn't answer her, Louise said, 'You took it from Mrs O'Shea, didn't you?'

Alice snatched the instrument from Louise's hand. 'And I think I'll take it back to Mrs O'Shea.' Her voice was low, growling, strangely threatening.

'Alice . . .' Louise looked around the landing, through the open bedroom door, and what she could see of the stairs and hall, in bewilderment. There was nowhere Alice could have gone. Yet she'd vanished. There was no sign of her.

'Alice!' she rotated in a circle. 'Alice, where are you!' Frantic, Louise screamed.

She ran into the other bedroom and the bathroom, before charging down the stairs, shouting Alice's name.

Halfway down the staircase she caught a glimpse of a

figure standing in the centre of the lawn. She stopped and stared. It was Alice. Even as she watched, Alice seemed to flicker in and out like a faded electronic recording on a broken disc. Then, before Louise's eyes, she literally disappeared.

# Nineteen

Louise was terror-stricken but fear for her daughter proved stronger than concern for herself. She ran out of the house and into the garden to the exact spot where she'd last seen Alice. She could make out imprints of Alice's shoes in the lawn but there was no trail of footsteps to follow. It was as though Alice had been spirited away upwards to the sky by a giant bird . . . or ghostly spirit.

She looked up. A flock of enormous black crows were cawing and circling round the trees.

Again the phrase sprang to mind just as it had done when she and Patrick had driven into Wake Wood on the day they'd moved into the town.

'A murder of crows.'

Sick with apprehension, Louise turned a full circle, crying out, 'Alice, where are you? Please, answer me, Alice!' as loudly as she could.

The only reply she received was the cry of the birds and the whisper of a winter breeze that carried with it the slightest hint of warmth and promise of spring.

'Alice . . . Alice, where are you? . . . Alice, please don't do this, sweetie . . . Baby, where are you?' Louise begged, still more afraid for her daughter than for herself.

The sun began to sink low, travelling through the sky at an accelerated rate, fading faster than usual. Darkness was falling, although the afternoon had barely begun. It was as though the earth's cycle had gone into overdrive, breaking every known law of physics.

Louise sank down on the cold grass and studied Alice's footprints. No matter what, she had to think calmly and coherently for Alice's sake. She had to begin a slow, methodical search for her daughter. That was it! If she looked everywhere in the garden and house she would find Alice. She simply had to!

Children didn't just disappear into thin air. It wasn't possible. It was true that some were abducted, but as no one else had been either in the house or garden except her and Alice, Alice had to be still here.

She walked to the kitchen door and, starting from that point, moved slowly and deliberately out in ever-increasing circles, searching every inch of the garden as she went.

On her third circuit she saw something strange that didn't belong in the ground. A patch of an unnaturally bright blue colour for the time of year, lying motionless, sticking out proud from the mound of earth on the grave that Patrick had dug for Howie. Had it really only been that morning?

Louise approached the splash of blue slowly and warily. When she reached it, she bent down and retrieved the piece of cloth. It was attached to Alice's doll. The one Alice had thrown at her on the landing. She picked up the doll. It was dirty, its limbs torn, hanging loosely from its body, its blue dress ragged and shredded. She looked down again. Beneath it lay Peggy O'Shea's abacus. She picked that up also, brushed the dirt from the bone beads and wooden rods and shook uncontrollably as something akin to an electric shock charged through her body. The beads were bone – but from what: animal or human? She forced herself to concentrate on searching for Alice.

When she was certain Alice was nowhere in the garden, Louise returned to the house and checked every room again, closing the doors and windows after she'd searched them. Eventually she was forced to accept that her daughter wasn't anywhere in the cottage or the grounds.

She grabbed her coat and picked up the keys to their other car from the key box. Patrick had bought it for her not long after they'd moved to Wake Wood, saying she'd need it now she was running a business.

Recalling what Alice had said about returning to the O'Sheas', she locked the front and back doors, opened the car and tossed the abacus and doll on to the passenger seat. Would Alice have gone to the O'Shea farm without the abacus when her intention had been to return it?

Since it was her only clue as to Alice's whereabouts, Louise decided to act on it and if Alice hadn't gone to the O'Sheas' there was always the chance that she'd pass her at some point on the road.

She headed down the drive, out of the gate and turned on to the main road. The O'Shea farm was the other side of Wake Wood. She drove slowly towards the town, looking behind every tree and into the hedgerows as she passed, reducing her speed every time she saw a ditch or the entrance to a field. She stopped the car more than once and left it to lean on gates and look into the fields, although logic insisted that there was no way Alice could have travelled as far on foot as she'd driven in such a short space of time.

The twilight was gathering rapidly; soon night would fall. And when it did there would be little point in continuing her search for Alice – she wouldn't be able to see her. Alice was wearing dark clothes, and dark clothes in shadow would make it impossible for her to spot her daughter.

Louise stopped the car at the crossroads just before the outskirts of Wake Wood. A mile ahead of her was the main street. Behind her, the road she'd travelled. To the left a track that led to one of the farms she'd visited once with Patrick when he'd ministered to a litter of piglets. To the right, a narrow country lane that wound the long way around the town, eventually meeting up with the road on the other side. From that point it was only a short distance to the O'Shea farm.

Louise left the car and looked down each road in turn, crying out Alice's name as loudly as she could. But there was no human reply.

Only the distant sound of the wind turbines grating in the wind, and the cry of night birds circling and congregating overhead. At midnight it would be time for Alice's return to the woods. What would happen if they couldn't find Alice for the feather walk?

Would Alice then be allowed to remain in Wake Wood? Tied to the place for ever, unable to take a step outside the town limits without suffering again from the old wounds that had killed her?

What had she and Patrick precipitated when they'd lied to Arthur?

What had they done?

'Alice!' Her cry echoed high into the sky. Loud, plaintive. 'Alice, please answer me, sweetie, where are you?'

Alice walked through the woods. Although scant light shone down through the trees from the moon, and virtually none from the stars, she walked as quickly and surely as if it were bright sunlight and she could see exactly where she was going. Way ahead of her in the distance she could make out a light burning in the O'Shea farmhouse kitchen and she aimed straight for it.

The discordant childish singing that had haunted her daydreams and nightmares for the past two days intensified as she drew closer to the lane that led to the farmhouse. She passed a tractor. Its large black wheels towered above her and she rested against one of them for a moment, covering her ears in an attempt to block out the sound, but it was no use.

The noise grew louder and louder, intensifying until she felt she could stand it no longer. Finally she snapped and screamed . . . and screamed . . . and screamed . . . but still the voices persisted . . . deafening . . . shrill . . . cacophonous.

When no one came out of the farmhouse she wondered if her screams, like the singing, only existed in her own head.

She looked around and then back at the house before straightening her back and walking towards it.

Peggy O'Shea had almost finished the chores she'd set herself for that day. Beds changed, washing and cleaning finished; now she lowered her Kitchen Maid – the clothes horse that hung on pulleys from her kitchen ceiling. On the table beneath it was a stack of sheets and towels. She picked up the first of the sheets, folded it neatly and hung it on one of the slats.

When all the sheets were neatly arranged, she started on the towels. The rack was fully loaded when she pulled the cord and hoisted the Kitchen Maid back up to the ceiling. She tied the cord securely to its hook and hesitated. There was a strange noise in the yard. A scratching . . . a scraping . . . rats or . . . She trembled, preferring not to think of Alice Daley and the alternatives.

She went to the window, pushed aside the curtain and looked out. The light was still on in the cattle shed and the vet's estate car parked outside it. She hoped that the vet would be able to do something for the bull. The animal had cost so much money. More than she and Mick could really afford at the time or now. They were still paying off the bank loan and would be for a few more years by her reckoning.

The yard yawned back at her, empty and deserted. The stables were shuttered. The doors locked. The pig pens closed up for the night. She listened hard. The dogs were quiet. Whatever she'd heard was obviously insignificant or they would have started barking.

She went to the range, opened one of the ring covers on the top and slid the kettle on to it. The water started to bubble the moment it was placed on direct heat. She smiled. As she kept telling her neighbours who favoured more modern electric stoves, the best thing about a kitchen range was that soups and stews stayed warm and required very little heating, and water was never far from the boil when you needed a good strong cup of tea.

She lifted a casserole dish from a covered ring, crouched down and opened one of the low oven doors. As an afterthought, she opened the door above it to check the heat. Satisfied there was sufficient coal and wood to keep the fire burning long enough to heat the dish through, she pushed the casserole on to a rack in the small oven.

The moment she closed the oven doors the kitchen lights dimmed and flickered.

'Not again,' she muttered. One of the downsides of living in heavily wooded countryside was an erratic electricity supply. High winds meant lines became caught up in branches. Or, even worse, falling trees brought down poles, which meant they could be off-supply for days, which gave her another reason to be grateful for her kitchen range. She was used to the inconvenience. But she hoped that the light would last long enough for her to fetch candles and matches from her store cupboard. She reached out and gripped the back of a chair to steady herself while she rose from her knees.

'Thank you for letting me ride your pony.'

The child's voice was robotic, high-pitched. Terrified, Peggy whirled around to see Alice Daley behind her.

'Alice, I didn't hear you come in.' Peggy forced a cough in an ineffectual attempt to conceal her fear and the quivering in her voice.

'I know you didn't,' Alice chanted triumphantly.

'Your parents will be looking for you.' Peggy failed to smile at the child. 'They have to take you back soon.'

'Will they?' Alice questioned in a sceptical tone that said they wouldn't. She held up the dandy brush and curry comb Peggy had shown her how to use when grooming the pony. Both were heavily matted with bloodstained hairs. She dropped them on to the flagstone floor. They fell with a loud, jarring clatter.

Peggy stared at them in horror. 'My pony! What have you done?'

Alice jumped on the elderly lady's back and laughed. Kicking her heels viciously into Peggy's sides, she shouted, 'Come on, horsey. Giddy-up . . . giddy-up, horsey. Come on . . .'

It took all of Peggy's strength to remain crouched upright. Gasping for air, breathing heavily, she crawled a few steps on her hands and knees and backed away from the range. She halted close to a chair. She tried to reach out to it but Alice kicked her hard in the ribs again and she fell forward, wincing in pain.

Still coughing violently, Peggy struggled valiantly to her feet.

'You're not supposed to rear up, horsey,' Alice shouted, digging her heels into Peggy's ribcage again and again and grabbing at the old woman's hair.

Peggy lurched across the room, aiming to reach a clutch resembling the one Mary had used on Deirdre and given to Louise. It was hanging from the corner of the dresser. Twice, she almost managed to grab it. But Alice kicked her hard and she fell back. The third time she almost touched it, then Alice yanked at her hair again and pulled her away.

The fourth time she managed to grip one of the strands of rope between her thumb and forefinger but she sensed Alice was toying with her and had allowed her to reach it. Fighting Alice's weight and the pain the child was inflicting on her, she turned.

To Peggy's amazement, Alice slid from her back. She allowed Peggy to place the clutch over her head.

'There now, Alice,' Peggy rasped hoarsely, arranging the clutch neatly around the young girl's neck. 'Doesn't that feel a lot better?'

Alice blinked slowly, then looked down at the clutch. 'That's very pretty,' she commented brightly.

'Yes,' Peggy agreed, straightening her aching back. She desperately tried to be positive. 'It is pretty, isn't it? Doesn't it feel good around your neck?'

The kettle began to boil on the range, activating the whistle. The noise seemed to irritate Alice. She lifted the clutch from around her neck and threw it to the floor. 'You keep it, old woman. It doesn't work for me.'

Peggy stared at her incredulously, then lifted her hands to her own throat. She gasped, struggling for breath as her fingers dug deeper and deeper into her own neck. She tried to wrench them away but they refused to obey the signals she sent from her brain.

She was lost, helpless, powerless – in thrall to Alice's will. The child was killing her without physically having to lift a finger against her. Peggy fought her own hands wildly. Black spots wavered before her eyes. She caught a glimpse of herself in the mirror that hung over the mantelpiece. Blood was flowing – pouring from her ears and nose.

The whistle from the kettle grew louder and louder, more and more painful to hear. The Kitchen Maid clattered down from the ceiling and hung suspended alongside the table.

Peggy struggled and fought her way towards it. She was breathless, on the point of blacking out. Hoping she hadn't miscalculated and the rack would support her and break her fall, she threw herself across the bars. Her hands still refused to move from her throat. Every time she tried to loosen her grip her fingers tightened, cutting off the supply of blood as well as air to her head.

She looked down. Alice was on the floor in front of her, watching her. Peggy could still see herself in a corner of the mirror. Her face was darkening by the second from red to black.

'Don't forget to say "hi" to your husband from me when you see him.' Alice ducked under the sheets that hung from the clothes rack and looked up at Peggy's face. It was pressed close to the bars of the Kitchen Maid, only inches away from her own.

Alice thrust her hands up through the bars and grabbed Peggy's head by the ears. She pulled it down hard towards her, pressing it as tightly as she could against the wooden slats – the only barrier that separated her face from Peggy's.

She continued to grip Peggy's head, practically swinging her whole weight on it, all the while staring deep into Peggy's eyes.

Not only Peggy's ears and nose but also her eyes began to bleed. Slight at first, then gradually the flow grew thicker and thicker, the blood changing colour from bright to dark red.

The old woman opened and shut her mouth but no sound emanated from her lips. Alice watched and smiled and waited.

She only released Peggy when she was sure that the old woman was dead. She left her body lying across the Kitchen Maid, swinging gently back and forth, back and forth, across the room.

'Bye, old woman,' she whispered as she went to the door and opened it.

# Twenty

L ouise drove slowly down Main Street. Lights shone from shop windows, doorways and houses but nothing moved. No people, no animals. The town was deserted and everything was quiet. She wondered if people were eating their dinners and preparing for the feather walk behind their curtains.

She had no idea of the time – she'd left her watch behind in the cottage. Was Mary Brogan already making her way to the cottage to fetch Louise, Alice and Patrick? Mary had promised to go with them. Would she forget?

She wound down both the front windows of her car and peered from side to side of the street as she dropped her speed to walking pace, all the while constantly looking for Alice.

The street lights and then the shop lights began to flicker. Slowly, gradually, they dimmed from bright to pale yellow, then light to dark dismal brown before finally blacking out altogether, plunging the entire town into darkness.

Shivering, Louise pressed the electric buttons that wound up the windows. She locked the car doors from the inside, turned up the heating and pressed the accelerator, driving out of the town as fast as she could.

She didn't know where she was going. She only knew that she needed warmth, people and all of Patrick's strength and sound common sense. She needed him to offer an explanation for what she had seen.

She could almost hear him say, 'Alice disappeared in front of your eyes. Louise? Really, you're imagining things.'

And there was Alice. Above all she had to find Alice. And when she did . . . what then? . . . The feather walk . . . the return . . . the loss of her daughter . . . for ever.

Bag in hand, Patrick left the cattle shed. He loved most aspects of his job but he invariably felt despondent whenever he was forced to put an animal down, especially one as young and valuable as the O'Sheas' bull. And now all the decisions about the bull had been made, he had to face the prospect of Alice's 'return'. An event he'd been dreading ever since Arthur had brought her back and given her to him and Louise.

He was stowing his bag in the back of his estate when Martin passed him in the yard, jumped into his car and drove off at speed.

He hoped the boy would be all right. The death of Mick O'Shea had hit his son hard. It hadn't been easy for Martin to accept the loss of his father's prize bull as well, especially in view of the violence the animal had suffered before its death.

Life could be so very unfair. When the phrase came into his mind, Patrick didn't know if he was thinking of Martin O'Shea or himself. He took a moment to look around. The wind was rising, rattling the doors and windows of the barn and stables. The barn door was closed but the top part of one of the stable doors was swinging back and forth on its hinges. He couldn't be certain but it looked like the stable that had been occupied by the grey pony Alice had ridden the last time they'd visited the O'Shea farm.

He delved into his pocket and pulled out the blood-stained chain. He stared at it for a moment, then called out, 'Alice.'

There was no reply and neither had he been expecting one. He reached into the back of his car for the large torch. He switched it on and walked to the stable, training the beam of light on the darkest corners of the yard as he went. When he reached the stable with the open door he called out, 'Alice' again.

He trained the light on the ground and stepped back in horror. The light picked out a darkly red, glistening slick of blood and gore running out from the stable on to the straw- and mud-strewn yard.

Patrick pushed the top half of the door that was swinging open and looked down into the stable.

Sickened by the sight that greeted him, he leaned on the bottom half of the door for support. The hide of the beautiful grey pony had been cut and slashed to bloodied red ribbons. Unlike the bull, he didn't need to get down beside the animal to see that it had stopped breathing.

He fingered the chain again, turned and looked around the yard. Leaving the stable, he crossed the farmyard and headed for the farmhouse. A glow emanated from one of the downstairs windows. Recognising it as the kitchen and seeing the curtains slightly open, Patrick approached it and looked inside.

Inside the room, the Kitchen Maid was swinging gently on its pulleys. Beneath it, half hidden by a blood-stained hanging sheet, was the lifeless body of Peggy O'Shea.

Mesmerised by the horror of what he was looking at, Patrick stared at the corpse. Surely all of this couldn't be down to Alice. It couldn't . . .

'Patrick? Patrick.' Louise had to touch his arm to alert him to her presence.

He turned, stared at her in bewilderment, then as recognition and relief coursed headily through his veins he murmured, 'Louise, Alice has done some terrible things. I don't know how I can begin to tell you—'

'Stop!' She held her finger over his lips.

'No, listen to me. Louise. You have to know—'

'Patrick,' she broke in quickly. 'I'm pregnant.'

Patrick stared at her as if she'd lost her mind. 'We both know that's simply not possible, Louise.'

'I know it's not possible,' she said hurriedly. 'But it's true. Alice found out. I mean . . . she knew. I don't know how she knew. But she was the one who told me. Then she ran off. She was upset. She insisted we didn't love her any more. That we didn't want her. She said something about coming here—'

'She did come here,' he broke in. He glanced through the kitchen window again, not wanting to look at Peggy, but strangely drawn to the horror of the sight.

Louise followed his line of vision. Tears coursed

down her cheeks when she saw Peggy O'Shea's corpse lying on the flagstone floor, steeped in her own blood.

She turned to Patrick. Needing support, she embraced him. 'What are we going to do? Patrick,' she whispered into his ear. 'What are we going to do?' she repeated in a mantra of despair.

He only wished that he had an answer to give her. But all he could say was, 'What the hell have we done, Louise?'

Arthur, Tommy and Ben were sitting around the table in Arthur's living room playing poker, but only Arthur was smiling. He laid down his winning hand with a flourish, scooped up all the cash in the pot, pocketed it and glanced at the clock. 'It's time to go to the woods, boys.'

The moment he finished speaking the television went dead.

'Strange,' Arthur muttered as the lights flickered before dimming to a feeble brown that darkened the room to the point where none of the men could see one another's faces.

The doorbell rang, shrilly and persistently.

'All right, all right, I'm coming. Just wait a moment.' Feeling his way, Arthur left the room, walked into the hall and opened the front door. He stepped out on to his drive and looked around but there was no one that he could see. Although it wasn't easy to see anything without the glow from the outside lamps. Just as he was about to re-enter his house, a car pulled up. Shading his eyes from the headlights, Arthur waited for it to stop.

Martin O'Shea parked alongside Arthur and wound down the window.

'Martin, how's the bull?' Arthur asked in concern.

'Dead – hacked up,' Martin snapped sourly. 'The vet had to finish off what his daughter started.'

'What are you saying?' Arthur demanded.

'You were wrong about those outsiders,' Martin pronounced vehemently. 'They're wrong, Arthur. And their daughter's wrong!'

'What do you mean, "wrong"?' Arthur questioned soberly.

'You're the expert, Arthur – you work it out.' Martin reversed his car, backed away from the house and headed down the drive.

Arthur rubbed his chin thoughtfully and looked up at the night sky before returning to the house and rejoining his company in the living room. The lights were a little stronger but not much. He eyed the two men still sitting at the table.

'There's a problem,' he announced.

'Really?'

The voice came from behind him. It was childish, tinny and electronic. Arthur whirled around. Alice was in the corner of the room, holding his case of antiquated veterinary instruments. Lifting it high, she opened it and tipped its contents out over the coffee table. The metal tools fell on to the table and floor with a loud clatter.

'Now, which one shall we use?' She picked up a rusty veterinary lance, ran her finger down it and then pocketed it.

Arthur shouted at her, 'Get out of this house.' He

turned to the others. 'Whatever you do, don't look at her.'

'Who's a bossy boots, then?' Alice goaded. She circled the sofa.

Tommy and Ben kept their heads lowered, their gaze firmly fixed on the floor. Alice stopped for a moment and shook in convulsions.

When she recovered, she walked over to Ben and pulled herself up on to his knee. She started to bounce up and down and sing. 'Ride a cock horse to Banbury Cross . . . Go on – do it!' she ordered Ben.

Ben muttered, 'Ride a cock horse. Ride a cock horse . . .'

Alice bounced hard on his knee. 'No, that's not right. Move your knee up and down and sing "to Banbury Cross".'

Terrified, Ben repeated, 'Ride a cock horse to Banbury Cross . . .'

'To see our fine lady . . .' Alice's bouncing became harder, more vicious. It was obvious that she was deliberately trying to hurt Ben.

'Look at me!' Arthur commanded Ben insistently. 'Not her. Whatever you do, don't look at her.'

Arthur's directions came too late. Ben was already in thrall to Alice. His gaze was riveted on her, his will subservient to hers.

As Arthur watched, hoping even at this late stage that Ben would be able to free himself from Alice's control, blood began to run from Ben's mouth and ears. Seconds later, Ben started to shake as blood streamed down his cheeks from beneath his eyelids.

'We've got to get out . . .' Tommy jumped up from his chair, ran to the door and wrestled with the door handle, but it refused to open. He fell to the floor, gasping for air. When he looked back at Ben, his brother was still sitting upright, but he was dead in his chair.

Alice kicked the dead man's shins as she climbed off his lap. She looked at Arthur and began to move, slowly, inexorably, towards him. For every step she took towards him he took one back, retreating from her as fast as she advanced.

'You want to send me away,' Alice reproached.

Arthur realised he was shaking. He gripped the table and forced himself to remain calm. He began to chant, softly, quietly, melodically, hoping to soothe her anger with the hypnotic power of his voice. 'Go back to the trees, lie among the roots . . .'

Alice started her own chant in competition with Arthur's. As she spoke, the lights in the room dimmed and pulsated with the changes in the tone of her voice. 'I won't lie down, I won't go to bed. I'll stay up as long as I like!'

Arthur's voice grew stronger, more insistent. 'Go back to the trees, lie among the roots . . .'

'I *won't* lie down, I *won't* go to bed. I'll stay up *as long as I like!*' Alice countered savagely, screaming the words.

The room began to shake, the vibrations and the duel chanting building to a crescendo that ended by plunging the room into complete darkness . . . and absolute silence.

\*

The first sound was a slight rustling from the area where Arthur had been standing. A cigarette lighter was struck.

Arthur held it high so it illuminated his face as well as the immediate area. He walked around the living room. There was no sign of Alice.

'She's moved on,' he whispered to Tommy.

'Too late for Ben.' Tommy crawled over to his brother's corpse and caressed his head.

Patrick drove his estate car slowly along the wooded road that led from the O'Sheas' farm into the main street of Wake Wood. Louise sat beside him, peering into the countryside.

'Where do you think she'll go?' she asked anxiously.

'The cottage. Sooner or later she has to go to the cottage. It's the only place she *can* go.' He hesitated before saying, 'You do know that we have to take her back to the woods as Arthur said?'

Louise nodded, but Patrick knew she could well fail when the time came to actually hand her daughter back in the 'return' ceremony.

'We've got to give Alice up. We've no choice, Louise,' he added firmly.

Louise didn't answer him. The car headlights dimmed and the engine spluttered.

'Not again.' Patrick turned the ignition but it refused to fire. He waited a few minutes, then tried turning the key again but the car was completely dead.

'I'll give it a couple of minutes.' Patrick and Louise sat in silence while the seconds ticked off on Patrick's watch. When enough time had passed, he turned the ignition once again. Still dead. He reached into the back seat and picked up his torch.

'Try your phone,' he suggested to Louise.

Louise took her mobile from her pocket and switched it on. 'Nothing,' she said. 'It's as dead as the car.'

They left the car and moved around the front of the bonnet into the dim beam from the headlights.

Louise kicked something. Something soft. She looked down and saw a dead crow at her feet. 'Lift the light, Patrick.'

'What?' Patrick turned to her in confusion.

'Lift the light so we can see what's on the road,' she urged him.

He did as she asked. All around them, up and down the road, lay dark mounds of dead birds. Patrick stooped down, picked one up by its claws and examined it. As he did, another bird dropped from the trees above them on to the roof of the car, landing with a bang.

Louise recoiled. Patrick dropped the bird he was holding and took the one from the car roof.

He looked at it for a few seconds, and then shouted to Louise, 'Get back in the car.'

'What is it?'

'Don't argue – just get back in.'

Even as he barked the order at Louise, the car began to shake. Both of them froze in terror. Then, as suddenly as it had begun to shake, the car stopped.

'Hey!'

They both turned at the cry.

'Alice?' Louise called out tentatively.

Patrick swept his torch beam around them, picking out a small pink hand waving from behind a tree. He kept the beam trained on the tree, then slowly, inch by inch, Alice slid into view.

'You were going to leave me,' she accused them angrily.

'Never,' Louise countered. 'We love you. We won't ever leave you, sweetie. But we didn't know where you were.'

'But I'm right here,' Alice replied logically.

'I was at O'Shea's farm tonight,' Patrick informed her.

'Were you?' Alice continued to watch her father.

'Do you want to tell us about what you did there?'

Alice looked at him blankly.

'I know what you did at the farm, Alice. Do you want to tell us why you're doing these terrible things?' Patrick demanded heatedly.

Alice slid back around the tree until she was out of sight. Then she giggled. Her laughter hung, disembodied, eerie and disquieting in the cold night air. 'If I put enough things in the ground, then maybe – just maybe – I won't have to go back again.'

Louise and Patrick glanced uneasily at one another.

'Da-a-ad?' Alice wheedled.

'Yes, honey,' Patrick answered, instantly wary.

'What's in your pocket?'

Patrick felt in his pocket, pulled out the silver chain and held it up so Alice would see it as soon as she turned around. 'Is this yours?' he asked.

Alice peeked around the tree. 'I lost it again.'

Patrick held it out to her. 'Would you like me to fasten it around your neck right now, honey, so you won't ever lose it again?'

Alice hesitated, as if she couldn't make up her mind to trust him. Then warily, one slow step at a time, she approached Patrick. She stopped in front of him and smiled. He returned her smile and stroked her hair before leaning forward and fastening the chain around her neck.

'Thanks, Dad.' She fingered the chain then hugged him. He hugged her back, but only with one hand. He thrust the other into his pocket and removed the hypodermic he'd filled with fluid in the cattle shed. He flicked the cap from the top of the needle with his thumbnail and it fell noiselessly on top of the birds' corpses that littered the road.

'I love you, honey,' he said sincerely.

'I love you too, Dad,' she replied, '. . . and you, Mum.' Alice buried her face in Patrick's shoulder.

'I love you too, sweetie.' Louise's voice was heavy, thick with emotion when she saw what Patrick was about to do.

Patrick pressed the hypodermic needle through the layers of Alice's clothes, deep into her thigh.

'Ow!' Alice cried out. 'What are you doing?'

Patrick pushed in the plunger. Alice pulled back, away from him. The hypodermic fell to the ground. Alice looked at it and started to sway.

Louise cried out, 'Alice.' She ran to her, grabbing her arms when Alice started to struggle with Patrick.

'I want to stay with you . . .' As the drug took effect,

Alice's voice grew fainter. She slumped and Patrick caught her.

'It's over,' Patrick told Louise quietly.

'It's not over . . .' Alice's voice had dropped to a whisper.

Patrick picked up his daughter and carried her to the car. He laid her on the back seat and checked her vital signs.

'Is she . . . ?' Louise couldn't bring herself to say more.

'She's tranquillised. As I said, we have to take her back, Louise.'

There was a sudden sound of flapping wings that rapidly intensified to a crescendo. Patrick closed the back door of the estate. The noise of the large black crows flying around them was becoming deafening. Patrick pushed Louise into the car and slammed the door, sealing her safely inside before running round to the driver's side. Ducking and weaving to avoid the birds, he fell into the seat and closed his door. As soon as he was safe inside he reached for Louise's hand. He needed reassurance, the knowledge that he wasn't alone.

They both stared at the windscreen but all they could see was a mass of flapping, writhing feathers.

Patrick tried the ignition. It fired, and those of the birds that could still fly whirled away. Crunching over the feathered corpses of the others, Patrick pulled away from the side of the road and headed for the centre of Wake Wood.

# Twenty-One

Louise persuaded Patrick that there was one person they could go to for help. She directed him to Mary Brogan's house. He parked the car outside.

Louise held the back door of the estate open while Patrick lifted Alice's limp body from the back seat and carried her to Mary's front door. A light burned in the hallway and Louise realised electricity had been restored to the town. She pressed the doorbell.

Mary opened the door almost immediately. She looked from Louise to Patrick and finally to Alice, comatose in Patrick's arms.

'What's happened?' One look at Patrick and Louise's stricken faces had been enough for her to know that whatever it was, it wasn't good.

'I lied to Arthur, Mary,' Patrick confessed, deciding the only course left to him and Louise was to tell the truth. 'Alice had been dead for over a year before Arthur brought her back.'

Horrified, Mary's eyes rounded. 'Oh, Patrick, what have you done?'

Pale, trembling, Louise placed her hand on Alice's chest. Panic-stricken, she screamed, 'Patrick, she's not breathing.'

'She won't stay that way,' Mary warned. 'You have the clutch I gave you?'

'Not with us, not here,' Patrick replied.

Mary looked skywards. 'May we all survive,' she prayed feelingly.

It was pitch black, impossible to see outside the circles of light beaming from the torches Patrick and Mary held. But the deeper Mary, Louise and Patrick went into the woods, the more they sensed life moving all around them. The sound of footfalls and the crackle of twigs breaking underfoot assailed them from all sides as their neighbours also headed to the spot Arthur had designated for the beginning of the short feather walk.

Louise and Patrick felt as though every inhabitant of Wake Wood was on the move, preparing to witness the ceremony of 'the return', as Mary Brogan had put it, to ensure that they really did place Alice back into the earth where she could do no more damage to Wake Wood or its people.

By tacit agreement, as the one most conversant with what was about to happen, Mary led the way. The path was uneven and she picked out her route carefully, stopping and shining her torch around the area every minute or so to check her bearings before moving on. Louise followed close on Mary's heels and Patrick, carrying Alice's dead weight on his shoulder, brought up the rear.

All three had to duck frequently when large black birds swooped dangerously low and close to their heads, their wings whirring, menacing in the darkness.

There was scurrying all around them as small mammals, disturbed by their presence, fled through the undergrowth.

Louise dreaded arriving at the designated place, but at the same time she was irritated because she felt they were making slow progress.

After half an hour of steady walking, Mary turned right and began to climb the side of a steep ravine. Louise grabbed the trunk of a birch for support and followed her, taking care to avoid the showers of small stones Mary was dislodging on her ascent. Patrick stood back for a moment, shifted Alice from his right to his left shoulder and took a deep breath before following them.

'I like Mary Brogan, Dad. She's nice, isn't she?'

Alice's whisper in Patrick's ear caught him off guard. He stumbled clumsily. Losing his footing, he fell into a bush, only just managing to keep a grip on Alice. If that had been the edge of the ravine . . .

The same thought had obviously occurred to Alice. She whispered, 'Careful, Dad. I know I have to go back but I'd like to say goodbye properly to you and Mum before I leave.'

Patrick fought a rising tide of sour bile and nausea that rose from the pit of his stomach. He was angry, yet he felt he had no right to be. Arthur had warned him from the outset that the rules of Wake Wood must be obeyed. He'd known all along what had to be done. Now the time had arrived, he had no choice. But neither had he known just how wretched he'd feel when the moment came.

He tried to concentrate his energies on the task in

hand and follow Mary without thinking further than the next step he was about to take. Head down, lips compressed, he started the climb. Already Mary and Louise were distant shadowy figures and he had to move quickly just to keep them in sight.

Alice moved her arms around his neck. He froze, expecting them to tighten. She hugged him, then released him. He weakened in relief.

'Please put me down, Dad. Then I'll go. I'll disappear into the woods. You won't ever see me again. I promise.'

It wasn't easy but Patrick managed to ignore her plea. He kept climbing in the direction Mary and Louise had taken, determined to stay strong for the sake of Louise . . . and – the thought warmed him – their coming baby.

Mary and Louise reached the top of the hill and entered a clearing that seemed to be full of people, although it was so dark, Louise found it impossible to estimate the numbers lurking silently in the shadows beneath the trees. An enormous bonfire had been built from dead wood, and it dominated the centre of the space, waiting to be torched.

'This is it. We're here, Louise. I told you that the feather walk would be short because of Alice's age. It will be three times around the bonfire and thirty paces to the east.' Mary patted her arm. 'Do you want to find somewhere that you can sit and rest until it's time?'

'I'll rest after Patrick gets here.' Louise walked to the edge of the ravine and looked down, hoping to see her husband in the darkness.

'He was just behind us,' Mary murmured. 'He'll be here any minute.'

'I know,' Louise answered automatically, but already she could feel a tight knot of apprehension forming in her stomach.

Patrick negotiated the steep path up the hill with difficulty. It wasn't easy to juggle Alice and the torch he was carrying but somehow he managed it. His daughter had never weighed so heavy, but he tried to quicken his pace in an effort to lessen the distance between him and Louise. It had been a good few minutes since he'd last seen her and Mary. He was barely aware of tightening his arms around Alice as he walked, until he felt her fighting back, punching and kicking his arms and body, resisting the pressure he was putting on her. Already he was loath to let her go.

'Dad, you're hurting me,' Alice protested.

Patrick kept on walking, taking longer and longer strides in his haste to reach the top of the hill.

Angry, Alice shouted. 'Dad, put me down!'

Patrick kept moving, all the while trying not to think of what he and Louise were about to do. For the moment Alice was still in his arms. Whatever she'd done, she was his honey . . . his little girl . . .

'All right then, Dad. Remember, you made me do this.' Alice's voice sharpened in exasperation.

She didn't move an inch but Patrick gagged as if he were choking on something caught in his throat. Spots wavered before his eyes. He felt faint and tripped but he struggled on . . . had to keep moving . . . to keep moving . . . to put one foot in front of the other . . .

'Don't make me do this, Dad,' Alice warned.

Unable to breathe, Patrick coughed. Blood trickled, warm, salt and stinging, down his cheeks from beneath his eyelids.

Alice slid from his shoulder the moment his arms fell slack to his sides. She stood back, facing him, watching as his entire body went into a paroxysm. He fought to draw air into his lungs, tried to call out to Louise and Mary for help, but all he managed was a weak groan.

And all the while he struggled to remain upright Alice stood in front of him, a few feet away, just watching – and waiting for him to collapse to the ground.

Louise paced impatiently at the top of the hill but she was careful not to move far from Mary. She studied every figure that appeared on the summit to join the knot of people assembling in the clearing, but none proved to be Patrick.

Concerned, unable to wait a moment longer, she went to the edge of the ravine, looked down, scanned the path and shouted, 'Patrick? Where are you? I can't see you.' When there was no reply other than the steady tread of people making their way up to the top, she turned to Mary.

'I'm going back down. Patrick could have fallen . . . He could have . . . Anything could have happened.' Louise tried not to think of Howie and Peggy or what Alice was capable of.

Knowing it was useless to try and talk Louise out of looking for her husband, Mary said, 'I'll come with you.'

The two women started their descent along the path they'd just taken.

Mary shone her torch either side of the route, checking every shadow. Soon she became as worried as Louise. She tightened her hands into fists and muttered a silent prayer. But when she saw Alice standing ahead of them, blocking their path, she abandoned her prayer and murmured, 'Alice . . . Please . . . no . . .'

'Hello.' Alice stared coldly at Louise and Mary, her eyes unnaturally bright, luminous icy pinpricks in the darkness.

Mary wanted to move but she couldn't. It was as though she'd been transformed into a firmly rooted plant. She was totally incapable of leaving the spot she stood on.

Alice crept towards Mary, taking her time, relishing the hold she exercised over her.

Patrick was lying on his side a few feet away from Louise and Mary. He'd heard Mary's voice but he couldn't see either her or Louise. It was too dark, although he sensed Mary and his wife were close by. He fixed his gaze on Alice. If he reached out to her, could he stop her?

He tried to move one of his arms but it lay limp, paralysed, useless. All he could do was remain on the ground, cursing his own impotence.

'Thank you for being nice to my parents, Mary.' Alice drew closer and closer to Mary, wrapped her arms around her waist and hugged her tight. 'You've been very kind to them.'

Alice began to convulse and, almost immediately, so

did Mary. The torch Mary was holding fell to the ground and she cried out as her shaking became more and more violent.

'I'm not going back, Mary.' Alice unbuttoned Mary's coat and slipped her hand inside. Mary sank down on to her knees.

Louise shouted her daughter's name to no avail. All she and Patrick could do was listen in horror as the ominous squelch of soft tissue being invaded filled the air. Mary didn't utter a sound but Louise watched Mary's eyes darken and glaze in agony in the pool of upturned light from the torch. Within seconds, rivulets of bright crimson blood began to stream down Mary's face from her eyelids, ears and mouth.

Louise thought that Alice would never end her lethal embrace but eventually she did step away from Mary, exposing a ghastly open wound in Mary's stomach. Triumphant, Alice smiled, turned to Louise and held up her hand. It was covered in blood and gore to the elbow.

Mary stared at Alice, swayed on her knees and finally fell, slumping sideways on to the leaf-covered dirt path.

Louise crawled to Mary and crouched beside her. She didn't need to feel for Mary's pulse. No one could survive the injury Alice had inflicted on her. Louise looked up at her daughter in horror and screamed, 'Alice!'

Alice stepped aside and for the first time Louise noticed Patrick's prostrate figure illuminated at the edge of the beam from Mary's discarded torch. His eyes were closed. Louise looked for signs of breathing but saw none obvious. Patrick was unable to help her because he was unconscious . . . or . . .

Louise closed her mind, unwilling to think of the alternative. Patrick couldn't be dead . . . not Patrick. Alice couldn't – wouldn't – kill her own father . . . But then this thing . . . this monster that looked, spoke and appeared to be Alice couldn't possibly be the daughter they had brought up and loved. The child they'd nurtured such hopes and dreams for.

Alice turned to Louise and said, 'Mum?' in a normal, conversational tone.

Terrified, Louise shrank back as Alice advanced on her. She felt herself beginning to tremble. The same violent convulsions that had held Mary and Alice in thrall were now beginning to take an insidious hold on her.

Alice lowered her head and hunched over. When she next raised her face, the expression in her eyes was cold, pure evil. 'Mum . . . why don't you answer me when I talk to you?'

Louise staggered back, away from Alice. Leaving the path, she turned and retreated, fleeing into the woods.

'Mum . . .'

Louise ignored Alice's cry and ran . . . and ran . . . and ran . . . She didn't know where she was running to. She only knew she had to get away from Alice and put as much distance as possible between her and the thing that was occupying her daughter's body, before she ended up dead and mutilated, like Mary.

Because she wanted to live. For the sake of the child she was carrying – she wanted to live.

*

Louise didn't stop until she was incapable of taking another step. She collapsed, weak and breathless, praying that she'd put enough ground between herself and Alice for her daughter not to find her. She crawled under a thicket of bushes and lay low, wishing she could momentarily disappear by dissolving into the earth.

Far below her on the fringes of the woods she could see car headlights travelling along the country road that wound past Wake Wood. Evidence that a world existed beyond the town; a normal world where people lived boring conventional lives; one where children went to school, adults worked in offices and stores, and in between they shopped, went to cinemas and visited friends and relatives – a world she was no longer a part of.

All around at a distance, faint beams of torchlight danced between the trees, twigs snapped and boots hit the ground as the stragglers among her neighbours made their way between the shadowy rows of tree trunks and headed for the gathering at the lip of the ravine.

'Mum . . .' Alice's voice carried sweet and low, heart-breakingly familiar as it echoed through the woods. 'Mum . . . where are you?'

Louise didn't move. She lay as flat to the earth as she could and waited for the black spots to stop wavering in front of her eyes while she struggled to catch her breath.

She froze when she saw Alice drift slowly past her hiding place. Her daughter was so close, if she'd reached out she could have touched her foot. Louise closed her eyes, too frightened to breathe any longer lest she alert Alice to her presence.

Alice called out, 'Mum? Ready or not, I'm coming . . . Where are you, Mum?' as though they were playing a game of hide-and-seek.

Louise continued to lie still. The earth was cold, damp. It smelled of winter's rotting leaves; death and decay assailed her nostrils. Yet Alice had to return there.

She recalled Arthur's words that night at the cottage when he'd told her and Patrick that he could bring Alice back to them.

*Alice's heart will beat, her lungs will breathe. She'll remember you and the life she had with you. Some of it . . . but she'll also be deceased – although that's something she won't be aware of. You'll need to bear that in mind the entire time you're with her.*

Even after everything that had happened – all that Alice had done – when the time came, would she be able to return her daughter's body back to the earth with its foul stench of putrefaction and the grave?

Louise finally breathed out when everything around her had fallen quiet. She counted to one hundred in her head, then rose cautiously. Alice had gone. The woods around her were still, unnaturally so, after the earlier movement and sounds. She looked around indecisively, uncertain which direction to take.

'Where are you, Mum?'

Alice's voice, light, disembodied by the night, floated towards her, eerie and threatening.

Louise took off again at speed. She wasn't even sure which direction she was heading. She only knew that she had to put as much ground as she could between her and Alice.

'I'm going to find you,' Alice shouted after her. 'Ready or not . . . I'm coming, Mum . . .'

Louise didn't falter, didn't hesitate for a moment. Head down, she continued to charge ahead into the pitch darkness beneath the trees.

# Twenty-Two

Patrick opened his eyes. He was surrounded by deep black shadows that shut out all shades of light. He could hear crashes, bangs, dead wood snapping and the low murmur of distant conversation. Sticks and stones dug uncomfortably into his flesh. He breathed in deeply and then remembered. He was in the woods. They'd been walking to the place where Arthur would hold the ceremony of the return. Him, Louise, Mary and Alice . . .

He raised his head and cried out, 'Louise . . .' then he saw Mary outlined in the faint glow of a torch. Her body was bloodied, wounded, broken just like Howie, the bull . . . the pony . . . and Peggy O'Shea.

He closed his eyes, unable to bear the pain of what his daughter had done.

'Patrick?'

He opened his eyes again and looked up. Arthur was standing over him, stony-faced.

'Arthur . . .'

'Help him to his feet,' Arthur ordered someone behind him.

Tommy and Martin came into view and hauled Patrick upright. They forced his wrists into a clutch that proved as effective as handcuffs. Patrick struggled, but once Martin twirled the sticks until the ropes cut deeply into the flesh, his arms were bound as securely as if he'd been manacled with chains.

Arthur drew close to Patrick and whispered low in his ear, 'Eleven months, two weeks and two days. You can't lie about these things and get away with it, Patrick. But I admit you had me fooled.'

'We wanted to see Alice again,' Patrick cried out, desperate to explain to Arthur why he'd lied. 'And you wanted to keep us here,' he reminded him.

'How long had Alice really been dead?' Arthur demanded.

'A year, a month and a few days. Let me go, Arthur,' Patrick pleaded with his partner. 'I can help you . . .'

Arthur shook his head. 'The clutch will release you, Patrick, but only when Alice is back in the ground. Not one minute before.'

'Release him?' Tommy queried in disgust.

'Only when Alice is back in the ground,' Arthur reiterated calmly.

Patrick lashed out with his bound hands, struggling to free himself. 'Arthur,' he shouted. 'She'll kill my wife.'

'I hope not,' Arthur said quietly. He walked away.

Martin and Tommy took advantage of Arthur's departure to beat, kick and punch Patrick. They forced him back down on to his knees. Thinking of Peggy and the O'Shea livestock, Patrick couldn't even blame Martin. But he was bemused when he heard Tommy mutter, 'That's for Ben.'

Had Alice hurt or killed Tommy's brother too?

'Arthur . . .' Faint, barely conscious, Patrick shouted a last appeal. But he was too late. Arthur was no longer even in sight.

Louise crouched low in a thicket of close-growing bushes beneath a copse of silver birch trees. Their trunks gleamed tall, straight and fairy-like in the gloom. Alice's voice, ethereal and ghost-like, reverberated, echoing around her.

'Mum, where are you? Ready or not, I'm coming . . .'

Louise looked up to see a black crow hanging in the branches of one of the trees above her. She couldn't be certain, but it looked like the very same bird that Alice had found so fascinating on her first day in Wake Wood.

'Mum . . . you'd better come out now . . .'

At the sound of Alice's voice the bird burst into life. Its wings started fluttering as if it were trying to fly, which was impossible given that its legs were still tied firmly together.

Terror-stricken, wanting to get away from the creature whether it was dead or not, Louise sprinted out of the undergrowth and crashed out of the bushes. Alice's voice wailed around her, eerie and unsettling.

'Mum . . . Mum . . . come out, wherever you are!'

Louise ran blindly, speeding downhill, lurching past trees and bushes. She fell, painfully skinning her hands. She clambered back on to her feet right away and continued hurtling downwards through the woods and away from Alice, charging headlong . . . until she slammed hard into a wire fence.

Pain ricocheted through her body as the breath was

knocked from her lungs. She winced, gasped and doubled over, too shocked and injured to move.

Ahead of her on the other side of the wire fence was pasture. Thick grass stretched to the horizon in the moonlight, totally devoid of trees. Could she climb the fence? Was it strong enough to bear her weight?

She tested the wire mesh with her foot – it sagged but held. Still hurting from the impact of her collision, she clambered awkwardly over it and jumped down the other side into the field.

Looming high above her a short distance ahead were the unmistakeable towers of the wind turbines that had been erected above a railway bridge. Below them she could see the square outline of the sign that marked the town boundary of Wake Wood.

'Mum . . . where are you? . . . Ready or not, I'm coming to find you . . .' Alice's voice drifted on the night wind, faint, distant, muted by the trees and yet clear and audible.

Louise walked on deeper into the field until she'd passed both the wind turbines and the WELCOME sign. Only then did she turn and cup her hands around her mouth to amplify the sound. As loud as she could, she called out, 'Alice . . . A-l-ice . . . where are you? I'm here, waiting for you. Come and find me.'

Above her the blades of the wind turbines whirled, grating and swishing in a rough, unmelodious, mechanical din that polluted the night atmosphere.

Louise walked on for a few more paces, increasing the expanse of clear open field between her and the woods. She stopped again, turned and shouted, 'Alice! A-l-ice!

Where are you? I'm here, waiting for you,' towards the woods.

The blades of the tallest turbine swept on.

'Alice . . . it's me . . . Where are you?'

Something small flashed on the edge of the woods. It moved from tree to tree, hiding behind them, before coming to rest on the very edge of the field next to an old oak on the wooded side of the fence.

'Hi, Mum. I'm here.' Alice waved to Louise.

Louise waved back. 'Hello, sweetie.' She couldn't conceal the sadness in her voice.

'Why did you run away from me, Mum?' Alice whined.

'Because I was scared,' Louise answered truthfully.

'Are you still scared?'

'No, not really, not any more.'

'I bet you are,' Alice goaded.

'Well, maybe just a little, sweetie,' Louise admitted.

'That's probably why you didn't answer me when I called you. You did know that I've been calling you? And calling you?'

'Yes, I know. I heard you. You've found me out,' Louise conceded.

'You could come to me now though, Mum.' Alice held out her hand in readiness to take hold of Louise's.

'I know I could, sweetie, but I'm tired. I've been walking a lot. I have no breath left. And I hurt myself running into that fence.'

'Well.' Alice stared at Louise, a menacing glint in her eyes. 'I'll come to you, then.'

'That would be nice of you, sweetie. Be careful when

you climb over the fence. It's not that high but it's not very stable.'

Alice put her foot on the mesh and hauled herself upwards. She climbed steadily, reached the top, hooked her legs over, and then suddenly stopped and looked at Louise. 'Mum?'

'What is it, sweetie?' Louise waited for Alice to reply.

'Can I have a hug?' Alice asked plaintively.

'Of course you can. But not there. Just get down and come to me, sweetie.' Louise brushed a tear from her eye before opening her arms wide to her daughter. Alice launched herself from the fence, landed and began to approach Louise.

As she watched Alice walk towards her, more tears poured down Louise's face. She knew what was about to happen, but knowing didn't make it any easier or prepare her for the full force of the impact when it came. She subdued a tide of panic, crouched and waited.

Slowly, infinitely slowly, as though the world was moving forward like a film in slow motion, a single frame at a time, Alice walked across the field towards Louise.

Behind Alice – slight at first, then, the closer Alice drew to her, appearing thicker – was an unmistakeable slick of blood that trailed from Alice's finger.

Alice walked past the sign that marked the boundary of Wake Wood, took another step, fell to her knees and screamed . . . 'Mum!'

Her cry was agonised, heart-rending.

Louise stood and watched as the hideous dog bites and deep, ragged, gouged teeth marks appeared once again on Alice's face and neck, tearing open her flesh.

Alice continued to scream . . . and scream . . . She rolled over . . . writhing in distress . . .

Louise was catapulted back to the old house, reliving every horrific second of the end of her precious daughter's life.

Her arms fell to her sides and she walked over the grass to where Alice lay, fatally wounded and bleeding. She reached her just as Alice became very still.

'I'm so sorry, sweetie.' Louise knelt on the grass, took off her coat, lifted Alice on to it and wrapped it tenderly around her daughter. She picked up Alice, cradled her in her arms, rose to her feet and started to walk back to the trees, struggling with Alice's weight as she carried her along the fence line, through a gate and up the hill.

Large black birds circled above them, but Louise didn't deviate from the course she'd set herself. She tried to imagine herself back in the old house. Putting Alice to bed as she'd done so often during the nine years her daughter had been hers to love and care for.

'Now, sweetie, we're off to bed,' she crooned softly. 'Off to Blanket Street,' she murmured, cuddling Alice close to her. 'The sandman is flying through the air, coming towards us with his bag of sweet . . . sweet dreams.'

She passed Patrick on the ground. Battered, bruised, bleeding from a myriad of small cuts, he looked groggily up at her. But she saw his eyelids flicker. He was alive!

She hugged the knowledge to her and suppressed her instinct to go to him and comfort him. He had to wait his turn. She had a more important task to complete first, for someone who needed her even more than Patrick. Someone who had no one else to turn to . . . someone who wanted to stay on this earth but couldn't . . .

When Louise reached the clearing at the top of the hill she saw a faint streak of colour on the eastern horizon. Dawn was breaking. She didn't look at her neighbours massed around the edge of the clearing, all wearing their black feathers, only at Alice.

Arthur was waiting. He guided her, once, twice, three times around the bonfire, before lighting it. Then he led her over to a spot on the eastern edge of the ridge.

He stepped back and Louise knew they'd reached Alice's final resting place. She knelt at Arthur's feet and placed Alice gently and carefully on the ground next to her.

'My angel, we're almost there. Almost home. I'll just make up the bed for you, all warm and cosy so you can sleep tight and safe.' Louise started to dig in the ground with her bare hands.

Patrick stumbled clumsily up the hill towards her. Tommy and Martin went to him and held him back. Louise looked up and saw him. She noticed that his wrists were bound in a clutch just like the one Mary had given them for Alice.

She looked away from Patrick and back at the hole she was digging. Oblivious to the damp earth clinging to her hands, clothes and arms, she continued to scoop out a shallow grave beneath the trees. The earth crumbled easily between her fingers. It wasn't hard to remove and the whole time she worked she talked to Alice.

'The bed will be warm . . . warm and comfortable, sweetie . . . You'll sleep like a princess . . .' When she considered the hole deep enough to hold Alice, Louise picked up her daughter, still wrapped in the coat, and settled her gently inside before dropping a kiss on to her forehead.

'Are you comfy, sweetie?'

Alice stirred, curling into a foetal position as if she were lying in her own bed between clean linen sheets. Slowly and gently, Louise began to pile the earth she'd removed from the hole on top of her daughter, settling it and smoothing it over her slim young body as if she were covering Alice with a swansdown-filled duvet.

'It's story time, Alice. Once upon a time there was a little girl who went for a long, long walk in the woods. She walked and walked and walked and then discovered that she'd lost her way and couldn't find . . .'

Louise concentrated on the story, ignoring the yellow beams of the torches moving towards them in the gloom, but she sensed people drawing closer and closer to her and Alice, and behind them – Patrick.

They halted a few feet away from her as she continued to fill in the grave.

No more than the lightest whisper on the wind at first, a chant grew in volume and intensity, becoming gradually more and more audible as the seconds ticked past and she filled in the grave.

'Go back to the trees and lie among the roots . . . Go back to the trees and lie among the roots . . .'

Arthur looked at Patrick and signalled to Martin and Tommy, who stepped up either side of him and brought him forward. They propelled him next to where Louise was kneeling, still piling earth into the grave. Alice was almost covered with dirt but she was still moving, her chest rising and falling with every breath she took, her outline clearly visible beneath the coating of earth Louise was heaping over her.

Louise was still talking but only to Alice, and Alice alone.

'. . . and although the darkness was drawing near, now the little girl knew she didn't have far to go. The cottage and safety were only a few short steps away, not far . . . not far for her to walk at all now . . .'

Louise finished piling up the earth she'd removed. Leaning forward, she patted the mound of loose dirt, flattening it until it was level with the surrounding ground and there was no trace left of Alice and nothing to indicate where she lay.

The clutch binding Patrick's hands suddenly sprang and dropped off.

Louise took her time over smoothing the surface of her daughter's grave, making sure it was weed- and stone-free.

'A few short steps and the little girl would be happy for ever and ever. The door would open and her grandma would take her into her arms and carry her into the warmth of the cottage, and the door would close for ever on the cold and the darkness and the night . . .'

Louise lay across the simple grave. Cold tears slipped down her cheeks. Around her the woods fell still and silent.

Patrick sensed Martin and Tommy loosening their hold on him. He moved forward. Martin patted his back reassuringly as if he were trying to tell Patrick that he'd been forgiven.

Patrick stooped down beside his wife and whispered, 'Louise?'

She looked up at him. Her eyes were empty, bereft even of hope.

He held out his hand to her to help her up from the ground. She took it.

But before Louise could rise, the earth erupted beneath her like a volcano. Dirt sprang up and showered, shooting into the air like a fountain, spraying over Louise and Patrick.

A hole opened. Alice's hand snaked up through it from beneath the ground and grasped Louise's foot in a vice-like grip.

Louise screamed. Alice's hold on her ankle tightened, pulling her downwards into the grave.

Louise looked up at her husband and pleaded, 'Patrick!'

Patrick grabbed hold of both Louise's arms. He pulled her upwards, closer to him with every ounce of strength he could muster.

Alice proved stronger.

Inch by inch, Louise was slowly dragged down until she was waist deep in the earth.

Tommy and Martin ran forward with Arthur. They grabbed hold of Patrick's arms and chest, gripping him tight.

'Help me to get Louise out,' Patrick begged.

Despite the combined efforts of all four men, Louise was still being pulled, deeper and deeper into the earth. The ground was level with her chest when her hands slid from Patrick's grasp.

He shrieked, 'No!' and tried to grab her by her shoulders but she slipped from his fingers.

She continued to slither downwards. Earth covered her up to her neck . . . her chin . . . her lips . . . her eyes . . . her hair . . . and then she disappeared completely as a second shower of earth shot up, erupting from the spot that had swallowed her.

Patrick wrenched himself free from the men who were holding him and flung himself headlong on to the grave.

He cried out, 'Louise!' He dug frantically with his bare hands, scrabbling with his fingers in the earth that had already settled. But no matter how deep he probed, he only found yet more earth.

He continued to excavate, emptying the grave Louise had made, piling the earth around him like a dog digging a hole. But he found only earth . . . and more earth . . . and more earth.

'They're gone, Patrick.' Arthur laid his hand on

Patrick's shoulder. 'They've both gone. You won't find them. Not now.'

'Louise . . . Alice . . . I have to . . .'

It was a long time before Arthur finally managed to stop Patrick from digging.

# Twenty-Three

'So sorry for your loss', 'How are you really?' and 'Are you coping?' were phrases Patrick came to loathe as the hours after Louise's disappearance evolved into days . . . weeks . . . and eventually months.

Awake, he felt as though he were trapped in a nightmare world. Asleep was worse because his dreams were laced with the scenes and knowledge of Louise's horrific disappearance. Again and again he relived that crucial moment.

The look of sheer terror on her face and in her eyes when she realised she was about to be buried alive.

He needed no reminder of how impotent and helpless he'd felt when he'd failed to save his wife. When all he could do was look on and watch the tragedy unfold before his eyes. That feeling hit him anew every single time he thought of it with all the force of his initial despair, devastation and misery.

Whereas once he'd loved mornings, now he dreaded them even more than evenings. Evenings meant firelight and memories he could lose himself in to the point where they seemed more real than the day he'd just lived through.

Mornings brought the bitter, harsh consciousness of

his solitary state. Louise may have no longer been in his bed, his house, his life, but she was his first thought on waking and his last at night – on the rare occasions when he was fortunate enough to sleep.

Locked into the backwater town of Wake Wood, imprisoned by the promise he'd made Arthur, for the first time since he'd been born he was completely and utterly alone in the world. And he hated it. It was almost as though he'd been dropped into a lonely limbo, where he continued to exist merely as an entity to mark time until the Fates decreed that he could be allowed to join his beloved wife and daughter.

His neighbours were sympathetic but not overly so. He knew there were some people in Wake Wood who would never entirely forgive him for the lie he'd told Arthur about how long Alice had been in her grave. And whenever he thought of Peggy O'Shea, Ben, Mary Brogan – every one of them valued and valuable people the community could ill afford to lose – and the violent and brutal way they'd died, he didn't grudge the townsfolk their anger.

The days when he had a lot of work and a number of animals to attend to were just about bearable. The worst were the quiet ones when he had nothing to do except potter around the cottage, where everything reminded him of Louise – and to a lesser extent, because she'd only lived within its walls three days, Alice.

Like Louise had been with Alice's possessions, he couldn't bring himself to touch, much less throw out, any of Louise's personal belongings. He left her clothes in her wardrobe and dressing-table drawers, her coats on the rack in the hall, her shoes in the cupboard and her jewellery in the case on her dressing table.

The only thing of Louise's he moved was her handbag from his car when he found himself clinging to it and crying for the third time in the week after she'd gone.

The freezer was still full of her favourite tuna steaks, the cupboard stocked with her preferred brands of muesli and biscuits. He knew she wouldn't – couldn't – return.

But that didn't stop him from looking to the door every time he heard a noise outside. Or jumping up whenever a car entered his drive. Or racing to the telephone if it rang – and always hoping for the impossible.

That Louise was about to walk back into the cottage and his life.

He took to driving around the back lanes so he wouldn't have to travel down the main street of the town and pass the shuttered door and windows of Louise's pharmacy. He ate most of his meals in country pubs so he wouldn't even have to go into town to shop for food.

Whenever Patrick saw Arthur – and Arthur took care to see that they met most days – his senior partner reminded him that the town desperately needed a pharmacist. Arthur suggested that Patrick consider either renting the place to another pharmacist or selling the shop and the stock – most of which, as Arthur pointed out, was rapidly going out of date.

Patrick did think about it, but doing something about

the pharmacy required an effort he wasn't prepared to make for months. He wasn't even sure where Louise had kept the keys to the shop.

As the weeks passed he made a few half-hearted attempts to find them. When he discovered that they weren't in any of the cupboards or drawers in the cottage he fetched Louise's handbag from the hall cupboard, where he'd stowed it after taking it from his car.

He placed it on the table and sat and looked at it for a long time before he finally gathered enough courage to unzip it, and even then he felt that in some way he was violating Louise's privacy. Prying into her personal effects when he had no right to.

He tipped the contents of the bag out on to the table. The keys were at the bottom. Louise's purse was heavy, as was her make-up bag that he'd seen her use so many times. He didn't open either. He set them aside along with her mobile phone, pen and notebook. He picked up a small, handbag-sized atomiser and sprayed it on his wrist. The room was instantly filled with Louise's perfume. He closed his eyes, revelling in the sweet familiar scent. He could almost believe that she was with him again, walking across the room . . . He could have sworn he heard her voice calling his name . . .

'Patrick?'

He replaced everything except the keys in Louise's handbag, zipped it up and returned it to the cupboard. He went to bed and tried to sleep. But it was hopeless. The perfume he'd sprayed had lingered in his senses – not that he needed any reminder to think of Louise. But somehow it made her presence all the more real and her absence all the more unbearable.

He left his bed, showered, dressed and drove into Wake Wood. He didn't even realise that it was five o'clock in the morning until he checked his watch as he parked outside the pharmacy.

He unlocked and opened the shutters and the shop door, went inside, switched on the lights and looked around.

A thick layer of dust had settled over the shelves, their contents and the counter, filming the entire interior of the shop a ghostly silvery grey. He picked up a box that contained a bottle of shampoo and looked at the neatly outlined square of clean shelf beneath it. He replaced the box in the exact spot where it had stood and went to the counter.

Louise's wooden hairbrush was next to the till. He imagined her brushing her hair before . . . He thought back to the last time Louise would have been in the shop.

Late afternoon before the night of Alice's return. Louise would have brushed her hair, slipped on her coat, emptied the till, picked up her handbag and hurried out to meet him so he could drive them both to Arthur's house, ready for the ceremony.

He crouched down to counter level and looked at the wooden hairbrush. Imagined Louise's fingers curled around the handle as she tugged it impatiently through her long blonde hair, pulling strands out by the roots . . . strands that he could see still caught up in the bristles. He tugged at one, stretching it out to its full silver-blonde length. And as he did so the germ of an idea entered his mind.

Louise had only been in the earth three months . . . only three months . . .

Patrick went behind the counter, found a clean plastic bag and carefully placed the hairbrush inside it.

For the first time since Louise had gone he was formulating a plan. Thinking ahead to the future, not back to the past, and it felt good. So good he didn't want to let the idea go.

He looked around the shop and decided that Arthur was right. He had no right to keep the shop as a shrine to Louise. For the sake of the town he had to move on. Either put the place on the market or find a qualified pharmacist who was prepared to rent it from him.

He left the shop, locked the door and the shutters and returned to his car, more animated than he'd been since Louise had disappeared.

He drove slowly down the main street and out to the road that led to the cottage. All that was needed was a fresh corpse – and as Louise had only been gone three months, he had nine months to wait for one.

When they had a body, Arthur could use the hairs from Louise's brush as a relic to bring her back. That would give him three more days with Louise. Days in which he could love her, tell her how much she'd meant to him, days in which they could say a final goodbye to one another . . . precious days . . .

It was while he was thinking of and planning for that time that another idea came to mind. One that, if it proved feasible, could change the rest of his life.

He slammed on the brakes, stopped the car and climbed outside. He was in the same lay-by he and Louise had pulled into when the car had broken down the first time. The breakdown the mechanic had been unable to diagnose once the car engine had started again.

He looked up at the field where he'd seen the boy who'd disappeared when the car had burst into life.

Had he been a ghost?

Someone like Alice who'd undergone the ceremony of 'the return'?

Louise was pregnant. He'd seen the stick on the shelf in their bathroom, '3+ weeks'. She'd been gone three months – in five months Louise would be coming to full term. If she was still with him they would have been making preparations, decorating the spare room as a nursery . . . buying a cot . . . Could he . . . ?

Thoughts whirled around his mind like dead dry leaves in a storm. He needed to talk to Arthur. And quickly.

Because if his idea could work and he planned carefully, he need never be alone or lonely again.

'Patrick?' Arthur answered Patrick's knock in robe and pyjamas. If he was surprised at the early hour Patrick had chosen to make a visit, he made no outward sign. He showed Patrick into his kitchen, switched on the light, brewed coffee and listened in silence while Patrick outlined his plans.

When Patrick finished, Arthur topped up their coffee cups, turned his back and went to the window to watch the sun rise.

'Could it work?' Patrick ventured, looking anxiously at Arthur.

'I don't know,' Arthur replied honestly without turning his head towards Patrick. 'To my knowledge no one has ever disappeared before in the same way that Louise did. And certainly no pregnant woman that I've heard of. Therefore nothing like you're suggesting has ever been attempted. But that's not to say that it could, or couldn't, be done. I simply don't know.'

Patrick dreaded hearing Arthur's reply but he had to ask the question: 'Will you help me?'

Arthur turned and finally looked at Patrick. 'You've really thought about this?'

'Yes,' Patrick answered.

'You know, it could go wrong, just like it did with Alice.'

'Yes,' Patrick confirmed. 'But the only thing I want to know is if you will help me,' he reiterated.

He had to wait five minutes for Arthur's answer.

# Epilogue

Five months later, Patrick joined his neighbours in Arthur's yard. It was two weeks earlier than he would have ideally chosen but a corpse had become suddenly available. A child – a particularly strong life force, or so Arthur assured him – had been knocked down by a car in the main street. The parents had been happy to donate the corpse once Arthur had promised them that the next available cadaver would be utilised to bring back their child for a three-day 'goodbye'.

As before, the bonfire was lit at twilight. The witnesses assembled as soon as the sun disappeared from the horizon. The JCB, tractor, rigging and harness were in place, the ancient veterinary tools laid out on a side table.

Patrick found the ceremony of Louise's 'return' less stressful than Alice's had been simply because he knew what to expect. He took the handful of Louise's hair that he'd extracted from her hairbrush and handed it to Arthur, who placed it in the corpse's mouth after he'd enacted all the preliminaries.

Patrick cut himself with a scalpel, his blood was burned, the chanting began. After what seemed like a lifetime of waiting, Louise emerged, bloodied and exhausted, from the cracked, burned and battered shell, to fall into his waiting arms.

There was so much Patrick had forgotten. The exact curve of Louise's jawbone; the precise shade of blue in her eyes; the intonation of her voice . . . just how much and how deeply he loved her.

As soon as the ceremony was over he drove Louise back to the cottage, where he helped her rinse the worst of the mess of blood and fluid from her body before she showered.

He was surprised by the sight of her naked body – by just how close to term she was. He placed his hand on her stomach and murmured, 'How much do you remember?'

She looked at him and smiled. 'I . . . I'm not sure.'

'So how is it with you?'

'Fine.' She smiled self-consciously at him. 'You?'

'Fine,' he echoed and she laughed. 'And Alice?' He kissed her neck, lovingly, intimately.

'Alice, she's great,' Louise said enthusiastically. 'She – we both miss you. Alice is hoping for a sister.'

'Really? A sister. I'm glad she's OK.'

Louise turned on the shower, stepped inside and Patrick went into the master bedroom.

He listened hard with every fibre of his being. Was it his imagination or was there really a tapping? Was someone knocking at his door? He checked his watch. Surely not at this hour. Not straight after the ceremony.

Arthur was his nearest neighbour and he was miles

away. Besides, Arthur had been with him, helping and supporting him throughout the ceremony. Surely now Arthur and all the others would respect his privacy.

The sound appeared to be coming from somewhere above him. He steeled himself, leaned back and stared. A skeletal tree branch was bouncing wildly on the skylight, hitting it intermittently and lightly. So lightly, the sound was reminiscent of a child's fingers drumming against glass – or the wings of a small plastic bird . . .

Tap tap tapping . . . the branches on the skylight . . .

The world had turned full circle. Patrick picked up a towel and hid the scalpel in the folds. Then he remembered. The cottage was well within the town boundaries – there would be no blood.

'Patrick?'

'Come in. I have a towel all ready,' he called back.

Arthur sat in his car beyond the bushes in Patrick's drive. Out of sight but not out of earshot. His car windows were open.

Then he heard it. A long drawn-out scream followed by the unmistakeable cry of a newborn child.

He smiled. Patrick would no longer be alone. Wake Wood's vet would be a more contented and dedicated man. And more tied to the town than ever.

ALSO AVAILABLE FROM HAMMER

# *Twins of Evil*

## Shaun Hutson

**One of Hammer's classic films, novelised by one
of the UK's best known horror authors**

Karnstein Castle stands like a bird of prey on the highest point of
the hills that surround the village below. A huge monolithic
reminder to all those who see it of the power of the family who have
lived there for centuries.

By day the village of Karnstein is a peaceful place, but by night, an
unimaginable evil roams free. Villagers are found dead, their
throats ripped open and bodies drained of blood. Young girls
disappear and are never seen again. Rumour has it that they are
taken to the castle for the pleasure of Count Karnstein, the last
surviving member of the family.

Into this strange place, come beautiful identical twins Maria and
Frieda. While Maria lives a blameless life, Frieda is drawn to the
castle and Count Karnstein. A man rarely seen in daylight, a man
steeped in Satanic ritual and the blood of beautiful young girls.

Before long Frieda and Karnstein unleash a reign of bloody
terror on the villagers, and no one, it seems, is strong enough
to stop them.

# *The Witches*

## Peter Curtis

**Based on this classic book by Peter Curtis (aka Norah Lofts),
*The Witches* was released in 1966 starring Joan Fontaine**

Walwyk seemed a dream village to the new schoolteacher, Miss
Mayfield. But dreams can turn into nightmares.

When it becomes clear that one of her pupils is being abused, Miss
Mayfield is determined to do something about it. But Ethel won't
say anything, despite the evidence of Miss Mayfield's own eyes,
and someone seems to be actively discouraging her from
investigating further. As she tries to get to the truth of the matter,
however, Miss Mayfield stumbles on something far more sinister:
Walwyk is in the grip of a centuries-old evil, and anybody who
questions events in the village does not last long.

Death stalks more than one victim, and Miss Mayfield begins to
realise that if she's not careful, she will be the next to die . . .

'Eerie . . . horrific . . . brilliant' *Guardian*

# HAMMER

Hammer has been synonymous with legendary British horror films for over half a century. With iconic characters ranging from Quatermass and Van Helsing to Frankenstein, Dracula, and now the Woman in Black, Hammer's productions have been terrifying and thrilling audiences worldwide for generations. And there is more to come.

Leading actors including Daniel Radcliffe, Hilary Swank and Chloe Moretz are now following in the footsteps of Hammer legends Sir Christopher Lee, Peter Cushing and Bette Davis through their involvement in new Hammer films.

Hammer's literary legacy is also being revived through its new Partnership with Arrow Books. This series will feature original tales by some of today's most celebrated authors, as well as classic stories from more than five decades of production.

Hammer is back, and its new incarnation is the home of smart horror – cool, stylish and provocative stories which aim to push audiences out of their comfort zones.

For more information on Hammer,
including details of official merchandise, visit:
www.hammerfilms.com